CRA

BROTHERLY LOVE

CRACKER

BROTHERLY LOVE

Jim Mortimore

First published in Great Britain in 1996 by
Virgin Books
an imprint of Virgin Publishing Ltd
332 Ladbroke Grove
London W10 5AH

ISBN 0 863 69994 4

Typeset by Galleon Typesetting, Ipswich
Printed and bound in Great Britain by
Mackays of Chatham PLC

FOR Jon and Alison and their as yet unnamed
Significant New Arrival

SPECIAL CONGRATULATIONS to
Mister David Uppington Esquire and his
Significant Other Life Form

AND Jo, Nacula, Huw, Esther, Martin, Martin,
Ollie, Michelle, Mel.

'When the going gets weird, the weird turn pro.'
Hunter S. Thompson

PROLOGUE

Mummy was singing again. It didn't happen very often. Chrissie was grateful for that. She didn't like it when Mummy sang. She always had a friend home when she sang like that, like a little girl. Chrissie didn't like Mummy's friends. They frightened her. Mummy frightened her too, when she brought them home, when she was with them. She frightened Chrissie now, even though she was only singing.

> 'How much is that doggie in the window,
> The one with the waggly tail?'

And there was another voice too. Mummy's friend. But he didn't sound like a friend. His voice was deep and loud. 'Slut. Filthy little slut. Tart.'

Chrissie rolled over in bed, careful not to make any noise. She didn't want to disturb her brother lying asleep in the next bed. He was only young; he wouldn't understand. He'd be angry. He was always angry about something. Still, that was because he was so young, Chrissie supposed.

Mummy was still singing.

Her friend's voice was louder. 'You've always wondered what it was like. Filthy little slut. Well now you're gonna find out, you little tart, you little slut.'

Chrissie felt tears sting her eyes. He wasn't Mummy's friend. He would never talk to her like that if he was. He wasn't Mummy's friend, so why did she bring him home? Why did she bring all of them home? Why did she sing to them sometimes, pretend to be a little girl?

'You're dying for it, aren't you? Twelve years old and

1

you're dying for it, you filthy little bitch.'

Mummy stopped singing then. And her friend stopped talking. For a moment it was quiet and then the other noises started. The noises that sounded like someone being hurt, even though Chrissie knew that wasn't what they were at all.

On the next bed Jim stirred and sighed restlessly. Chrissie reached for her teddy bear, JS, to give it to Jim to help him sleep. JS wasn't on her bed. Mummy had taken him again.

MONDAY

ONE

Jean McIlvanney ran a shower. Hot water then cold. Out of the bathroom and towel dry. Rub colour into the skin. Foundation. Rouge. Lipstick. Mascara.

Who will it be tonight?

The feather touch of a makeup brush against her lashes. Another at her cheeks. Fake silver clasped at her wrist and ankle.

What will he want me to do?

Stockings and shoes. Short skirt. No bra.

Will he want to talk?

Will he look at me afterwards?

Her leather jacket, the short one that showed off her bum.

What will he think of me?

What will he say to me?

How much will he pay?

No. Stop that. Stop that right now. Ask yourself questions like that and you just let them use you. It's my choice to work this way. It's my body. I am in control. I work for my kids and I earn a reasonable wage. I'll charge him my rate and to hell with his night-out-with-the-lads-hide-it-from-the-wife-beer-money. No pay, no play. I'm not doing this for him. I'm not even doing this for me. For Chrissie. Chrissie and Jim. I'm doing it for them.

Any mother would do the same.

Ignoring her reflection's silent voice, Jean McIlvanney checked out her face one last time. It would do. Her legs were her real selling points. Hence the short jacket and skirt.

Makeup and dress complete, Jean made the last stop in her nightly ritual. In the kids' room Jim was fast asleep. Three and a half, blond hair, blue eyes. Nothing could wake him. He'd slept through a fire alarm once, then sternly told off the fireman who'd carried him from the flat, for waking him up. Chrissie was different. Three years older but lacking her brother's robust build, Chrissie was slim like her mother. Slim and apparently fragile. Jean's own fragility was an illusion, a come-on to the punters; Chrissie would grow out of hers soon enough. It was in her genes. A gift from mother to daughter. A tool she would someday use to make her way in life.

Jean bent to brush a lock of brown hair from Chrissie's temple. The child turned away from her mother, snuggled up against the wall.

Repressing guilt, Jean said, 'I've got to go out, honey-buns. I'll be back soon.'

Chrissie hunched her shoulders against her mother's touch. Jean felt anger stir in her, somehow managed to let it go, let it drown in the love she had for her kids, the fear she experienced every time she left them alone. Her voice was a whisper as she said, 'I'll be bringing a friend back.'

Chrissie said nothing. Pretending to be asleep. But her breathing was fast, thready. She was angry. Another genetic present from her mother.

Jean understood that anger. 'I'll bring you back some chocolate, hons.' Even as she spoke Jean knew the words for the platitudes they were. Chocolate. I'll bring you chocolate. *Some messed-up punter who couldn't get a hard-on without a broom handle and some Vaseline, more like. Or an S&M freak with the face of a choirboy and a thing for Marks and Sparks rainwear.* Jesus. What she wouldn't give for one night of straight sex with a man she could love, respect, relate to. If he only jumped up and screamed when United scored it would be a start.

Ignoring Chrissie's stubborn silence, Jean McIlvanney

6

tucked in her daughter and walked to the front door. As she left the flat she made certain the door was double locked and the hall light was on. You couldn't be too careful these days.

Outside the night was warm, muggy. Stars poked sparsely through a sheet of umber cloud which coiled restlessly above the buildings of central Manchester like some smoky dragon. Jean unbuttoned her jacket. There. A few more wares for sale. A couple of cars passed her as she walked towards town along the main road. One driver revved his engine suggestively. Another grinned at her as he passed. Was he interested? No. Just his way of showing off to his mates. Or being friendly. Offering support. Part of a society that condemned women like herself, another sad bastard with enough associated guilt to sink a battleship.

Well he could stuff his support, his sympathy. She didn't need it.

Jean walked on. Overhead the streetlights glimmered faintly, orange on darkening clouds. Lowering her eyes to the ground, Jean walked on. A taxi passed, then a bunch of teenagers in an open-topped Land Rover. They all waved to her and some whistled, even the girls. Despite herself Jean smiled back. The Land Rover was followed by a quick succession of cars, a purple Mondeo, a gold Cavalier, a restored Hillman Imp. Jesus. She could be a traffic assessor working one day a fortnight and be earning more pro rata than tonight.

Jean walked on.

A man on a bicycle bumbled past. Raleigh Nirvana. Ten speed. Useless handgrips. Stupid plastic thing round the chainset that kept falling off. Jean watched the man as he skimmed past, avoiding eye contact. Another guilty one. Sheep. They did it to themselves.

Jean walked on. Half an hour. A succession of cars and faceless eyes in the night. She laughed to herself when she realised she could reel off the make and model of every

7

vehicle that passed her but couldn't remember a single detail about any of the drivers beyond the one thing that linked them all: the guilty expression whenever she challenged them with a look to pull over and conduct a transaction.

Turning a corner Jean began to walk along City Road. Her beat. *Think of yourself as a copper, love,* some old-timer had told her when she first went on the game. *Clark Kent patrolling the streets and keeping them free of pervs.*

Jean had frowned. *Yeah, right, Marge,* she'd replied in a cutting voice. *All the pervs'll be in my bed, right?*

Over the years Jean had found she wasn't wrong. And when Marge died of an overdose less than a year after they met, Jean was surprised to find how little it bothered her. Marge was an idiot. There wasn't a vein in her body left unscored by needle tracks at the end. The game had got her, hook, line and sinker, was using her. Marge was a victim.

Not Jean. As far as she was concerned it was the other way around. She was clean, sharp, on the button. She didn't use drugs, had no vices. She'd kicked Jim's father out when he turned violent shortly after Jim was born. He went with threats of violence and a final punch that bruised her cheek for a fortnight, but he went none the less. Jean had a couple of friends meet him after his weekly night out with the lads. Pissed, all he could do was succumb to the blows. He never found out who was responsible for the attack, assumed his broken jaw was due to a mugging. Jean never felt the need to tell him, to gloat. Why make problems for yourself? She'd had the satisfaction of hurting him the way he had hurt her. It was over. Except it wasn't over. Because that was how she'd got on the game. A violent husband who'd made her give up any chance she might've had of a real future, a country so deep into a recession that it was in danger of vanishing up its own behind, and the pittance the Social coughed up to help her; all these had driven her to a life society condemned. They'd taken away her choices and then made her a criminal. As far as Jean was concerned she was doing a job, plain and simple. Bread on the table for the kids. That was it. It wasn't her fault. She hadn't screwed the country. Just a few hundred sad blokes with slightly more money than sense.

Footsteps behind her. Jean turned, smiling. It was Denise Fletcher. Denny was the closest thing to a friend Jean had. On the streets anyway. Well, when you took away the rivalry; Jean kept herself sharper looking than Denise, although the other woman had more dress sense. Well, she had classier clothes anyway. And Jean had to admit, she looked sharp in them. *Sharp as a doctor's brand new pin*, as Marge would've said, then giggled aloud at the deliberately crude reference to abortion.

'Denny,' Jean said. 'Much doing?'

Denise smiled a little half smile. 'Nothing. There's been another march.'

By the tone of her voice you'd have thought Denise was talking about something that crawled in the gutter and begged for a freebie. The Reclaim the Night marches were growing ever more popular with the religious, the pious, the guilty-by-association. The marches were composed of mainly white, catholic, middle-class women and couples; were sanctioned by the local government and given a vaguely amused but none the less solid boost by the press. It was music for the masses. But it was popular. And it made total nonsense of your income.

Jean sighed. 'For God's sake. The kids need their dinner money. The rent's due.'

Denise kicked her heel absently against the pavement, striking a seductive pose without even seeming aware of it. 'I could lend you a tenner.'

Jean uttered a short, humourless laugh. 'I'm up to my eyes as it is.'

Denise sighed, bounced her handbag against her hip. She looked up and down the street and her expression said it all. 'What's wrong with them? Where are they all? I should be on the catwalk, not the flaming street. Come and get me!' She wiggled her bum suggestively at a passing motorist, grinned at Jean when the car pulled over and parked. But as she turned to walk towards the car the passenger door opened – exploded might be a better word – and a woman charged out screaming abuse at the driver.

Denise sighed and looked back at Jean, who hadn't moved because she'd already recognised the car, a dark blue Renault 5 with a slight dent in the nearside wing.

The woman who had left the car walked unsteadily towards them on high heels and Jean saw that it was Joyce Watkins. She was only twenty-two. The new kid on the block. Catholic upbringing. Everything shocked her. A classic case. Still, she'd get over it – or she'd get out.

Joyce hurled one last obscenity at the driver of the car and flounced away. She shook her head as she passed Jean and Denise. 'Flaming pervert. Thinks 'cos I look like a school-girl I've got the sense of one.'

Jean caught Denise's eye, nodded at the Renault. 'Shirley.'

Denise stifled a laugh. She walked up to the car and bent down to the passenger window, which was open. There was a momentary exchange of words, then Denise leaned backwards and said in a loud voice, 'Carry on dreaming, love,' and, with a flip of her hand to Jean, began to walk slowly away along the street.

Jean sighed. The Renault remained still, the window open. Jean stared at the car. Walked towards it. Bent down to the window. 'Hello, Dave.'

The driver looked sideways at her. Glasses, a weak chin, watery eyes above a thin body. 'Shirley Temple without a condom.' His voice was pitched a little high. Nerves shot, probably, after two rejections. Then again what did he expect? Joyce was right. If he did it with them he might've done it with anyone. And if, as seemed to be the case, he'd come over all faint with the thought of doing it in the buff, God alone knew what diseases he might be harbouring.

Then again, Dave was a punter, a regular who had never yet failed to pay up, and who, despite his sexual eccentricities, seemed harmless enough.

Jean stared at him through narrowed eyes. 'Shirley Temple. With a condom.'

Dave adjusted his glasses. 'Without.'

Jean sighed. 'With.'

'There's a girl round the corner who'll do it.'

'Then she's a fool.'

Dave frowned. Jean stepped back from the kerb, anticipating the moment of rejection. The Renault drove off suddenly. Turning away from the exhaust fumes, Jean saw Denise climbing into a Ford Sierra. Great. How was she going to feed the kids now? How was she going to get their dinner money?

A squeal of brakes. She turned. The Renault had pulled up a hundred yards along the road, braking lights gleaming in the darkness.

For the kids.

She walked up to the car, which reversed part way to meet her. Once again she was looking at Dave. This time he seemed calmer. As if he'd sussed her out. Well if he thought that he had another think coming. 'Shirley Temple without a condom,' she said to him. 'Hundred quid. Take it or leave it.'

Dave smiled. It was an odd, disconnected kind of smile. As if Dave were thinking about something else entirely while bartering a price for using her body. 'Thirty quid. With a condom.'

Jean sighed with relief. Now they were talking the same language. 'Fifty.'

'Forty.' Dave seemed to think about it. He tapped the steering wheel absently. 'There's not much doing tonight, is there?'

Jean sighed. 'OK, forty. But you better be one hell of a tipper.' She climbed into the car.

David drove them back to her flat. He drove carefully,

11

observing all road precautions. A responsible guy. Distant but responsible. He didn't make conversation, but that was OK. She wasn't there to discuss the finer points of life.

Once in her flat she made a quick visit to Jim and Chrissie. Both asleep. Gently hijacking Chrissie's bear JS she closed the door to the kids' room and led David into her own bedroom. There she undressed for him, posed naked with JS. David followed her into the room, stood beside the bed. Watched as she undressed. He told her to sing. How much is that doggie? She sang quietly. He told her to sing louder. With a thought for the children, she notched the volume up a little. She posed seductively for him. He told her not to. He told her to sit on the chair beside the dresser. She sat. She did everything he told her. Then he began to swear at her, his voice never rising above a dull monotone. How could he do it? Eradicate all feeling from words meant solely to express anger, fear, loathing? His voice never changed. On and on. Slut. Bitch. Filthy. Teach you. Begging for it. Twelve years old. Gagging for it. Show you. Come here. Now. Now. Now. Open wide, baby, here comes Daddy.

She clutched Chrissie's bear as David surrendered to orgasm. *Thank Christ*, she thought. *Thank Christ and all the little angels I'm not his kid.*

Afterwards he dressed quickly. He didn't look at her as she dressed herself. When they were both ready and she'd checked on the children once more, she found Dave groping in his wallet for money.

His expression of pathetic concern and embarrassment when the wallet turned out to be empty was laughable. Almost.

'I've got no money.' It was the first time she'd ever heard feeling in his voice. He sounded lost, a little kid in a big shopping mall, hunting for Mum. Well he'd get no sympathy from her. She'd been Shirley Temple for him, hijacking Chrissie's bear to do so. She'd sung for him and let him

12

use her and now he was going to pay. One way or another.

She stood before him, looked up at him. 'What are you saying? You got no money? I can't believe you said that.'

David shook out his wallet in a pathetic gesture. 'I had a fifty slotted down the side here. My wife must've taken it. Shopping. You know.'

'You're damn right I know. That money was for my kids' dinner money tomorrow. And the rent.'

'I'll drop it by in the morning.'

'In your dreams.' Jean reached out and plucked the wallet from David's fingers. 'What have we got here? Barclaycard? That'll do nicely.'

'You can't have that, it's Maggie's. It's –'

'It's what you *owe me*, David.' Jean reached for David's jacket and threw it at him. 'Now take me to your cash machine before I do something you'll regret.'

Jean took the bear back to Chrissie's room. The girl was awake. Pretending to be asleep again. 'I'll just be five minutes, hons.' Chrissie ignored her. Feeling more and more angry by the minute, Jean left the room, closing the door gently behind her.

She grabbed David by the hand and dragged him through the flat. 'Get a move on will you.'

David allowed himself to be hustled out of the flat and into the Renault. If Jean had thought about it she might have felt the first edge of tension in his body then; the set of his limbs, the resistance, the colour draining from his face to be replaced by his former bland politeness. She didn't, though, because she was too concerned with getting the money he owed her. For the rent. For the kids.

The high-street banks were five minutes' drive towards town.

When they got there she made him get out of the car first, then followed him to the cash machine. She shoved in the card. She looked at him. 'Well? What are you waiting for?'

He tapped in a number. The machine bleeped. She tapped

13

in the request for fifty pounds herself. The machine bleeped again.

INSUFFICIENT FUNDS AVAILABLE TO COMPLETE THIS TRANSACTION.

Jean swore, tapped in a lower figure.

INSUFFICIENT FUNDS AVAILABLE TO COMPLETE THIS TRANSACTION.

With a bleak look at David, Jean tapped in a request for the lowest cash amount you could withdraw. A tenner. A lousy tenner.

INSUFFICIENT FUNDS AVAILABLE TO COMPLETE THIS TRANSACTION.

Jean uttered a short humourless laugh. Beside her David was growing more and more agitated by the moment. When she thrust his card contemptuously back into his hand he flushed bright red.

'Well?' she demanded in a loud voice.

'That's probably why she took the money from my wallet . . .'

Behind them a middle-aged couple waited impatiently in line for their go at the terminal.

'What about your account?'

David began to stutter. 'My wages went in on Wednesday. It was a cheque. It can't have cleared yet.'

A young man with a punk-style haircut and torn leather jacket joined the queue.

Jean glared at David. 'What're you going to do then?'

'I don't know.'

' "I don't know?" "I don't know!" ' Jean cast a look around at the people waiting for the cash machine, then quickly back to the man shivering beside her. 'I dress up like Shirley Temple and screw your brains out for an hour and then you tell me you've got no money? Jesus Christ, David, what are you going to do about it?'

'I'll. I. I'll sort it. I'll –'

Another figure had shambled up by now. A wine-sodden

14

tramp, huge, dressed in filthy clothes, his face terribly scarred on one side; half-empty bottle clutched in one hand, the other outstretched for a possible handout. 'Never put yer faith in technology.' A foul stench of uncleaned teeth and inner rot brought the man's words to Jean. She curled her lip in disgust. Some people had no self-respect.

David looked wildly round at the new voice. 'Yes, thank you,' he said politely to the man. Turning to Jean he added, 'It'll clear by tomorrow . . .'

'I told you. I need it *tonight*. You're going to have to borrow it.'

The tramp added usefully, 'Technology. No heart. No soul. Can't tell a machine you're desperate for cash. Can't tell a machine about the kids, the mortgage.'

'Right on, baby,' said the punk.

Behind Jean the woman coughed impatiently.

Aware he had an audience, the tramp told Jean, 'We're all gettin' replaced by machines. Machines are makin' machines. This machine was made by another machine. And that machine was made by another machine and that one by . . .' Losing his thread momentarily, the tramp took another hit from his bottle and began again. 'Japanese machines. German machines. Korean machines. Classy them ones are. Not like English machines. They're a load of old rubbish. It's the recession. We'll be buyin' in machines from all over soon just to run the country, you mark me –'

Jean glared at the tramp. 'I'll mark you all right if you don't sod off.' She stared at the three people waiting in line behind her. 'You got kids have you?' she said to the woman. 'Well, I'm doing the best I can by them, so don't you judge me.'

The woman frowned, turned and dragged her husband back to the waiting car.

Jean called after them, 'What would you do if your boss screwed you over for fifty quid? Go to the bloody union, that's what. Well, I ain't got a union, have I? And who's fault is that?'

15

The couple got into their car and drove off. Jean turned to glare at the punk.

He grinned. 'Fancy a quick shag then, do ya?'

'Jesus Christ!' Jean dragged David away from the cashpoint and back to the car. 'I need that money or I go straight to the cops and scream rape. Right now. 'Cos that's what it is. Rape. We had an agreement. I did my bit; you won't do yours.'

David spluttered. Whatever he might have said was lost as the tramp sidled up to them again, warming to his theme nicely.

'We the people have been made redundant by the machines. Everything's untouched by human hand. Nobody working. Nobody earning money to buy the machines the machines are making. A solution is needed. Wipe out the redundant people. How do you wipe them out?' The tramp paused as if consideration of this point was of vital importance, then hit a less than interested Jean with his punchline. 'Use the machines, that's how. Ships, planes, tanks, bombs, guns. Use the machines to kill the people.'

Jean turned to the tramp with such a look of anger that he took a step backwards, bolstering his courage with another gulp from the bottle. Jean couldn't believe it when he continued, 'The machines will win, you know. Machines are making better machines and those machines are . . .' he thought a moment, 'making better machines and they're all getting better at wiping us out and one day they will.'

Jean felt a lot like wiping the tramp out herself. Managing to hang on to her temper by the skin of her teeth, she shoved David back into the car and climbed in herself.

'You borrow the money, David. From a friend, a beer-buddy, from your wife if you have to. It's that or we're straight off to the nick now and I'll claim you raped me.'

David looked at her then. 'You made me use a condom. There's no evidence.' His voice was no longer calm, just a hint of excitement, like someone testing out a new theory to see where it might lead.

16

'*Will you please just get me the money you owe me, David!*'

Abruptly David started the car and pulled away. The acceleration caught Jean by surprise. She rocked back in the passenger seat, then spent a confused thirty seconds grappling with the seatbelt.

'Where are you going?'

David did not reply. He did accelerate. The Renault sped along the main road out of town.

'What are you up to, David? Are we going to get my money? We'd better be or else it's rape, you know. And I don't care who knows it.'

David said nothing. He said nothing as they turned onto the ring road and accelerated again. By this time the first tingle of uncertainty was jittering along her spine, fizzing out through her nervous system and goosing her brain.

David turned off the ring road then. Drove through roads that narrowed until they became a dirt track leading into the green belt land.

Jean laughed nervously. 'Hey, David, your friends live miles away, do you know that? I could let you have a couple of quid off for petrol if you like.'

David made no reply, hands clenching the wheel, turning gently to guide the car through the maze of woodland. She became aware for the first time just how big his hands were. In fact they were enormous. And calloused. Was he a carpenter? Why hadn't she noticed that before? Why hadn't she even thought of that before? Because he'd been just another punter, that's why. Another sad bloke with slightly more money than sense. So she'd thought.

The Renault bounced over tractor ruts. They were in a field. The city lights spread out to one side, a river of bright yellow ochre and white. Above her cloud dragons fumed silent umber. Above them distant stars promised nothing except the overwhelming knowledge of isolation. Jean had a sudden image of herself alone in this field, alone in the night

17

on a planet which itself was alone in yet a larger night. And that was when the flicker of nervousness she'd been feeling turned into full blown fear.

'OK. That's it. Stop the car, I'm out of here. Right now, David! Stop the car!'

He turned to look at her then. 'You made me use a condom. There's no evidence.'

Jean looked at him, felt her mouth open in stunned realisation. Then she was scrabbling at the door and the seatbelt catch simultaneously, screaming abuse as she did so.

The car juddered to a stop, the door flew open and Jean tumbled out into the night. Her foot caught on the seatbelt strap and she fell. Cold, hard earth pressed into her cheek. She could feel the heat from the Renault's engine inches from her head. A ticking sound came from the car. Metal cooling in the night. She began to crawl. Her shoe came off. There was dirt in her stockings. Dirt in her clothes, her hair, her mouth.

A hand on her shoulder swung her round. She swung a fist wild in anger; felt her arm jerk as she missed completely. A moment then a blow rocked her head, sent her reeling onto her back.

David loomed over her and she knew what he was going to do to her.

'David,' she mumbled through numb lips. 'I'll do anything. Shirley Temple without a condom. Only please stop. OK? Stop now. Please.'

David stopped.

She began to sing. 'How much is that doggie?' David put his head on one side and listened closely.

Oh God, thank Christ, he was listening. She'd got him. Now with just a little more effort she'd be away from him and back with the kids –

He said, 'You made me use a condom. There's no evidence.'

Jean screamed then.

He bent down beside Jean, his breath sweet against her cheek, held her down with those big hands of his; held her down and pounded her face until hot blood bubbled out of her mouth and the pain took her somewhere far away.

She never felt him rise from her, leave her, return a moment later with something taken from the boot of the Renault. This time it wasn't like before. She felt something cold inside her. Something cold and hard and icicle sharp.

He shoved again, harder this time. Shoved. Twisted.

Something tore inside her.

And there was pain; cascades, a cataract of pain that swept her away from her life, her children.

Jean McIlvanney summoned the strength to cry out but death stilled the scream in her bruised throat before she could utter a sound.

TWO

Afterwards they would say it began with the rape but in truth, for Jimmy Beck, it began long before that. It began in Belfast, when Beck had been just a kid. Just one among hundreds dossing around, bunking off school, playing footey in the fields instead of doing his homework. Just some kid, no-one special. Except that Daddy had thought he was special. Very special. And it had taken little Jimmy Beck a long time to get used to just how very special Daddy thought he had been.

Daddy was dead now, and Mother. And Beck had moved to the mainland. Manchester, via Liverpool. On the way he had collected a number of qualifications and the rank of Detective Sergeant in the Manchester Met. Infrequently, Beck had wondered whether his parents would have been proud to know that. The truth was when your daddy told you he loved you while hurting you the way he had and your mother stood by and allowed it to happen, then nothing was clear-cut any more. But although Beck hated his parents – had hated them, he now realised, for more years than he was comfortable remembering – there was still a part of him, the part that had heard the words *I love you, son* and responded to them with acceptance, that was glad his parents weren't alive to see his shame, to know that they were at least as responsible for the rape as he was himself.

During the last thirty years little Jimmy Beck had grown into an insular man, powerfully built, aggressive, unforgiving and relentless. Until very recently he had been an angry man; the anger had been growing in him for years, planted

21

there by his father and nurtured, among other things, by his mother's refusal to acknowledge the truth of little Jimmy's fear. But Beck also knew that he had been responsible for the growth of that anger himself.

In the months since the rape he'd stayed away from work; done a lot of thinking, a lot of reading. The rape had begun with the seed of anger, true, but what had blossomed into violation was equally due to bad healing of his own wounds, and for that no-one was responsible but himself. Oh yes. Beck had read the books about rape. He understood himself now. He was an infection. An old wound that had not been properly tended, one from which the infection had crept insidiously throughout the rest of his life, contaminating everything he did, everything he was, until the Jimmy Beck that was the host for the disease simply no longer existed, and he had become the disease, become the fear.

Become the anger.

And now he was shut in with the anger, into his darkened flat, a hot zone of infection where a week's washing up mouldered in the sink, where a fortnight's dirty laundry festered in the bathroom, where the windows hadn't been opened to let out the smell of tobacco and whisky for nearly a month.

Where the gun still rested on the Welsh dresser.

Her prints would still be on the gun, even after a month. Still be there as evidence, a connection. He hadn't touched the gun in all that time. But he kept it there, refusing to put it away or clean it. He needed it there. The gun belonged to his father. And Jimmy Beck needed that gun now more than ever. It was like a time machine. A link to the reason he had raped. Not that Jimmy Beck needed reasons any more. He had reasons and understanding enough from the books. The gun represented a solution. A month before, when he had attempted to implement that solution he had lacked the strength. But strength came through understanding. And the one thing Jimmy Beck knew about himself now was that

22

this infection that he was, this viral colony of rage, had to be cleansed. No matter who it affected, no matter what effort it took.

The sound of the front door bell interrupted his indul-gently masochistic chain of thought. Irritably he rose from the sofa, dodged a week's accumulation of pizza delivery boxes and opened the door. 'What do you know.' Beck's voice cracked, as if he hadn't spoken for a month, as if getting the words out was the hardest thing he'd ever done. 'Mister Blobby.'

He stood in the doorway, a huge man squashed into a space ample for an average-sized adult. Edward Fitzgerald, clinical psychologist. Brilliant clinical psychologist. Also fat, irritating, misogynistic, smug. In Beck's book, a man to hate for a great many reasons.

Fitz squeezed through into the flat when Beck didn't shut the door in his face. 'Thought I'd come and see you on the eve of your return to work. Check out the old psyche, make sure everything was ticking along hunky dory. Wouldn't like to think you were some time bomb about to be let loose on an unsuspecting society, now would we?'

Beck suppressed his desire to swear with an effort. 'You know as well as I do why you're here and it's got nothing to do with how fit I am to return to work.'

Fitz didn't acknowledge Beck's words, merely continued with his own vaguely condescending babble. 'Thanks for letting me in, Jimmy. I was expecting to have to carry on a conversation from the other side of the door, like last time.'

Annoyed, Beck said nothing, moved back into the living room.

Fitz followed. 'I've brought you a present.' He produced a bottle of whisky and two glasses from a Valubuys carrier bag, brushed aside a week's worth of dirty cutlery and overflowing ashtrays from the table and set the items down. 'Actually I brought you two presents.' Fitz groped in his pocket and produced a plastic ball of air freshener, which he

23

set beside the whisky. 'I couldn't decide which you'd need the most.' He stared around the flat and wrinkled his nose. 'Well, I suppose that's one question answered.' He twisted the airball fully open.

Beck sighed as the sickly scent of roses filled the room. Fitz made him want to puke. His irrepressible compassion and irritating humour. He was pathetic. That he was almost invariably correct in his assumptions was a source of unending frustration to Beck. Beck was a copper, the old school. Thump 'em 'til they bleed or confess. They understood that. Not Fitz. Fitz liked to empathise. To visualise. To understand. While seconded to the police he had scored an impressive, though mixed, track record of cases. Now Beck himself had become one of Fitz's cases. Not officially. But in the month following the rape Fitz had butted into his life so often that Beck simply found it easier to see him than not. Last time he had visited, Fitz had left a book he had co-authored about the psychological link between rapists and victims for Beck to read. Fitz had told him the book was a bestseller. After reading the accounts of trauma victims, Beck could see why. It was more entertaining than *Brookside*.

Fitz opened the bottle and poured two generous measures into the glasses. Beck took his without comment.

'Scunthorpe.' Fitz downed his drink in one, filled the glass again. Beck felt Fitz's eyes rake across his own untouched glass. 'Careful, Jimmy, you'll leave me standing if you keep drinking at that rate.'

Beck swung angrily on Fitz. 'Everything's a contest for you, isn't it?'

Fitz sipped his drink and smiled infuriatingly.

Beck said, 'Even finding out if your bit on the side was raped or not.'

Fitz's smile faded, his lips thinning to a line. 'Detective Sergeant Jane Penhaligon was not my "bit on the side". She was my lover.' He set down his glass. 'Why did you rape

24

her, Jimmy?' Fitz's voice was flat, no anger, no concern; a robot.

Beck laughed inwardly. With Fitz everything was a game. Beck was a rapist and yet Fitz had come to him for absolution. Because when Penhaligon'd asked Fitz for help he hadn't been there for her.

Still, if he wanted to play the game . . . 'You've never raped anyone?' Beck asked pointedly.

Fitz stared at Beck then reached for his glass. 'No.'

'You're a liar.'

'I'm not.'

'How old are you?'

'Forty-six.'

Beck grinned then, sipped his own drink. 'Got your end away for the first time, what . . . thirty years ago?'

'Thirty-one. Thelma Edison.'

Beck studied Fitz then. Studied Fitz the way he himself had been studied so often in the recent past. 'And the ones after Thelma? Back alley, back seat of a car, they struggle a bit but you're full of booze, won't take no for an answer.' Beck stared narrowly at Fitz. 'But then what's your left hand for? It's to grab their wrists while your right hand roams free, isn't that it, Fitz? And you keep on doing it, don't you, until you're sure, until you're bloody positive you're going to get nothing. Only then do you stop.'

Fitz swallowed his drink and poured another. Beck watched him. Fitz looked up. His face told Beck everything he wanted – needed – to know.

'We've all done it. Everyone my age and over. We've all done it. We could all be had up for rape, right?'

Beck saw Fitz relax suddenly. The psychologist smiled.

'You said, "Everyone my age".'

'So?' Beck put down his drink, made a roll-up, jammed it between his lips.

Fitz watched him do all this.

'So?' Beck asked again.

'You were talking about me. You should have said, "Anyone *your* age." Or "Anyone *our* age." But you didn't. You said, "Anyone *my* age." '

Beck felt the old anger rise inside him. 'Don't you dare take that tone of voice with me. I know what you're thinking. Well I'm not some bit of muck!'

But Fitz wouldn't back off. 'We're not talking about date rape, Jimmy. You wore a mask, carried a knife. You knocked her about a bit.' Fitz took a step closer to Beck and his voice hardened. 'She thought you were going to kill her.'

Beck locked eyes with Fitz, saw how desperately he wanted Beck to agree, to acknowledge that Fitz was right. He sucked on his roll-up and said nothing.

After a moment more Fitz turned away, went to the window. 'Mind if I open this?'

Beck shrugged.

Fitz turned back from the window. 'You've been to the hospital. I've read your case notes. Stress. Depression. Prone to anxiety attacks.' A moment, a penetrating look. 'Guilt does that to a man.'

Beck blinked, sucked on his roll-up. 'Why should I rape her? I've screwed her. I got sick of screwing her, so why should I rape her?'

Fitz pursed her lips. 'Convince me.'

Beck smiled, blew smoke. 'There's a little heart. Tattooed on the inside of her thigh.'

Fitz's expression hardened. 'Now I know you raped her.'

And suddenly Beck felt laughter bubbling up inside. 'A rapist is going to see that is he? Rip 'em off, stick it in, a dark field in the middle of nowhere and he's going to see a little thing like that?'

Fitz reached for his empty glass, filled it again.

Beck said, 'You kissed her little tattoo, Fitz, yeah? Felt her hair tickle your cheek as you kissed it?'

Fitz lifted the glass to his lips, swallowed hard.

'For God's sake, you've been there. If a fat piss artist like you can screw her, anyone can.'

Fitz smiled wryly. 'She said something similar.' It was obvious to Beck the words hurt.

Beck blew smoke at Fitz. 'There you go then. Surprising, isn't it, Fitz? A nice bit of stuff like that and she's so . . . well, willing. When I was a kid I'd cop off with the dog. You know the way there was always a nice one and an ugly one. Well, I'd cop off with the ugly one, the dog. I thought I'd have more chance of screwing the dog, you see. I was wrong. You've got just as much chance with the nice one.'

'You've been at the *Guardian* again, haven't you?'

Beck grinned, blew more smoke. 'Your book, actually.' He studied Fitz, waited for a response. When there was none, he continued, 'Bilborough screwed her.' The lie hurt Beck just as much as Fitz. But it was all part of the game. The sacrifice you made to win. 'He was my best friend and now he's dead. Do you think I'd lie about something like that?'

'I think you're capable of anything.'

'You don't want to hear it, do you, Fitz? Screwing Penhaligon was the highlight of your life and now it means nothing because we've all been there before you. It means absolutely nothing.'

Fitz made an abortive attempt at a grin. The empty whisky glass was shaking in his hand but he didn't think to put it down. Beck caught his glance for a moment and was unsurprised to see the rage there. 'If you want to do it, Fitz, do it. Don't just stand there looking menacing. Do it!'

Beck was assaulted by a savage memory. DCI David Bilborough lying in the gutter in a lake of blood, back arched across the kerb, stomach ripped open and steaming in the late afternoon sunlight.

He grabbed onto the image, used the guilt and anger to fuel his own stance against Fitz. 'Whoever did it, whoever raped her deserves a medal. She ponces around, flashes it about, she wants you to look, what do you see?'

27

Bilborough being zipped into a body bag, himself on his knees, blood all over his hands, begging Penhaligon not to tell anyone that it was his fault, that it was his, Jimmy Beck's fault that his boss and best friend was dead –

'She's looking at you like muck, that's what. And all that come-on, that chat, the eyes, was all so she could put you down. Because she enjoyed that. Putting you down.'

As he'd enjoyed putting her down later. Putting her down and raping her. It was as clear as daylight in his mind. The rape. And afterwards: the break-in. The gun in his mouth. His own gun held in his mouth *and she was bucking on top of him, raping him with the gun as he had raped her and he was begging her to kill him, to pull the trigger and kill him but what came out were platitudes, excuses, because in the death he was terrified that she had the strength to do to him that which he couldn't do himself –*

'Impotent. You can't get a stiffie, they call you impotent. They're wrong. You're impotent when you do get a stiffie. You're at their mercy then. They've got the power. And they abuse that power. They're tarts. Every single one of them. Tarts.'

There was a long silence. Then Fitz said slowly, 'I want you to tell me you raped her. She needs that. Needs you to acknowledge your guilt.'

Beck uttered a humourless laugh. 'I've had that for weeks, Fitz. Counsellors and therapists, psychologists, psychiatrists, all coming out with bullshit like that. I've got an A level in it. I'll tell you what you want, shall I? I'll tell you what you really want. You want to go back to her like the all-conquering bloody hero and tell her I admitted it and for her to be so damn grateful she'd let you get your leg over right then and there. That's what you really want, isn't it Fitz?'

Fitz grinned then, a casual, friendly grin, and Beck realised the whole thing from beginning to end had been a set-up. A way of getting him to talk. And he'd fallen for it.

Fitz hadn't wanted him to admit to raping anyone; only to decide if he was capable of rape.

Fitz's grin widened as he realised Beck had twigged on. 'You find sex a rather interesting subject, don't you, Jimmy?' he asked in an insufferably smug voice.

Beck felt anger bloom inside him again. 'I know what you want to do to me, Fitz. Well, if you want to do it, Fitz, do it. Come on, do it!'

Fitz was a big man. When he butted Beck, Beck knew about it. He fell heavily onto the sofa as Fitz stomped out of the flat, fell and squashed pizza boxes and grinned as he felt blood burst from his nose and run down his face. He felt like laughing but didn't. Because although the pain brought a kind of absolution it wasn't enough to balance the guilt he felt. Not nearly enough. Yet.

THREE

In the presbytery of St Catherine's church a fire roared to dispel the damp gloom of the evening. The flames painted swathes of orange across the wooden table and chairs, the old-fashioned wallpaper, the comfortably faded rug and sofa. Father Michael Harvey had his feet up in front of the telly, watching *Hill Street Blues* while preparing the sermon for the following morning. Michael was a thick-set man, prematurely bald, with piercing blue eyes and a ruddy complexion. Those unfamiliar with him could often be heard to say his was the face of a drinker, but Michael only smiled when he heard these rumours. He was a drinker no more; in truth had really only ever gone for the odd Malibu, and then only because he liked the taste of coconut. These days a good chunk of Bounty satisfied his craving as much as any devil's brew. God had shown him the way and chocolate was it.

St Catherine's was a small parish located in the heart of Manchester. He had inherited the parish from Old Man McGruder, who had run the church before him and to whom he'd been apprenticed. Michael smiled when he thought of his apprenticeship – and that was when the knocking came at his front door.

Not just knocking.

Frantic, wall-shaking hammering.

His plans for a quiet evening frustrated, Michael abandoned both television and sermon to answer the door. When he did so he felt the curiosity on his face change to alarm – felt the muscles spasm in involuntary surprise.

31

It was his brother, David.

'Dave?' There was no tremor in his voice, but he felt himself begin to shake none the less. Shake inside where it counted most. Where it frightened him the most.

David was shaking too. 'Bless me, Father, for I have sinned.' His voice was thin, wavery, as if squeezed out of a body unwilling to let it go.

Michael stared closely at his brother, could see nothing apparently wrong. 'Dave. What's the matter, lad? What's wrong?'

'Bless me, Father, for *I have sinned*!'

Michael held the door open, but still had to practically pull his brother into the hall. As for David he was repeating the same phrase over and over, mindless reiteration of his desperate plea for forgiveness, understanding; and more, the need for confidentiality that came with a parishioner/priest relationship – something that was dubious at best in their relationship as brothers. The words began to run together, his mouth pushing spittle down his chin until Michael did the only thing he could do; dragged David into the kitchen and sat him at the table, poured him a double shot of Old Man McGruder's last half bottle of brandy and made him swallow it all.

David fell silent, then blinked. He looked at Michael, stared right through him.

'Dave –'

'Bless me, Father, for I have sinned. Bless me, Father, for I have sinned! *BlessmeFatherforIhave –*'

'Right, then, lad, that'll be enough of that!'

Michael poured another shot of brandy into his brother's glass and made him swallow it. At last some colour began to appear in David's pale cheeks.

'Right. Are you hurt? No? What about Maggie? The kids?'

Silence.

'Well, what's up then?'

Again, no reply from David. He just clutched the glass and shivered.

Michael sighed. 'Here, lad, give me that glass, look you've spilt it all down yourself, and you know how it'll stain –'

Michael stopped as he reached for the glass. The stains on David's coat weren't brandy. They were darker. Shaking, he opened the coat and pulled it off.

The stains were blood.

David's clothes were covered with blood.

'Holy Mother of God.' Michael's eyes widened in amazement.

'Bless me, Father, for I have sinned.'

Michael suddenly found himself seated opposite David. Brother opposite brother, between them the brandy, the bloodstained coat and a growing sense of fear.

'May the Lord help you to confess your sins with true sorrow.' Michael licked his lips. The terror building inside him left him no recourse but to clutch vainly at his own faith; the two of them playing out the game of religion, the game of understanding and forgiveness, each a crutch to the other's weakness.

'Michael . . .' David began to cry. His head went down on the table, scattering the glass and brandy bottle. Alcohol flooded the table and dripped onto the floor. 'I've taken a life. I've murdered someone.'

And Michael listened while David confessed to him the evening's events; horror layered upon horror, until he felt like crying out for relief from the pain. And through it all not once did David raise his eyes to meet those of his brother, not once did he lift his gaze from the table or from the floor, where the remains of the brandy fell, drop by drop, into a slowly growing puddle. Only at the end did he look up, as if talking, telling the tale had given him strength enough to ask the final question.

'Michael . . . what shall I do?'

33

Michael didn't hesitate. 'Tell the police.'

David looked away again, a sob caught in his throat. 'I can't!'

'How can you expect to live with a thing like this on your conscience? If you don't report it they'll catch you and it'll go the harder for you.'

'I've got kids.'

'From what you say she had kids too.'

'I'll go to prison. For life. I can't do that, Michael. I can't, I just *can't* . . .'

'You selfish –' An angry sigh. 'David, she's *dead*! Do you hear me? Dead. She's dead. You killed her!'

The anger in Michael's voice had David in tears again. The tears just made Michael even angrier. And frustrated. Nothing in his past had prepared him for this.

David was looking at him again, eyes shining with renewed hope. 'I'm not thinking of me. I'm thinking of Maggie and the kids. Someone's got to look after them.'

Michael felt himself sickened by his brother's self-serving justification. 'You've murdered another human being!'

'Only a prostitute.'

'There's nothing only about it! She was a person. A woman. A human being. God made us in his image, David. He made us all, he made us equal!'

'But she was just a prostitute!'

'Who's more worthy, David? A woman who sins by prostitution, or a man who sins by murder?'

David began to shake. 'Whatever I do it's not going to bring her back.'

Michael felt a rage build inside him, felt his stomach shrivelling up with tension. 'Come with me to the church. We must pray together for guidance.'

'Yes, Father. Yes, of course.'

'And call me Michael will you? I am your brother.'

The church was dark, gloomy with shadows, wood-panelled walls, pews, pulpit, nave that were cheerful during the day seeming displaced somehow now. Or maybe it was Michael that felt displaced. As if he'd taken some sideways leap into an alternative dimension where people you knew and loved suddenly turned out to be monsters lost beyond any hope of redemption. He shook off the feeling, lit some candles, led David to the font.

David dipped his hands into the water to bless himself. Blood from his hands mixed with the water, swirled gently until it vanished completely.

Michael wished the problem would vanish as simply. 'You're sure she's dead?'

David nodded dumbly. He stared at the water dripping from his hands, the blood running into the water and dripping into the font. 'Help me.'

Michael frowned. 'I'm not going to absolve you, that's for sure.' He stared at David, lifted his eyes from the font to the image of Christ hanging from the wooden cross. He closed his eyes. What should he do? His brother had committed the first sin, that of murder. But David was his *brother*. And did the Lord not teach that all should be responsible for their brothers? Oh for crying out loud, why was the path so unclear! A touch of neon, Lord, the odd catseye to show the way. These signs he could understand. But this? This crisis of morality? *What in the name of the Lord was he to do?*

Michael remained in a state of prayer until David shuffled sideways a step and broke his concentration. He opened his eyes. He'd reached a decision. Good or bad, he'd be judged on it when the time for judgement came. He caught and held his brother's gaze. 'For the rest of your life you've got an obligation to her kids. You look after them. That's time and money and effort. Can you promise me that?'

'Yes, Father.' David spoke without looking up.

Michael sighed. 'Break that promise and I go straight to the police.'

'Yes, Father.'

'OK.' Feeling himself slip ever further from the path, Michael told David what he wanted him to do. 'We'll get rid of those clothes. Every stitch. I've some that'll fit you. Scrub the car from top to bottom. Spotless. Then we'll drive to the field where you left her.'

'No . . .'

'We'll drive to the field where you left her and we'll bury her –'

'No, Michael, don't make me I can't do that I just can't –'

'You've got to do it, got to bury her, you've got to!'

'You don't understand, I can't, please don't make me Oh God Our Father Who art in Heaven Hallowed be Thy Name oh please don't make me Michael, *I can't do it I can't!*'

'Jesus Christ, David!' Michael struggled to regain his breath. He was flogging a dead horse here. 'Then ditch the car. Walk home. I'll come with you. Report the car stolen in the morning.'

'And Maggie?'

'Tell her everything.'

'Oh God help me. How can I do that?'

The pathetic whine in his brother's voice made Michael want to be sick. 'If you won't bury the body, it's going to be discovered. You'll need an alibi.'

'She was a *prostitute*. I can't tell Maggie I've been with a –'

'Yes you can, David, you can. Because if you don't you'll go to prison and I'll be damned forever for supporting your lies, if I'm not already. You need an alibi. Maggie will have to be it. She'll have been watching telly. You need every detail of every programme she watched. That's your alibi. You sat in all night and watched telly with Maggie.'

David swallowed, bowed his head even lower. More water from his clutching hands dripped into the font, and more blood with it. 'I can't.'

'Oh yeah, right. You can't tell your wife you've been with

36

a prostitute, but you're capable of killing another human being?' Michael squeezed every ounce of contempt he possessed into his voice; the pay-off was worth it.

'I'll do it.'

'Amen to that.'

So they burned David's clothes, and they cleaned the car with Chlorox and a number of other industrial products, cleaned until the fumes reeked in the upholstery and the carpets threatened to dissolve. Then Michael drove David home and waited while he went inside. A few moments later, when the sound of Maggie's angry voice came from the bedroom, Michael lowered his head to the steering wheel and prayed as he had never prayed before in his life. Prayed for guidance, for strength. But most of all he prayed he'd done the right thing in advising David to confess to his wife.

Though he sat in the car for another two hours he found no comfort in his prayers, no love, no strength. Just the cold ache of loneliness and a bitter sensation of guilt growing in his heart.

And over the next two hours Father Michael Harvey became gradually possessed of the most terrible fear; the utter certainty that he had made a great mistake, perhaps the greatest in his life; and that as a result of this a great many others would suffer. Try as he might he could not dispel this fear, this certainty.

When he could bear the sensation no longer, he started the Renault, drove it ten miles out of town and abandoned it, and then walked home. He walked all night but could not leave behind the fear.

FOUR

At about the same time that David Harvey was confessing the most awful sin of his life to his elder brother, Jane Penhaligon, Detective Sergeant in the Manchester Metropolitan Police, was also screwing up her courage, but for a very different reason.

She was looking at herself in the bathroom mirror. Looking at herself and wondering, was this the face of a victim? Were these small ears and these green eyes and this pale skin and this tightly bound red hair those of a *victim*?

She had been asking herself the same question for more than a month. Actually, that wasn't quite true. Actually, wouldn't it be more true to say she had been *avoiding* asking herself that question for more than a month?

That was the key word here. Avoiding. As, say, she was avoiding hearing the ringing of her flat door bell right now. A soft tone but insistent, one that had been buzzing gently now for nearly five minutes while she had been staring fixedly at her reflection in the bathroom mirror.

Avoiding because she knew who would be there. And why.

Giving in to the noise, she donned a dressing gown and answered the door. A mountain of a man was standing in the corridor outside. Edward Fitzgerald, doctor, psychologist. Her lover. Her friend. Her betrayer.

Fitz stared at her as the door opened, said nothing as she stared at him, gauged the reaction on his face. Guilt. She could smell it. As if the emotion were whisky and someone had upended a bottle over his head.

'Panhandle,' he said eventually.

She didn't allow herself a reaction.

Fitz held aloft an invisible hat, rubbing his flat-top with his fingers and screwing his face up into a ridiculous impression of Stan Laurel.

She didn't smile.

Eventually he allowed his hand to fall back to his side.

'Panhandle, please.'

His voice was deep, held a northern lilt. The voice, like the man, could be by turns sarcastic and seductive, deliberately obtuse or bitingly intelligent. Penhaligon knew this of old, but whereas the knowledge once turned her on, now it only angered her. Once she would have sparred verbally for a couple of hours over a bottle of Chardonnay while anticipating some of the best sex she'd ever had, now she felt only a faint revulsion. Fitz had used her, had never loved her. She had been committed to him and he had dropped her like a hot brick when his estranged wife had breezed back through the door. In truth, Penhaligon knew she was hardly being fair to Fitz, things hadn't been as simple as that. Judith was pregnant. Penhaligon herself had been raped. But her hate wasn't any less because of that. Her thoughts for this man, her ex-friend and ex-lover, were coloured now by an anger that ran far deeper than any petty betrayal of her love.

Fitz had betrayed her as a friend. She had needed him and he had not been there for her.

A month ago under circumstances she was only just learning to deal with, she had been raped by a colleague, DS Jimmy Beck. Later she had broken into his flat to find proof of the rape, held his father's gun in his mouth when he had discovered her there, had been utterly set in her resolve to kill him.

And Fitz, the one person who could have eased the rage out of her, sucked out the poison Beck had put into her, chose to be with his wife instead.

She remembered sitting astride Beck as he lay cringing on the floor, holding his own gun in his mouth, raping him as he had raped her, using the fear, the penetration, and Jimmy Beck had gone somewhere over the edge of fear, mumbling about having been raped as a kid himself, and she had pulled the trigger because right then, more than anything else in the world, and in defiance of both her training and her own ethical code, she had wanted to take a human life, take it and end it; wanted that so badly she could taste it as she had tasted him in her mouth with the blood when he had hit her and filled her with his seed of terror and rage.

And Fitz could have stopped it. Even after she'd pulled the trigger on Beck, Fitz could have saved her. Saved her from her own anger. Because the fact that the gun was unloaded was irrelevant. Because it had never been about Beck, it had only ever been about her. Her anger, her way of dealing with the rape. And she had messed that up utterly, she now realised. Rage wasn't the answer. It felt good, it felt right, but it wasn't. Understanding was the answer. Understanding that the rape wasn't her fault. That it was a problem of Beck's. Understanding that the guilt and self-loathing Beck had put into her could be taken and used to fuel the healing process. Something she had been unable to do on her own. She had needed Fitz's help.

But Fitz wasn't there for her.

Because of Judith.

When she'd rung him moments afterwards, from Beck's flat, he'd been with Judith. Judith who seemed to feel she could walk in and out of his life exactly as she chose with any amount of emotional baggage, and expect him to walk on eggshells around her and pick up the baggage she left and carry it around after her like some kind of emotional slave. And in truth the most annoying thing about the whole affair was that Fitz seemed willing to allow that to happen to him. Fitz was as much a victim of Judith's manipulation as she herself was of Beck's violence.

41

Fitz looked at her now, with eyes she had seen screw tightly shut at her touch, the lips she had once kissed with such passion thinning determinedly. 'You've got a cheek if you hate me that much Panhandle.'

' "Fitz, it's me, Jane. We need to talk." ' Penhaligon quoted herself from the phone call and then stared at Fitz, challenging him to say anything but what he had said that day.

And she saw that Fitz was overcome with guilt and pain. And he finished the quote. ' "I can't talk right now." ' Fitz pursed his lips, struggled with the words. 'But you never let me tell you why.'

'Because of Floyd, right. But I didn't care why. I wouldn't have cared if harpies from the seventh level of hell had carried Judith off to the everlasting flames.'

Fitz smiled. He obviously thought they were back on familiar ground. No way. No more familiar ground. Not now, not ever.

He started to speak.

Penhaligon shut the door in his face.

From the other side of the door a muffled voice said, 'I've been to see Beck. He's been reading, but he's got it all wrong. He's feeling guilty. We can get him.'

How could he do *this to her!*

Penhaligon swung round, whipped the door open and dragged Fitz through into the living room.

'Oh yeah. We can get him. Like he raped you too, right?'

Fitz stood by the drum kit, a childish grin plastered across his face. 'Fight it,' he said smugly.

'What?' Penhaligon allowed some contempt to mix with the anger in her voice.

'That urge to bundle me into the bedroom, rip off all my clothes. It'll pass. Keep fighting.'

Penhaligon felt her shoulders and arms tense. 'I told you to keep your nose out!'

The smug look on Fitz's face vanished in a moment. 'I couldn't.'

42

Penhaligon felt her anger fade with his smugness.

Fitz licked his lips. 'Look. I've got to ask you this.'

'What?'

'Did you and Beck ever . . . you know?'

'Kiss? Go to bed? Is that what you want to know, Fitz?' A moment when she felt like screaming out at the terrible, restless injustice of it all. 'How could you ask me that? *How could you!*'

Fitz said nothing. 'You're right. I'm sorry. I just – I had to . . .'

Penhaligon took a step nearer and pushed Fitz so hard he took a step backwards. 'Get out, Fitz. You don't care about me. You never cared about me. This whole thing is about you, not me. It's about your guilt. You don't care how *I* am. You weren't there for me. You were never there for me and now you've been to see Jimmy Beck when I expressly told you to keep your great nose out of my business!'

'I –'

'Sod you, Fitz. Now sod off. Just sod off. Before I hit you with . . .' Penhaligon looked frantically around the room, trying to get the frustration, the sheer anger he provoked in her under control. 'Before I hit you with my old dad's snare drum!'

And she took Fitz and, though he was nearly double her weight, pushed him effortlessly through the hall, the door, into the corridor outside the flat.

He turned for one moment as she clutched the door. 'He's back to work tomorrow. Beck. Will you –'

He looked as if he might be about to speak further, but she gave him no opportunity, slamming the door in his face before stomping back to the living room and pouring herself a large whisky and downing it in one gulp.

She felt like screaming. *No you stupid idiot! I'm not going to be all right. Not while Beck's anywhere within a hundred miles of me. So why don't you just take your guilt and your platitudes and your pious brotherly love and your wretched, manipulating wife and kids and stuff the whole kit and kaboodle right up your arse!*

She sank another whisky, took a bath that was much too hot and went to bed. Tomorrow was going to be – oh, the hell with it. Tomorrow was tomorrow. She'd deal with it in the morning.

FIVE

Fitz slouched towards the bus stop and wondered how much of his feeling for Penhaligon was due to love and how much to guilt. As a psychologist he found it easy to separate the two in others. In himself the task was more difficult. Did he love her? She'd asked him that once. A little over a month ago he had had no answer for her; now he had no need of an answer. He was in a no-win scenario. It was Captain Kirk and the blasted *Kobayashi Maru* test. There was no way to win; the only thing possible was to die. Or reprogramme the test. But Fitz was no fictional hero. Reprogramming the test came hard to him. Oh yes, once it had been easy, then life and everyone in it had been a game to Fitz. A game in which he wrote the rules. Manipulating the players had been a principal aim in his life, an end in itself, rather than the means to one. A joy. Now it was different. Now Judith had come back. Now he had betrayed Panhandle. Now Judith was pregnant. Now Panhandle had been raped. Mark and Katie, his kids, were growing fast; he was losing them. His job was becoming boring, his interest in it waning.

His whole world was going to the dogs.

Fitz concentrated on the business of putting one foot in front of another until he reached the bus stop. It was pathetic but there seemed nothing more important than that right at this moment. Just one foot in front of the other, plod, plod, shuffle, plod.

Somewhere deep inside he knew the depression was caused by Floyd Malcolm's attack on Judith. Floyd, a serial rapist, had been Fitz's last case on secondment to the

Manchester Met. Fitz had been working on the case, forming a profile of Floyd. An interview had made him certain that Floyd, a half-caste, was killing white women in an attempt to purge his hatred for his mother. So when Floyd had been released – insufficient evidence – Fitz had sat vigil with Mrs Malcolm. Only to find out that Floyd had anticipated him, had gone to Fitz's own house.

And Judith.

Judith, pregnant, had just re-entered his life after a five-month separation. Arriving at their home with Mrs Malcolm, Fitz had been terrified to see Floyd holding Judith at knife-point. Even as he tried to talk Floyd out of it, tried all the old tricks, all the old gambles, he had been shaking with fear. This time it was Judith's *life* he was gambling with. He had won but Mrs Malcolm had paid the price, killed by Floyd as she had run to comfort him after he had let Judith go.

Fitz had been right, but he'd done everything wrong. Gone to the wrong places at the wrong times. It had all ended wrong, with Judith and Penhaligon both betrayed. And Mrs Malcolm dead.

Since then Fitz had been on a downward slide. He had not laid a single bet. Whisky, his favourite blanket to hide behind, had practically taken over his life. He had betrayed the only two women he ever felt capable of loving, he'd screwed up the case and been responsible for at least one death. He should be in jail himself. Instead they were calling him a hero. The man that caught the Manchester Monster. Women loved him. He'd done radio and TV slots. But beneath all the glitz and glitter, Fitz knew the truth. He had failed. Judith knew it, had hated him since he had told Floyd to go ahead and kill her, finish the job he'd wanted himself for years and never had the strength to complete. Penhaligon knew it, had hated him since the phone call when he had not been there for her as she'd held Jimmy Beck at gun-point.

46

Fitz stared up at the sky then, peered at the restless clouds through the broken roof of the bus shelter, and metaphorically flipped God the bird.

A pigeon which had settled on the roof of the shelter shit on his sleeve.

Fitz glanced at the irregular white splotch on his crumpled suit and then looked up at the pigeon. 'How does it feel to be the vengeful arse of God?'

He looked down to see a pair of teenagers staring at him. They turned in examination of the timetable and hid their smiles.

He waited an hour for the bus and then when it came it was full.

Ten minutes later his piles began to ache.

By the time Fitz reached home his brain was well and truly fried and his arse was on fire. Mark and Katie were sitting together on the porch step, both staring blankly into the night. Katie looked as if she'd been crying. Fitz shot them a glance as he walked up the garden path. That their behaviour was about as atypical as a couple of kids could get seemed not to register at all. But if Fitz felt a little tremor of apprehension in his gut at their presence there in the garden, he ignored it. After all, what else could possibly go wrong on a day like today?

He grinned at Katie. 'Contemplating the whichness of the why, my little rose-Buddha?'

Katie smiled a teary smile but said nothing.

Mark added quietly, 'Hey Dad, you got shit on your suit.'

'Thanks, son.' Fitz stepped between the kids and cruised along the hall, into the living room.

Judith was there. She was still pregnant. That was OK then. Aliens hadn't kidnapped the sprog yet. Hang on though. Something was wrong. Something was different. Fitz peered around the room.

'Hello, Danny.'

Danny Fitzgerald. The slimmer, handsomer, slightly less

irritating Fitzgerald brother. Danny was slumped in the TV chair nursing a large whisky. Danny. His brother Danny. Whom he hadn't seen for eight years. In his own living room. Now.

Fitz made a run for the scotch that would have nailed him striker's position in United. 'It's Mum, isn't it?'

Danny nodded.

Fitz felt his world slide slowly out from under his feet. The room began a quiet fandango around him, Welsh dresser, furniture, curtains, telly, Judith, Danny. Only the whisky was still, the bottle rock solid in his hand. He didn't drink from it though. Just clutched it as Katie clutched her Axel Rose doll when she was just a kid. For comfort. And of course his mouth was running away all the while, the only thing moving faster than the room. 'Don't say anything. It's bad news, yeah, but I don't know how bad. I'm clutching at straws. A serious illness. An operation required. A colostomy, something like that. Women her age have them all the time. It'll be hard. A bit embarrassing, right, but what the hell. She never was the life and soul of the party. And she's tough, right? She can learn to live with anything in time. Isn't that right? She had us, didn't she? And after Dad, she could live with anything. Couldn't she?'

Neither Danny nor Judith answered the questions. They were all rhetoric anyway. Still clutching the bottle of scotch Fitz sank onto the sofa beside Judith.

'She's dead, isn't she?' Fitz's voice was a strangled yelp. No control. Tears sprang from his eyes. He crushed the whisky bottle so hard he felt it must surely burst in his hand, slash his fingers to release a flood of alcohol and blood onto Judith's fox-cream shag.

Judith reached out. He stared at her through a film of tears. Six foot four, with the finely tuned physique of Mister Blobby and she gathered him in and held him against her like a little kid that's grazed his knee. And although she was only half his size he grasped at her, gasping, needing the

48

comfort, the sympathy. Needing her strength. Because suddenly he had none of his own, not one iota. Suddenly he *was* a little kid again. A little kid who didn't know what to do or say, how to react to this shattering news, was not even sure he understood it.

He blinked back tears, took a slug of whisky from the bottle.

Slowly he fought his way back to rationality.

'How?' The single word was almost a shriek. A whispered shriek, some nightmare thing from a Lugosi film. No-one seemed to notice.

Danny put down his glass. 'Stroke. Half eight tonight. I've come straight from the hospital.'

Fitz managed the maths in two slugs of whisky – quick for him. 'That's nearly four hours.'

Danny said nothing.

'I said that's nearly four hours. In hospital.'

Danny nodded, faint irritation showing beneath the veneer of concern. 'I heard.'

And Fitz was on his feet, swaying gently, feeling the room begin its two-step around his head. 'That's nearly four hours. Why didn't you phone me?'

'Nobody knew where you were.'

And that was certainly true. He'd been at Jimmy Beck's pushing for a confession to rape in order to assuage his own guilty conscience while all the while his mother had been in hospital, lips blue, skin pale, breathing via a machine while her heart slowly gave up its hold on this world.

Something else to feel guilty about.

'*Why didn't you phone me!*'

And Danny was up too, contempt burning in his eyes, and the brothers confronting each other across a space loaded with alcohol and guilt. '*I* didn't want to leave her! And you've seen her once in the last six months so I thought you must be busy.'

Busy wanking off a guilty conscience. For all the good it did you.

Fitz felt the truth sting tears from his eyes again. 'You always were a self-righteous shite.' And he was out of the room, heading for the bathroom where the contents of his stomach had an appointment with the tiled floor because he didn't make it as far as the sink in time.

And later as he lay in bed with Judith and she held him again, and her strength filtered into him again like a bright light in the night, he remembered the mess of undigested whisky and food that had splashed across his shoes and prayed to a god in whom he hadn't believed for years, that one day he would have the strength to rid himself of his guilt as easily.

SIX

And in another bed not half a dozen miles away David Harvey snuggled close to Maggie and cried because no matter how he turned and how many blankets he brought from the airing cupboard he could not escape the bitter cold of guilt, a guilt that stained his conscience more indelibly than Jean McIlvanney's blood had stained his clothes and car, a guilt that marked his life as surely as any cancer. And though just before David Harvey eventually slipped into a fitful, dream-slashed sleep, he begged the Lord repeatedly to let the awful feeling in him ease, he knew that, like a cancer, it had only just begun to grow.

TUESDAY

SEVEN

DS Jane Penhaligon zipped her jacket right up to the neck and scuffed idly at the ruts in the field where, at 5.34 a.m. that morning, Jean McIlvanney's body had been found. Penhaligon looked around the field, took in the distant line of trees, the cows idly watching from the other side of a barred fence a couple of hundred yards away. The field was wide and flat; a cold, lonely place to die. Especially the way Jean McIlvanney had died.

A voice brought her back to reality; Penhaligon realised she was supposed to be taking a statement from Bruce Charnock, a local farmer and the man who had discovered Jean's body. Charnock was a ruddy-complexioned man, weathered, not much taller than her own five feet seven, a man built very much along the lines of the tractor he now leaned against. His hair was as red as his face, and stuck out from underneath a tweed cap. He was dressed in a windcheater, corduroy trousers and thick green galoshes.

Despite the extent of Jean McIlvanney's injuries, Charnock was smiling.

For some reason this annoyed Penhaligon. 'A bit of unlooked-for excitement, I suppose, Mr Charnock?' She couldn't resist the dig. Jean McIlvanney was a terrible mess. That, coupled with the fact that Jimmy Beck was lurking around the site as well, and that she hadn't yet managed to scrounge a good cup of Red Mountain from anywhere, all combined to make Penhaligon as irritable as hell.

Charnock didn't know quite what to make of her question. In the end she let him off the hook. 'Rhetorical, Mr

Charnock. Don't you worry about it. Why don't you tell us how you found her?'

'Well, I tell you. The amount of blooming kids I have strolling across the fields every night – especially at weekends when the clubs have shut – it's enough to drive you to distraction. Beer bottles and fag ends and contraceptives all over the show. Think they own the blooming place they do. Frighten the cows no end.'

'Oh? I thought cows didn't mind that sort of thing. As I remember from my own schoolgirl nocturnal activities they'd sleep through a police raid – that lot over there look as though they're still asleep.' And Penhaligon threw a nod towards the cows peering over the gate some way distant. 'In fact I'd have thought you'd be the last person to anthropomorphise about how your animals are feeling.'

Caught out with the truth, Charnock squirmed. 'Yeah, well. They don't really mind. 'Course not. But it's still irritating. I was bringing Old Yeller – that's me tractor by the way – up to the north field to get set for a bit of work when I saw her – the body. I didn't know it was a body then, of course. Thought it was some crusty having a snooze in me corn. Got down from the tractor and raised hell so I did. No blooming crusty's gonna scare me –' Charnock cleared his throat and had the grace to look embarrassed. 'Anyway. When I got to her I saw she was dead, like, and that thing stuck in her. Looks like a chisel, by the way.'

'Yes, thank you.'

'Anyway, I saw her, saw she was dead, called you lot on me mobile and waited here for you to turn up.'

'I see.' Penhaligon jotted in her notebook. 'Did you touch her, Mr Charnock?'

'No.'

'So how did you know her name when you reported finding her?'

'Oh yeah. Her bag was all spilled open. There was a family credit book there.'

56

'Did you touch the book?'

'No. It was lying face up. I could read the name.'

Penhaligon nodded. 'Did you notice anything else unusual?'

Charnock shook his head. 'No. It was just like I said. The body. That stuff scattered around. The ground's too cold and hard to take tyre tracks or footprints.' Charnock stroked an imaginary beard with his hand. 'Looks like someone brought her here then killed her. A classic disorganised murder.'

Penhaligon looked up at that. 'I beg your pardon?' *Who did this guy think he was, Sherlock Holmes?*

Charnock coughed in embarrassment. 'Sorry. I read a lot of procedural crime. Miss Marple. You know.'

Penhaligon snapped her notebook shut with a click. 'Miss Marple?'

Charnock looked like he was about to expound on the subject.

Penhaligon shook her head. 'Never mind. Oh and by the way – before you leave see that man over there wearing the "Police Forensics" jacket and let him take a cast of your boots. Better still let him have your boots.'

Charnock nodded, climbed back onto his tractor, opened a flask and sipped from it. Penhaligon smelled something suspiciously like a good Red Mountain brew. She licked her lips, wondering if he'd offer her some. No chance. Charnock was watching the hive of activity around Jean's body with bemused interest while waiting for the forensics team to call for his boots. She supposed if Miss Marple never felt the need for refreshment while on site then real policewomen shouldn't either.

Penhaligon said loudly, 'And don't forget to get a receipt.'

Charnock looked at her in surprise. 'For me boots?'

She nodded. 'For your boots.'

'OK.'

'And thanks for the coffee.'

Charnock gave her a peculiar look. 'Oh, sorry. Never thought.' Charnock offered her the flask.

Thank you. Penhaligon reached for the flask.

An irritable, grumbly voice called, 'Oy, lass, quit hobnobbing with the natives and come here a bit, will you?'

Penhaligon froze with her fingers an inch from the flask. She licked her lips. She offered a tepid grin to Charnock and turned to face her boss. She raised her eyebrows questioningly.

Detective Chief Inspector Wise was a bear of a man in his late forties. Large in every sense of the word. A big, furry animal of a man. Wrapped up in a Russian Army greatcoat that looked like it was out of date in World War Two, with only his beard and curly hair and bespectacled blue eyes peering out from a monumental collar, Wise rather resembled an out-of-place yeti. He beckoned to Penhaligon. She walked towards him, towards Jean McIlvanney's body.

'Get Farmer Giles there to cough did you?'

Penhaligon frowned at Wise's none-too-professional turn of phrase. 'I got his statement, yes, sir.' By now Penhaligon was in the thick of the activity around Jean McIlvanney's body. Forensics. The boys from the Nuthatch; Scene of Crime probing and snipping and bottling and labelling. She tried to avoid looking down over their shoulders. One glance earlier at the state of the body and the placement of the handle that was all she had been able to see of the chisel had been enough to make her feel like throwing up her breakfast – if she ever got a chance to have any.

She became aware that Wise was watching her closely. 'Y'all right, lass?'

She nodded.

'It's been a while, but I know how these things come back to you sometimes.'

Well thank you, sir, that's very sensitive of you considering how many times you must have been raped in your life.

58

'I'm fine, thanks.'

'Good. Now listen. We found a family credit book in the handbag. So the poor cow must have had kids. That means someone's going to have to go round to her house, right?'

Penhaligon nodded. 'I'll go now, sir.'

'Take DC Temple with you, eh? Give the lad something to do.'

Penhaligon stared at Wise uncompromisingly. 'Actually, I'd like Jimmy Beck with me on this one, sir, if that's all right with you?'

Wise looked surprised. 'You sure about that?'

Penhaligon forced her most normal expression. 'Quite sure. Back on the horse, you understand.'

'You know how he'll take it. As an admission you were wrong.'

Like I give a monkey's what he thinks.

'Nothing was ever proved, sir. And as you said, Beck's a popular officer. I think I'm ready to start dealing with that now, sir.'

Wise seemed pleased by this. 'Right then, lass. You drive, I'll take Beck's car back to Anson Road myself.'

'Thank you, sir.'

Wise nodded. 'Oh by the way, have you seen Fitz? I called him nearly an hour ago.'

Sure, we were in bed together with his wife.

'Is there any reason I should?'

Wise had the grace to look faintly embarrassed. 'No, just wondered, that's all,' he said quickly.

At that moment another police car bumped over the field and slid to a halt. Fitz got out. He was wearing the same suit as he'd been wearing when he'd visited her last night. It was as creased and crumpled as he looked himself; with some kind of stain on the sleeve, badly smeared by an effort to clean it off.

He plodded over to them, habitual high tar jammed into his mouth, looking like some enormous puffing billy. As he passed Jimmy Beck, busy with a number of evidence bags, the detective looked up with a humourless smile. 'Hey, Fitz. You know you got shit on your suit?'

Fitz ignored Beck.

Wise glanced at Fitz and shook his head sadly. 'I've seen some terrible things in this job, but –'

' "She's not a pretty sight"?' Fitz didn't smile.

'I'm talking about you, lad.'

'My mum died last night.'

This stopped Wise in his tracks. 'Sorry, lad. I didn't know.'

Fitz leaned right over the backs of the crouching forensics team, glanced briefly at Jean McIlvanney's body. Penhaligon watched his eyes. Normally sharp as lasers, this morning they were dulled with a mixture of sadness, guilt, lack of sleep. Probably booze too, if she was any judge of character. Even so, even working so obviously on autopilot, Fitz nailed every piece of evidence with perfect clarity. 'A classic disorganised murder. But he's used a weapon, not his bare hands. Probably that chisel you're holding there, Mister Nease. Maybe it was just lying around? No – no rust on it. Maybe it was in his car. There had to be a car this far from town. But why a chisel? A jack, yes, a tyre lever, even a torch. But a chisel? Is he a builder, or joiner? Maybe, but he'd keep his tools out of sight in the boot. They wouldn't lie conveniently to hand. Maybe the chisel belonged to her – but in that case why not a can of Mace or something like that? The chisel's much too big to fit in her bag. How would she carry it? And look at the state of her face. She's been hit. Given a good account for herself probably. So, she knows how to look after herself but this time got in over her head. And look at the way she's dressed. And what he did to her with the chisel. She's a prostitute. Brought her out here, possibly screwed her, beat her up, went to the boot, got the chisel . . . poor cow. Poor bloody cow.'

Fitz glanced in passing at Wise as he turned to leave.

'You're going to need me on a retainer on this one. Cash, please, as refusal of credit often offends.' And without another glance Fitz turned and walked back to the police car, got in and allowed himself to be driven away.

From the tractor Charnock waved his flask at Penhaligon. ' "Classic disorganised murder." That's exactly what I said. Miss Marple, you know.'

Penhaligon swapped looks with Wise, headed for Beck. At the address printed on the front of the family credit book, Jean McIlvanney's kids would be waiting for their mum to come home. She wasn't looking forward to what she had to do next.

Penhaligon went with Beck to Jean McIlvanney's flat. They took the duty social worker with them, which delayed them by a further twenty minutes. All in all forty minutes passed between leaving the site of the murder and arriving at the flat.

Penhaligon did not spare Beck a single glance throughout the journey. For his part she thought he was behaving overly normal – for the social worker's benefit she supposed. Not that she really cared. She and Beck had a reckoning coming – but not yet. Not when there were children involved.

Penhaligon rang the door bell. After a few moments a sleepy-eyed girl answered the door. She seemed to be about eight years old. The social worker, a sensibly dressed woman in her middle thirties named Pam Andreson, took charge of the encounter.

'Are you Chrissie McIlvanney?' she asked in a friendly voice.

The little girl cast a suspicious look past Pam at Beck, then looked back to the social worker and nodded.

'Is your mum home?'

Chrissie shook her head.

'What about your dad?'

'No.' The girl's voice was firm. The father reference didn't upset her then.

61

Pam crouched beside Chrissie and looked at her very seriously. 'Chrissie. My name is Pamela and your mum asked me to come and look after you for a while. This is Jane and Jimmy and they've just come to have a quick look around your house. I know that must be scary for you, but I promise we won't hurt you and I promise we won't break anything. OK?'

Chrissie frowned thoughtfully. 'Mum said if anyone weird came to the door while she wasn't here I was to call the police.'

Penhaligon knelt beside Andreson. 'Honey, I am a police officer.' She produced her warrant card and showed it to Chrissie.

'I suppose that's all right then,' said Chrissie, holding the door further open. 'But can you be quiet 'cos my little brother Jim is still asleep.'

Andreson smiled and followed Chrissie into the flat.

The child led them through to the living room.

Once there Penhaligon looked around, taking in the neat home, the shelves of books, the ancient TV and stereo, the little fishbowl. A perfectly normal home for someone living not terribly far removed from the breadline. On a table was a neat stack of paperwork. Bills, some paid, others not, some correspondence, a letter from the DSS.

Pam asked Chrissie, 'Do you have a nan, an auntie or an uncle?'

Chrissie nodded.

'Do you ever speak to them, on the phone?'

Chrissie dug in the table drawer and produced what turned out to be Jean McIlvanney's phone book. Penhaligon flipped through it, noted down the phone number from the page labelled simply, 'Mum'. There was no address. That was bad news. She'd have to talk to the mother herself; a phone call was never the best way to receive bad news. Especially news of the death of a daughter.

She looked at Pam and held up the phone number. 'I'll

sort this if you can deal with the kids.'

Pam nodded.

By now Chrissie was looking from Penhaligon to Pam and back again with wide eyes. She interspersed these looks with other, darting glances directed at Beck, who was running a finger along the books on the shelves and seemed unaware of the child's nervous interest.

Pam exchanged a quick look with Penhaligon, then asked the girl, 'When did you last see your mum?'

'Last night.'

'Does your mum bring friends in?'

Another look at Beck. The answer was obvious. Chrissie nodded.

'Men friends?'

'Yeah. And I don't like them! They make noises and they hurt Mummy and sometimes they steal JS – that's my bear that Daddy bought me before Mummy kicked him out.' She thought for a moment. 'I don't like them but Mummy likes them. And she always buys us stuff, me and Jim, when they've gone.'

Penhaligon looked at Chrissie and felt her heart come close to breaking. She left the child with Pam and made the phone call. Helen McIlvanney took the news just about as well as could be expected. Between tears she promised to contact her local station and have a car bring her to Anson Road. As Penhaligon put down the phone she was aware that Chrissie was watching her intently.

The little girl was on the brink of tears. 'When's Mummy coming home?'

Penhaligon didn't know what to say. Pam came out from the living room at that point and scooped the child away. 'Come on, love. Let's see if we can't get this brother of yours to wake up.'

'Why?'

'We have to go for a little drive.'

'To see Mummy?'

'Actually we're going to see your Nanny Helen.'

Chrissie's face fell. 'But we'll see Mum later, right?'

Penhaligon turned away from the child and re-entered the living room before she heard Andreson's reply. Either she was getting old or her job and her life were turning into the mother of all nightmares.

Leaving Pam to take Chrissie and Jim to the Family and Child Protection Unit at Anson Road station to await the arrival of Jean McIlvanney's mother, Penhaligon drove herself and Beck directly to the Nuthatch – the pathology unit situated half a mile from the station. By now Jean's body would be undergoing a formal post mortem. The results were going to be crucial to the investigation.

This time Beck was silent the whole journey. He avoided Penhaligon's looks, responded to no conversational gambits. Penhaligon secretly admitted to being a little puzzled. If Beck was this unresponsive towards her she wondered why he hadn't kicked up a fuss when Wise had assigned them together at her request.

Like I really care.

She parked the Volvo in the Nuthatch car park. As Beck turned without a word to get out she grabbed him by the shoulder and shouted 'Boo!' as loudly as she could to the back of his neck.

Beck leapt out of the car as if booted up the behind. He hit his head on the doorframe on the way out, adding to Penhaligon's amusement. She followed him out, laughing quietly to herself. But there was a dangerous edge to her laughter and that she fully intended Beck to hear.

'That wasn't funny.'

Neither was raping me.

'Feeling a little delicate are we, Jimmy? Fancy a little time off?'

Beck frowned, didn't bother to reply. He stomped off into the Nuthatch leaving Penhaligon grinning to herself as she locked the Volvo. Beck knew the truth. She was the one who'd been raped, yet he was the one who had gone sick. He was guilty as sin and he knew it, and he knew that she knew it too. Everything else was just a game.

Upon entering the pathology unit Penhaligon and Beck were given surgical smocks and taken through to the lab where Albert Copeley was busy conducting the post mortem.

Jean McIlvanney was laid out on one of three metal examination tables, naked, the top of her skull removed to reveal the brain beneath, the skin and muscle of her lower stomach reflected and clamped back to reveal a glistening mass of internal organs; the inside of Jean McIlvanney, open to the world for examination.

A wheeled trolley full of surgical instruments was beside the table. The room was tiled, bare, smelt strongly of antiseptic. A glass wall divided the main lab from the observation room, where a tripod-mounted camera watched the proceedings with electronic impartiality.

Albert Copeley was working on the corpse. He was a tall, angular man given to sudden, precise movements. Birdlike. An Ichabod Crane for the nineties. A man of science, a man of God. Sometimes Penhaligon thought he got a little mixed up as to which was responsible for the arrival here of some of his corpses.

Penhaligon hesitated as Copeley beckoned her forward, glasses gleaming over the top of the surgical mask. His hands and forearms were streaked with blood. More blood lay in droplets on the instrument tray and ran in a slow trickle from the table onto the tiled floor and down to the central drain. Later the floor would be hosed down with antiseptic. For now the smell of blood was overpowering. It brought images to mind. Images of the rape. Of being held down, helpless, face pressed into the mud. And afterwards the medical examination, the fingers inside her. The swabs. Again. Again. The doctor had been as sensitive as it was possible to be under the circumstances, yet still the ordeal had been humiliating, terrifying.

Penhaligon became aware she was the subject of some scrutiny herself. Beck. He was here. Watching.

Beck was watching *her*.

As if gauging her reaction to the post mortem.

Penhaligon felt anger flare inside, replacing the painful memories. So he wanted to come the voyeur did he? Well two could play that game.

She caught his eye and held it until he looked away, back to the human wreckage on the examination table. The wreckage that had once been a living woman named Jean McIlvanney. A woman who loved and laughed and shopped and brought up her kids and paid her rent and went to the pictures when she could afford to. In short a woman much like Penhaligon herself. A woman who was now dead, her skin cold and pale, the blood pooled in her extremities; limbs that had once held her children and bounced them as she sang to them, cuddled them, bathed them. Never again. She looked at Beck and saw his face change. Knew in an instant that he had seen all this, seen it and dismissed it. For him Jean McIlvanney was nothing more than a woman-shaped lump of meat; evidence.

Copeley looked up then, absorbed in his work so that he missed the interplay between them. He knew Penhaligon and aimed his words at her. 'Early thirties. Smoker. Given birth at least once. Five or six blows to the skull. Brain haemorrhage. That's what killed her. No traces of semen but there's other evidence she had intercourse prior to death. Tearing of the vagina. A knocked ovary. See the displacement? Only slight but you have to really be going at it hammer and tongs to get that sort of injury. I've excavated through the muscle wall a bit here, as you can see. The bruising there is consistent with intercourse, so the chisel could have been inserted after death.'

Penhaligon felt her head swimming. *You're wrong. You didn't see her expression when we found her. She felt everything. Oh God she felt it all, knew the end was coming.*

'Why?' That was Beck, with another sly glance at Penhaligon.

'I beg your pardon?' Copeley blinked behind his glasses.

'Why was the chisel inserted at all?'

Copeley studied Beck as if he were some kind of lab specimen. 'How the hell should I know? You're the copper. You tell me. Probably a sex thing.'

'A sex thing.' Beck savoured the words while staring at Penhaligon.

For a moment the image of Chrissie McIlvanney sprang into Penhaligon's mind, a tiny genetic icon of her mother. Was it her destiny to grow up to fulfil this image too?

Abruptly she smiled. 'Yeah. You remember sex, don't you Jimmy? That thing you do when there's no footey on the box.' *And no desire in your partner.*

Beck frowned. He tried for a riposte but nothing seemed to come. Verbally impotent. Penhaligon's smile widened. To Copeley she added, 'Keep us posted on the chemical series, yeah? We'll need to know if she was intoxicated or using drugs.'

Copeley nodded and grinned behind his surgical mask. 'I'll send them straight over. Couple of hours all right?'

Penhaligon nodded and left the lab.

'You want a lift, Jimmy?' she called from the sliding glass door. 'Or are you going to stay here a bit and catch up on the stuff you missed at school?'

Beck followed her in a moment, pulling off his smock and mask, face like a thundercloud.

Fitz, you'd be proud of me, Penhaligon thought as she led the way to the Volvo. *And I'd be pleased that you were if I didn't hate you so much.*

Back at the station a party was going on in the duty room. A balloon tree made out of condoms after the *Lethal Weapon* joke and a cake. Several six packs. Beck and Penhaligon stared around in bemusement as they walked into the duty room to a chorus of back-slapping, party hooters and cheerful 'Welcome back's.

Beck allowed himself to be dragged into this madness, stuffed a slice of cake into his mouth and munched happily for a moment. Then his face seemed to freeze up. Penhaligon, watching, sensed a tension there. Sure enough he caught her eye after a moment, turned, brought her a slice of cake.

What was this then? An apology? Guilt? What?

She studied the cake, looked at Beck, looked right into his face, his eyes. No. No apology there. No contrition. Maybe some guilt. She turned away from the cake, from Beck, forged a path through the mess of slightly intoxicated officers to Wise's office.

'Hello, lass.' Wise looked up from his desk as she entered. In one hand he held a plate of cake, in the other an open bottle of Newcastle Brown. 'Come in. Didn't hear you knock.'

'Shouldn't think so with that lot out there.'

'Yeah. Jones's idea. Spring a little surprise on our Jimmy. Cheer him up a bit.'

Penhaligon struggled hard to maintain her temper.

Sure, like he's the victim around here.

Wise must've caught her look. 'Look, I've got to say this. Jimmy Beck's been through a bad time. His nerves and that.'

Yeah, right.

'So go easy on him, y'know what I mean? No sudden shocks. Y'know. Like getting a round in or anything.' Wise giggled.

Penhaligon shrugged. 'Whatever, sir. But look. Do you think it's appropriate right now? We are conducting a murder enquiry. For crying out loud, the woman's kids are up on the third floor in the CPU.'

Wise waved his hand in an expansive gesture. 'Ten minutes won't hurt.'

Penhaligon frowned irritably. 'Well then I ought to tell you I saw the Area Chief Super parking up just as I came in. Wouldn't want to give the wrong impression, would we?'

Wise finished the Newcastle Brown, gulped down his cake and binned the paper plate and bottle. He went to the door. 'Right lads and lasses. That's it for now. We have got a murder enquiry to sort out, you know.'

The silence was punctured as Bobby Skelton burst a balloon behind Beck. Penhaligon grinned. Beck jumped half out of his skin. It was a moment worth the whole stupid party.

Ten minutes later the duty room was its usual chaotic self, *sans* condom tree, balloons, cake and beer. The cake and beer had been consumed in double quick time, the balloons had been burst in a fusillade. Heaven alone knew where the condom tree was.

Wise was holding court.

'This is the picture. We've got Jean McIlvanney, thirty-one, two kids, time of death around ten p.m. last night; method of death, multiple blows to the front and rear of the skull, chisel shoved up her . . .' a glance at Penhaligon. 'Sorry, lass. Insertion of chisel into vagina, possibly after death. It's possible our Jeannie was a prostitute. The two kids are in the Child Protection Unit waiting for their nan. Jane?'

Penhaligon took out her notebook. 'We interviewed the kids briefly with a social worker present. Apparently mum brought men home. Last night there was one who liked her to sing. Then there were what Chrissie describes as "hurting sounds"; that was when intercourse took place. Then silence for a bit. Then an argument about money. Then they left. Mother and friend.'

The door opened during her speech just long enough to admit Fitz. He stood just inside the door, listening intently. When Penhaligon had finished speaking he remained silent for a moment, then said confidently, 'He was a regular. If it's a stranger, it's money up front. But she trusted this man to pay up afterwards. A regular.'

Beck grinned as he sucked on a roll-up. 'How do you know the difference between a stranger and a regular then?' Beck waggled his eyebrows suggestively at Fitz and was rewarded with a round of titters.

Fitz smiled wearily. 'I talked to the kids, Jimmy. And that's your job.' Now his grin widened. 'Perhaps I ought to claim some of your salary, eh? Let you ease back into the job slow, like.'

Beck scowled, chewed on his roll-up. 'Are you insinuating something?'

'I never *insinuate*.' Fitz grinned. 'A good manly *thrust*, that's me.'

More laughter this time, now directed at Beck.

Despite herself, Penhaligon grinned. Then he glanced towards her with a little grin of his own, that crumpled smile he knew she found irresistible. Well this time she would resist it. She turned back to Wise.

'Cash machines, sir.'

Wise nodded. 'Good idea, lass. Bobby – get me a list of all cash-point machine transactions last night between eight and ten, within, say, half a mile of the victim's address.'

'On it, boss.'

'Jones. Set up a TV broadcast. Six o'clock news, the works. Get the mother in on it if you can.'

Jones nodded.

'The rest of you see me for assignments.'

In moments the duty room was bustling with activity.

Penhaligon went to her desk to find some blank paper to type up her report. Rummaging in the drawer she found the limp remains of the condom tree.

Great joke. Stuff it in Jane's drawer, watch her squirm.

She looked around for Jimmy Beck, found him grinning at her from the other side of the room.

Fitz cruised up then, took the offending object from her

and offered it to Beck. 'Think you might be looking for this.'

Beck snatched the tree and flung it in the bin with an angry scowl.

Fitz grinned at Penhaligon, but somehow his actions just seemed to make her angrier.

The duty phone rang, breaking the moment. Beck picked it up. 'Anson Road, duty room. Yeah. Yeah. Good. Send her up. No. I'll come and get her myself.'

He replaced the phone triumphantly. 'That was Dennis downstairs on the front desk. Apparently we've got a Denise Fletcher down there claiming to be a friend of Jean McIlvanney.'

He shot Penhaligon a glance that said, *Are you up for this or are you just gonna dick around with the other wets?*

She returned the stare, moment for moment.

Anytime, anyplace.

'The kids are upstairs. We'll have to talk to her in the interview room.'

EIGHT

When Fitz was called to the murder site earlier that morning he'd had a hangover the size of Queensland. Aboriginals were singing a map of their world in his head. Three cups of double strength coffee, a pint of Alka-Seltzer and an icewater shower couldn't shift either the hangover or the guilt. Still, what was new? Only the songlines. He had Chatwin's book on his bedside table. Mum had loaned it to him to read weeks ago; he'd never found the time. Ironically he'd begun to read it the day before she died. Now what he'd read of the prose was jammed in his head more immovably than the Coca-Cola jingle he'd heard over a decade before.

'I against my brother.
I and my brother against our cousin.
I and my brother and our cousin against our neighbours.
All of us against the foreigner.'

A terrible indictment of society when a Bedouin proverb dating back centuries still held true – even if only in part.

Arriving on site with the words still ringing in his mind, Fitz had drawn the obvious conclusions, uncaring as to whether the police had already formulated similar theories themselves. He was pretty sure they hadn't. Only Penhaligon had the smarts to see beyond the gore and she was displaying all the classic symptoms of displacement anger. It was clouding her thoughts. That was down to Beck. Oh, how Fitz would've loved it to be Beck lying in that field with a chisel up his arse. That would have brought a smile to Fitz's lips.

When he'd left the murder site Fitz had the police driver drop him back at home. He and Danny had business to sort out. The funeral. Mum's parish priest was a guy called Michael Harvey. Danny drove them there after breakfast. At least, Danny, Judith and the kids had breakfast. Fitz was still too hungover. He remembered mumbling something about poached kangaroo on toast and a glass of refrigerated Coca-Koala, but no-one had laughed.

When they arrived an hour later at St Catherine's Fitz was surprised to find the place familiar. It took him a moment to place the church, the canal-side setting. Then he got it. His first case on secondment to Anson Road had showed its initial blossoming of information here. Kelly, the amnesiac priest everyone thought was a serial killer. Fitz shook his head as Danny led the way to the presbytery. Proving Kelly's innocence had brought him into conflict with a belief he thought he had left behind years before. Lapsed catholic or no, somehow Fitz just couldn't seem to escape the faith.

'Once they got you, they got you by the balls,' he muttered.

Danny shot him a glance.

'Well they got you, didn't they? And Mum. Catholics. They're worse than the Mafia.'

At that exact moment the door of the presbytery opened and they were confronted with a stocky fellow with a carefully neutral expression. Danny shook his head and introduced the two men.

'Michael Harvey, Eddie. Edward Fitzgerald. My brother.'

'Ah yes. Mrs Fitzgerald's other son.'

Fitz shook his head as he followed Danny into the house. 'Dazzling.'

'Pardon?'

'The sunlight today. The way it comes off the canal and hits the church walls. Dazzling.'

Michael shot him a narrow look. Then they were in the

74

living room and faced with a pot of lapsang souchong and
another slightly frazzled-looking man.

'Eddie. Danny. This is my brother. David.'

'Fitz.'

'Pardon?'

'Call me Fitz.'

Michael nodded affably. But Fitz had scented something
going on in the room. Some bit of tension. He dismissed it
from his mind as unimportant. Later he would regret that
decision, but for now the quite disgusting burnt-sausage
smell of the tea mixed uneasily with his hangover and drove
all other thoughts from his head.

David rose abruptly. 'I'll . . . er . . . excuse me.'

Fitz nodded distractedly, although David's comment was
obviously aimed at his brother.

'I'll see myself out.'

Michael nodded. 'I'll be in touch.'

After David had gone Michael turned to Fitz and Danny.
'What'll it be, then?'

Fitz answered without hesitation. 'Scotch.'

Michael laughed. Nervously? 'I mean coffee or good old
PG Tips? Lapsang isn't to everyone's taste.'

When the drinks had been served Michael settled down to
the business of the day. He recorded the details of the service
on a portable laptop he took from a drawer on the Welsh
dresser.

'We've arranged the basic service. Now. Would you like
to read something?'

'The Sermon on the Mount.' Danny stared at Fitz as if
challenging him to refute his brother's choice.

Michael also looked at Fitz. 'Fitz?'

'I'd like to talk about her. Plain English. No platitudes.'

Danny was unhappy about that. Tough.

Michael made notes on his laptop. 'Fine. Holy
Communion?'

'Yeah,' said Danny.

'No,' said Fitz at exactly the same time.

Fitz stared at Danny. 'I'm not taking Communion.'

'Mum would want you to.'

That's right. Pour the guilt on. It's not enough that I wasn't there when the poor cow popped her clogs. Now I'm going to mess up her departure to the afterlife as well.

'Tough.'

'Fitz!'

'It means nothing to me.' Fitz felt his brother's contempt fizz out into the room like electricity. 'Stop looking at me like that!'

'Anything else?' Michael tried to act as peacemaker but it wasn't going to happen.

'I said stop looking at me like that, Danny!'

Michael persisted. 'Is there anything else, gentlemen?'

And Danny blew it. 'A game of bingo. Halfway through the ceremony.'

Fitz stared at his brother, began a laugh, aborted the attempt, tried to find words to describe the monumental inappropriateness of the suggestion – then stopped. Actually – the more he thought about the idea the more appropriate it seemed. Somehow, beyond all hope, Danny had nailed the one thing their mother *would* have wanted.

The thought of his mother made Fitz feel like crying again. Leaving Danny to arrange the final details, Fitz stepped back into the crisp morning air and lit up a high tar.

By the time he got back to the station, in time to hear Penhaligon's account of the interviewing of Jean McIlvanney's kids, he was in a royal temper. Only showing off seemed to help and even that backfired on him as usual, earning him the irritation of both Beck and Penhaligon. Beck he couldn't have given a toss about, but Penhaligon. Ah, Panhandle. Could he have been wrong about her all this time? Had she ever really loved him? Or was it one of those sad personality mismatches, the kind where you think

76

you're getting on really well, the kind where whatever turns you on about the person you fancy just makes them want to be friends with you? As little as two months ago, Fitz would have been on this thought like a hound, ferreting it out, dragging it kicking and screaming into the light of day for examination if required.

The truth was he was just too tired.

Now Fitz was sitting with Beck and Penhaligon and Denise Fletcher in interview room one. The room was plain, tiled in white, with no windows to offer a distraction to the frequent visitors to the room. Now the cold edge to the room had been softened deliberately with a pot of tea. Three cracked Flintstones mugs steamed on the table at which sat Penhaligon, Beck and Denise. Fitz had declined a mug, with a crack of his own about scotch. Now he stood beside the door, to one side of Denise as she spoke.

She was a striking woman; a strong, angular face which on many would appear ugly or masculine; somehow she had managed to turn it to her advantage. Her clothes spoke of confidence, as did her body language. Fitz could tell she was very comfortable with herself.

'I worked with Jean. I came here to report her missing. We were supposed to meet for lunch today after she dumped Chrissie off at school. There's been some right nutters around lately. You know. Pervs. So all us girls have got a pact. Anything dodgy and we go straight to you lot. We might get a fine but at least . . . well, you know. Violence is on the up. With some punters, anything can happen.'

Beck sucked suggestively on his roll-up. 'And what would someone of your profession consider "dodgy"?'

Denise shot Beck a look that had Penhaligon grinning from ear to ear. 'Axe-murdering maniac, maybe? Gunshots in your neighbours' flat? What the hell do you think I mean? We phone each other, tell each other who we're with and when we expect to be back. Well. Now Jeannie's gone missing. I can't even get a reply from her flat.'

77

'Perhaps she's taken the kids off for a holiday.'

Denise laughed. 'You men are all the same. You think we get to keep everything you pay us. That we're living in the lap of luxury. Well, I hate to disillusion you, but it ain't like that.'

Penhaligon stepped in when she saw Beck tense at Denise's verbal aggression. 'And Jean contacted you last night? Told you who she was with?'

'No. Didn't need to. I saw who she was with.'

Beck leaned forward eagerly. 'And you know this man?'

Denise shrugged. 'Sure. We all know him.'

Even Fitz felt the tension escalate in the room. Could it be that simple?

'What's his name then, love?'

'I dunno. We call him Shirley Temple. Drives an old blue Renault.'

Beck slumped. Fitz sighed. Only Penhaligon kept the questioning going.

'Why Shirley Temple?'

Denise shrugged without a hint of embarrassment. 'He likes you to sing "How much is that doggie?" Flutter your eyelashes a bit. It turns him on.'

'Oh yeah?' Beck wrote quickly in his notebook.

'Registration?'

'I wish we could. We'd have a union then and we could really earn all the money you blokes think we do.'

Fitz almost laughed out loud at Beck's expression. One more day like this and Beck would be ready to hurl himself off a tower block.

Beck sighed. 'I meant the car's registration. Did you get it?'

'No. Shirley's a regular. A weirdo but he wouldn't harm anyone. Blimey, I've done him myself. It's a bit of a laugh if you can get your head round it.'

'Singing songs, pretending to be a schoolgirl and selling sex. "A bit of a laugh." ' Beck stared hard at Fletcher.

She mirrored the look perfectly. 'Got to keep it in perspective, haven't you?'

Beck uttered a harsh laugh.

Fitz stared at Penhaligon, wondering if she'd ask the right question.

She didn't disappoint. 'You say he was a regular. Is it always cash up front? Even with the regulars?'

'Well, that would've been up to Jean, I suppose.'

'Suppose I couldn't pay?' Beck picked up on Penhaligon's line of thought. 'You'd come across but I couldn't pay?'

Denise fixed Beck with a sexy smile. 'What you, a copper? Everyone knows coppers are loaded.'

'That's a pile of –' Beck stopped, aware he'd fallen into her trap. 'So what about it, then? We've just done the business and now I've no money.'

Penhaligon sighed. Fitz noted the reaction. Empathy. She was identifying with Denise. One woman to another, common enemies against common Jimmy Beck. The old Bedouin proverb was still holding water.

'You wouldn't get out the door. Not in one piece anyway.'

Beck scribbled. 'What about a cheque?'

'Do me a favour. No. I'd go with you to the cash machine.'

Inside his head Fitz was weaving triumphantly past the defence for a shot at goal.

But Denise was staring narrowly at Beck. Fitz noted the glance. She was beginning to catch on.

Denise said. 'Look. I've answered enough questions to sink a battleship. I only came in here to let you know Jean hadn't showed up. So why the third degree?'

Beck settled himself back in his plastic chair, content to let Penhaligon handle the hard part.

'Denise, what I have to tell you will be hard for you to hear. I am very sorry, but Jean was killed last night.'

Denise was silent, staring in dumb amazement from Penhaligon to Beck and back again. A nervy laugh bubbled into words. 'That's a load of old . . . I only saw her at nine. She can't be dead. What about her kids? What . . . Oh God . . . Not Jeannie, Christ no. No!'

Fitz felt tears begin to slide from his own eyes. Not for Denise Fletcher or Jean McIlvanney. For his mum. For Danny. Himself. He had to get out of there!

Fitz quietly left the room as Penhaligon leant forward to comfort Fletcher. His last sight was of Fletcher sweeping all three Flintstones mugs from the table to smash against the floor in a flood of steaming tea.

The sound, and that of Denise sobbing, followed him out of the room, drilled into his head; it felt like it was his own psyche shattering. Fitz leaned against the nearest wall and tried to compose his thoughts. This was no good. He was losing it. He was losing it. How to get it back, control? How?

A moment's thought and a good long drag on his high tar gave Fitz the answer. It was time to sing Chrissie McIlvanney a song.

The third floor of Anson Road station was entirely given over to the Family and Child Protection Unit. Essentially it was like a well appointed flat, with a living room, bedroom, bathroom and kitchen. The only difference was that there was an en-suite medical examination room, with supply room and tiny office attached. The flat part of the unit was decorated much along the lines of any normal middle-class home. It had a dining table and three-piece suite in the lounge, cupboards stocked with food in the kitchen. There was a row of fluffy toys on the picture window sill and drawing books and colouring materials in a drawer beneath the table. The only things missing were a television and stereo. A video camera was bolted to the wall high in one corner of the living room. Two walls held seascapes by

Turner while a third held a Cretaceous triptych by Keable.

When Fitz entered the suite Pamela Andreson and Chrissie McIlvanney were drawing dinosaurs on paper spread across the dining room table. Jim was in bed, asleep.

'See the crest? That's a hadrosaur,' said Chrissie to the social worker. Her voice belied her words; it was subdued, almost a whisper. Fitz knew the sign. Chrissie was getting scared waiting for her mum or her nan. Scared, depressed, withdrawn. Where was her nan, anyway?

Pam answered that one quietly, so the child wouldn't hear. 'Coming from Newcastle, ASAP.'

Fitz nodded. He sat beside Chrissie and studied her pictures.

The girl looked up. 'Do you like dinosaurs?'

'My little girl Katie did when she was small. We used to have a joke. What do you get if you take a great big dinosaur like that one you've drawn there and bash it over the head until it's so small you can hardly see it?' Fitz grinned his crumpled grin. 'A tiny sore diney-saur!'

Chrissie shook her head. 'Heard it.'

Fitz shook his head too. 'Figures. I'm Fitz by the way.'

'I'm Chrissie.'

Fitz shook hands solemnly. He sniffed, looked around the living room. 'D'you know it's awful quiet in here.'

'Uh huh.'

'Well, do you like pop music? My Katie liked pop music when she was your age.'

' 'S'all right. Take That are dishy. Well Mum says so anyway. But I like rave.'

Fitz grinned. 'My Katie was into Nirvana at your age.'

'Naw. They're old-fashioned.'

Fitz nodded sagely. 'That's what I told her.'

'And whassisname killed himself. The singer. Didn't he?'

Fitz nodded. 'Me, I like old songs. *Annie Get Your Gun*. *The King and I*. You heard any of them, Chrissie?'

81

The girl shook her head. On the table another dinosaur was taking shape. This one had three horns and was built low to the ground.

'That's a stegosaurus, right?'

'Naw. It's a triceratops. Three horns, see?'

'Oh right. What about, "How much is that doggie in the window", Chrissie? Do you know that one?'

Chrissie dropped her colouring pencil with a clatter and stared at Fitz, shaking. She began to cry. Her voice was loud, startled, afraid. *'They took my bear, Mummy took my bear and sang to him, to her friend. She sang that song. The doggie song. I hate her. I hate her!'*

And she turned as Pam gathered her into her arms and held her while she sobbed. 'Where's Mummy? *Where's Mummy!'*

Fitz mouthed an apology to the social worker as he turned to leave. Then he turned back for one last question. 'Did your mum call her friend by his name, Chrissie? It's important. Last night. Did your mum use her friend's name?'

Chrissie looked at Fitz through tear-stained eyes. 'She shouted at him. Mummy shouted at him. He didn't have any money. She shouted at him. She called him bad names.'

'Did she call him anything else? Peter? Gerry? Thomas?'

Chrissie looked down at the floor, pursed her lips, then stared back at Fitz with unblinking eyes. 'David. When she shouted at him she called him David.'

Bingo!

'Thank you.' Fitz searched for more words of comfort but found he had none. Chrissie had confirmed all that Denise Fletcher had said and more.

He left the third floor, took the lift down to ground level. What should he do now? Everything was a little fuzzy round the edges. Not as fuzzy as with a good scotch or three in his belly though. Now there was an idea. Perhaps he'd go to the Robin Hood, sink a quick couple of shorts, just get his head together for later, for Danny and Judith and the kids. And Mum. Yeah. Just a couple of shorts. That'd be OK, wouldn't it?

But Fitz didn't go to the pub. Somehow he ended up in the little chapel on the ground floor at the back of the police station. Jean's body had been transferred there for viewing by her mother. When Fitz arrived Helen McIlvanney was already there, a tallish, thinnish woman in her fifties, stifling tears as she stared at her daughter's face – all that could be seen of her body beneath a silk shroud. Fitz stood quietly at the back of the chapel for a moment. What the hell was he doing here? He didn't know her. He should let the woman grieve. Leave her alone with her grief. But something stopped him leaving. Right down deep in his heart he knew what it was, but he wasn't prepared to acknowledge it – yet.

Helen turned, saw Fitz. 'You knew her?'

Fitz shook his head.

'Policeman?'

'I'm a psychologist.'

Helen nodded. 'You're supposed to know what people like me are thinking.'

'Yes. No. Sometimes. If you pay us enough.'

That got a smile. Just.

'Why are you crying? To make me feel better?'

'No. My mother died yesterday.'

'I'm sorry.'

'It's OK.' A watery grin. 'She owed me a tenner, too.'

Helen returned the smile. Beckoned Fitz to join her in the pews. 'It's not the same thing, a mother dying.'

'Yeah. You see a person grieving, you sympathise, but you're thinking of your own grief, that's all.'

Helen nodded. 'Go on, then.'

Fitz blinked. 'Sorry?'

'Tell me what I'm thinking.'

'Well right now you're thinking, "I hope he gets it right. It's too selfish, too sick for me to even start talking about it." '

83

Helen studied Fitz closely, the creases in his face, the fat, the eyes. She offered him her handkerchief.

He took it gratefully. 'Beats Andrex doesn't it?'

'Yes.' Another smile. 'I didn't know she was a prostitute. They told me all about it when I got here. A nice woman called Jane. Jane Penhaligon. Jean's lying up there, on the slab, my flesh and blood, my daughter, but all I can think is: what'll the neighhours think?'

Fitz uttered a quiet laugh. 'They'll think she was a good woman. She had to put food on the table, shoes on the kids' feet. She did it the only way she could. If they don't think that, they're stupid. And who cares what stupid people think?'

Helen nodded, seeing the truth there, lowered her head and prayed. Fitz watched her for a moment, thought about leaving. Something still made him hesitate. Some force was tying him to this room, this moment. Guilt? His mother? Probably both. He wouldn't put it past the old bat to *haunt* him back into the catholic faith.

The door clicked then, quietly, and Denise Fletcher entered. She had been crying. 'Hello?' Her voice was shaky. 'They said Jean was here. You must be her mother. Um . . . would you rather I came back later?'

Helen shook her head.

All three stood or sat in quiet contemplation for a while. Fitz thought about his mother, Danny, the songlines. Finally Denise rose, turned to leave. Fitz stopped her with a look. 'She had unprotected sex with him?'

Denise glanced at Helen, looked back at Fitz with something like contempt. 'I dunno. I got a punter before she went with him. Shirley asked me first. I knocked him back.'

And Fitz saw the unspoken addition to that speech. *If I hadn't Jean wouldn't have been killed. But maybe I would.*

He understood that very well. More guilt. *Breeding like a level four filovirus these days. Circle the globe in six weeks. Kills ninety-nine point nine per cent of all known bleeding hearts.*

'Why didn't she knock him back?'

Now Helen was looking up, attention held, eyes weeping and more than just grief coming out.

Denise said, 'I don't know that she didn't. But she needed the money more than me. There was nothing doing. There'd been a march – you know, Reclaim the Night. All the punters were scared off. It was a buyers' market. You get nights like that.'

Helen stood abruptly. 'She could have asked me for money you know. She could have asked me.' Fitz and Denise both looked at her. 'Will they catch him?'

'Yes.' It was clear from her tone of voice that Denise didn't really think that.

'Will they?' And now Fitz felt the guilt coming in waves off Helen like sweat off a long-distance runner, a palpable force fizzing out into the chapel, meshing with Denise's guilt, his own, a critical mass of pain that threatened to explode out of all control.

'Will they?' Helen asked again.

Denise sneered, 'She was on the game. Murder's an occupational hazard, that's what the police think. No big deal.'

And Fitz couldn't have that. The truth was wildly at odds with that. 'That attitude is ten years out of date, Denise. You're prejudiced. The police do care.' He stared at Helen McIlvanney and made a promise inside his own head, a promise he was determined to keep come hell or high water. 'We'll catch him.'

And then he made himself another little promise. An internal one nobody else but him could hear.

Time for that drink, I think.

NINE

Beck entered Wise's office to find Penhaligon deep in conversation with the DCI. Both looked up as he entered, Wise, particularly, fixing him with an unnerving blank stare. Beck sucked on his roll-up and tried to ignore the looks and the abrupt silence.

He waved a handful of paper sheets at them. 'Three cash machines in the area. This is everyone that used them last night.'

Wise took the sheets and glanced quickly through them. 'How many names?'

'Eighty-three.'

'Luv a duck, it'll take us a month of Sundays to sort through that lot.'

'I could get some of the lads started now if you like?' Beck offered.

Penhaligon took the sheets from Wise and scanned them. 'Can I make a suggestion?'

Wise shrugged. 'Go ahead.'

'Well . . . the argument was over money. If he'd got money out of the machine, he'd have paid her, not killed her. Nine names on that list put their cards in but got no money out. We should talk to them first.'

'Smart thinking, lass. Now I know why they never made you tea-girl.'

Beck grinned at Wise. Oddly, Wise did not grin back.

At that moment Fitz put his head round the door and said, with no preamble whatsoever: 'David. I talked to the kid.

His name's David. I'm off to sort out some stuff, I'll look back in later.'

Wise nodded his thanks. Penhaligon scanned the sheets eagerly. Her face fell. 'None of these nine names have the initial D.'

Beck felt himself grinning inwardly. It was nice to know Penhaligon could make mistakes too. 'Perhaps we'd better put you back on tea duty, eh, love?' He smiled over-widely.

Penhaligon shot him a venomous look. 'All it means is that the kid was wrong about the name, or that he used someone else's card. Maybe his wife's card. Isn't that right, sir?' Penhaligon looked at Wise for support and, to Beck's disgust, got it immediately.

'It certainly is,' Wise said. 'You'd better check it out, lass. And take Jimmy here, with you, eh? Looks like he could do with a smidge of fresh air.'

Penhaligon nodded.

The next hour passed in a bored blur. Beck marked the addresses of the nine names on the list and they visited them in order. Three weren't home, four were and insisted on chatting over tea about the awful state of crime in Manchester, one card turned out to be stolen.

Galen Jones, a middle-aged clerk, had just arrived home after three days in hospital recovering from salmonella poisoning. The card had been stolen from his wallet while he had been in hospital, hence he had only noticed it was missing that morning. He had reported it stolen less than an hour ago.

When asked if he kept his pin number written down in his wallet, Jones smiled and recited a page and a half from Macbeth. 'I've got a memory like a computer,' he said. 'Bloody nuisance at times, especially birthdays – I remember them all, you see – but where things like credit cards are concerned, it's a godsend.'

Penhaligon thanked Jones and led the way back to her car.

Beck was scowling.

'Thought we were on to something there, did we, Jimmy?'

Between Jones's house and the place where Penhaligon's Volvo was parked was a street-corner chip shop. Beck ducked in and emerged a moment or so later with food. Penhaligon was in the car already, engine running pointedly.

Beck waited for her to unlock the car door and then got in, munching contentedly.

'Want some?' He stared at her. 'Chips, I mean?'

Penhaligon turned and looked at him. Then she pulled away from the kerb and accelerated out onto the high street. Beck studied her closely while munching on chips and saveloy. Shoulders tense, face set in an expression of sheer determination. Why was she so angry?

'Open your window. The car stinks enough with you in it, without your bloody grub as well.'

Beck shrugged and did as he was told. He looked at Penhaligon and grinned. 'You want a bit of my saveloy?' He waggled the item suggestively and then pushed it into his mouth.

That was too much for Penhaligon. She jammed her foot onto the accelerator. Beck was slammed backwards into his seat, chips and saveloy flying everywhere. Gulping for air and trying not to choke on the half-eaten food, Beck abandoned the chip bag to clutch with vinegar-stained fingers at the dashboard. *What did the silly cow think she was playing at?* 'You're going too fast!'

'Oh yes, Jimmy, like you did when you raped me? Over pretty quick for you, wasn't it? It was different for me. Lasted a lot longer. But then you wouldn't know about that, would you?'

'What the hell are you talking about?'

'Oh don't give me that, you know exactly what I'm

talking about. Face down in the mud, legs open, begging you to stop because it was hurting, you were hurting me, and you didn't stop, you did it again and again; and afterwards, the humiliation, the guilt, the anger, and all down to you, Jimmy, all down to you!'

The car leapt forward again, ran a red light, turned right against traffic already beginning to move.The side of a bus loomed over Beck. *We're going to hit it, we're really going to hit it!* Beck jerked in his seat, already fearing the collision that would end both their lives.

'You're mad! I could report you for this! You're a police officer! You're exceeding the limit!'

Penhaligon's lips thinned to a line but she didn't answer. Her hair, tied back in a ponytail, lashed sideways at Beck as if it had a life of its own.

'Penhaligon – Jane – for God's sake!'

She looked at him then, turned that stare on him, the one she'd cultivated over the years of hurt, the isolation from her brothers, the constant contempt from her parents, her mother and dead father, Fitz's betrayal and the rape – enough hate for a lifetime and she turned it on Beck like a searchlight.

He shivered at her glance, seeing in her eyes pain of his own; his father's perverse love, his mother's disbelief, years of his own pain wrapped tightly into that one moment – and for that moment – as the Volvo tore along a residential street at more than forty miles an hour – they were joined. Joined together at that part of the human brain where love and pain and fear and hatred melt together into a seething chemical lava from which there can be no escape.

'Why did you rape me, Jimmy?' Her words were a scream above the engine noise.

'You're going too fast!' His own words were just as loud.

'I just want to hear you say you did it, Jimmy. That's all.'

'There's a crossing!' In front of them, black and white stripes approaching with frightening speed.

'I want to hear you say sorry. And I want to hear you say

you won't do it again – to anyone.'

'There's someone there! A woman with a pram!'

And Penhaligon looked then, and slammed on the brakes. The Volvo screeched to a halt three feet beyond the crossing. A whole pile of loose trash came bouncing from the back seat. A couple of magazines, the chip wrapper, chips, a half-eaten saveloy, a tin sewing box which burst open to reveal about thirty guitar plectrums and a somewhat dented cowbell from her drum kit.

And something else. Something that clattered and broke with a plastic rattle and trail of wiring. Something that Beck looked at with growing astonishment and horror. He picked it up.

'Taping me. You scheming bitch, you were taping me!'

Penhaligon said nothing. She sat, gripping the wheel, staring directly ahead into thin air.

'What did you hope I'd do? Incriminate myself in your paranoid fantasy? Christ, love. You're pathetic!'

Penhaligon said nothing.

Beck looked past her then, became aware of three pedestrians, one a mother with a pushchair, who were watching open-mouthed from the pavement as he yelled at the unresponsive Penhaligon.

Leaving her pram for a moment, the mother stepped nearer and banged on the driver's side window.

'Bloody idiot! You could have killed us!'

Without changing expression, Penhaligon slammed the Volvo back into gear and drove on. But she drove at a more sensible speed.

Beck threw the tape recorder out of the window.

Bitch. Scheming bitch.

Ten minutes later they pulled up outside the home of the last name on the list.

Beck bolted from the car as soon as it stopped. He sat on the Harveys' garden wall for a moment, gathering his wits.

Penhaligon strolled past with a breezy smile and rang the door bell.

The door was answered by an attractive woman who seemed to be in her middle thirties. Penhaligon introduced herself and Beck, flipped open her wallet to show her ID.

'Mrs Harvey?'

'Yes.' The woman brushed back a mop of curly brown hair. She looked tired and stressed, thought Beck, as he finally got his breath back and joined Penhaligon. Probably just been shopping. Still, damned attractive though. Bit of makeup, the right clothes. Not bad at all.

Penhaligon referred to the list she carried. 'Have you recently had a credit card stolen?'

'No. Why do you ask?'

Penhaligon was about to reply but Beck interjected, 'Just routine. Is your husband in?'

'David? No. He'll be in later. About six or seven. He works late today.'

Over Penhaligon's objections, Beck said, 'We'll drop by later on then. Thanks for your help.' He smiled as Mrs Harvey shut the door.

Back in the car, Penhaligon turned furiously on Beck. 'Wise put me in charge here.'

Beck shook his head. 'You don't get it, do you? Wife like that, would you go out on the pull?'

'What?' Penhaligon almost choked on the word. 'Looks aren't important if you need something your partner can't give.'

'Right. I suppose she likes to be tied up and raped. That what you mean? I suppose you're right. I wouldn't respect my wife if she let me do that to her.'

'You're sick.'

'It doesn't matter. Unless she's a dyke she didn't kill Jean McIlvanney.'

'That's bollocks, Jimmy, and you know it!'

Beck smiled at Penhaligon and mimed stirring a cup of tea.

'I get it. You're the guy. You've been off with nerves. You've got something to prove. Well, riddle me this, Batman – what did our friend Mrs Harvey say her husband's name was?'

Beck stared, silenced by her words. *How in God's name did I miss that one?*

'I'll tell you: it was David. Just like the kid said. David. If we find out he used her card, or they've got a joint account, then we've got him!'

Beck scowled. He hated to admit it, but she had a point. 'How do we get proof?'

'What about a description?'

'Good plan. Got a TARDIS, have you? Just slip back in time and catch him at it?'

'You're an idiot today, Jimmy. No. We cross reference the times that the cash machine was used. Find out whoever was the next person to take money out of the machine – go see them – get a description of whoever was in front of them in the queue . . . not too hard for you to follow, is it?'

Beck lit a roll-up and jammed it in his mouth.

'I'd appreciate if you didn't smoke in my car, Jimmy.'

Beck sighed and shoved the roll-up back into his tobacco pouch. 'Well, come on then. Who's next on the list?'

'Nigel Gant. Aged nineteen. Twenty-eight Egerton Avenue.'

Nigel Gant answered the door of his housing association flat wearing a bath towel and five rings shoved through various visible parts of his anatomy. He sniffed. 'Fuzz, right?' He grinned when Penhaligon produced her ID, looked her up and down with a friendly smile. 'Ratted you out straight away, didn't I?'

Penhaligon scowled.

'Impressed are we?'

Penhaligon sniffed. Beck grinned inwardly at her discomfort, told Gant what they wanted to know.

93

Gant shrugged. 'Well, you're right, as usual. I was there just as you say. I used the machine and all. There were two couples in front of me actually. Them and old Barney the pisshead. The couple directly in front of me were old, at least forty. The ones at the front were younger. Arguing. About money. Think his card wouldn't work. Barney was giving it some bleeding wellie and all.'

'Could you tell us what the man looked like?'

'What d'you think I am, a bender? No. Copped a load of the tart though. Bit old like, but nice legs.' Here a glance downwards at Penhaligon's legs to complement his words. 'Reckon she was on the game, myself.'

'Why's that, then?' Penhaligon's voice was quite cold. Beck's inward grin widened just a bit.

'Well, her clothes like. You can tell, can't you? Leather jacket and miniskirt, high heels. And the old body language. Know what I mean?' Gant wiggled his hips suggestively and the bath towel flapped around his knees.

Penhaligon sighed at Gant's reference to clothing. Beck wondered why. The descripton fitted that of the clothing found on or near the body. 'Would anyone else have seen them enough to get a description of the man?' he asked.

'Oh yeah. Barney was giving it some, as I said. He'll know everything you want. Used to be in the army that one. 'Til he fell in the bottle. Hangs out round Egerton's warehouse a lot. Probably find him down there about now. Probably get more sense out of him if you took him a bit of slosh, and all.'

Penhaligon thanked Gant. As they turned to leave a female voice screeched from inside the flat, 'Nigel! That Open University thing you wanted's on!'

Gant shrugged, faintly embarrassed, as Penhaligon fixed him with a triumphant grin. 'Er, yeah, well, caught me out there, didn't you? Doing a course, ain't I? Well, two actually. Philosophy and Physics. Keep getting 'em mixed up, see, 'cos they begin with the same letter.'

94

With a last grin, Gant shut the door.

Penhaligon seemed to be flustered somewhat by the conversation with Gant. Beck watched her run her fingers through her hair and then retie it more tightly as she led the way back to the car. He smiled to himself. She was losing it.

Egerton's warehouse was actually a row of old abandoned engineering workshops which adjoined a siding of the main Manchester–London railway. Huge buildings, caked with grime, brickwork crumbling, overgrown with moss. Stacks of rotting timber lay in piles in the grounds, on the other side of a chainlink fence. Grass had exploded through the concrete and, together with a huge growth of nettles and other bushes, was busy turning wood, fence and buildings alike into a kind of surreal, Dali-esque hedge sculpture.

Beck left Penhaligon in the car, made sure his R/T was functioning and climbed over the fence. His feet crunched on broken glass beneath the grass and moss as he walked between the stacks of wood towards the main building. As soon as he lost sight of the road two things happened. Firstly, it became very quiet, with just the odd bird and the distant rumbling of trains to break the silence. Secondly, he began to feel calmer. In the car with Penhaligon he had been wound as tightly as a coiled spring. The thing with the tape recorder. Scheming bitch. Trying to catch him out was she? No chance. No chance at all. You'd have to get up with the larks to catch out Jimmy Beck.

Then again she had been right about the name, the description, the punk. And the cash machine list had been her idea in the first place. She definitely had a brain on her today, and no mistake. Beck scowled, lobbed the butt of his roll-up away, ground it under his heel and lit another. He was out of it for a couple of weeks and the whole department went to hell. Women everywhere. And the others. Bobby Skelton's lot. Christ, he wasn't so old. Thirty-six. It wasn't old. Where had the time gone? Blink and before you know it the good old days of bash 'em till they squeal had been replaced with sensitivity, compassion, psychology. Christ. Compassion had killed David Bilborough. Sensitivity had been the root of the rape. And psychology was embodied by that irritating fat bastard, Fitz. They were ganging up on him. On him, Jimmy Beck, old-time copper, the only one in the department who knew the value of good old-fashioned police work.

Beck paused for a moment, tried to get his breathing under control. By now he had wandered round to the back of the main building. A row of low concrete sheds mouldered in the sunlight, their metal doors rusted or pulled away by vandals.

Beck stepped as quietly as he could towards the sheds. He peered into the first in the row. Blank concrete floor, piles of dust and crap, some kind of overhead joist which had fallen down bringing a chain pulley with it to crack the floor. The second. Same. The third. Nothing. The whole line was gutted. Whatever had been stored there was gone, probably nicked and sold years ago.

Then he hit paydirt. Peering more closely into the last shed Beck noticed a black smudge on the concrete floor. Someone had lit a fire in here. He raked soot with the toe of his shoe. Someone had lit a fire in here recently. And there were empty bottles scattered over the floor. And cigarette butts. Lots of them. Some with a coating of soot from the fire, some much more fresh and clean. Beck grinned. It was obvious the shed was in fairly constant use as someone's home. A filthy mattress and some stinking blankets piled haphazardly at the back of the shed confirmed the supposition.

Beck backed slowly out of the shed, stood blinking in the sunshine. He looked around, letting his eyes become accustomed once again to the light. He turned to look at the main building. It was a wreck, a mouldering corpse of a building. Shattered concrete with metal girders showing through the brickwork like bones through rotting flesh. At every floor gaping holes through which could be glimpsed the interiors of rooms. Shattered glass everywhere. At the corner of the building was a staircase. It had obviously once been walled in with glass. The walls were gone now, together with the hand rail, leaving nothing but a free-floating set of concrete stairs winding upwards through the air around a couple of thick metal posts from which the brickwork had long since fallen away. Every second turn they connected via a short stretch of concrete to the adjoining floor.

Beck studied the building. Was there anyone there? He stood quite still and listened. Lit another roll-up and sucked on it.

And waited.

And then into the sunny silence came a faint echo of noise. A voice singing *Rule Britannia*.

Old Barney.

It was coming from inside the building.

'I gotcha now.' Beck walked towards the staircase, climbed in through a hole in the wall where several large blocks of concrete had been removed.

Inside the building was shrouded in gloom. Shafts of sunshine dripped through holes in the walls and floors above, to leave scattered puddles of light on a treacherously unstable layer of broken glass, shattered brick and bits of twisted metal structural members. The place stank of birds. Pigeon shit added another crumbling layer to the floor, rising in powdery white puffs as he walked slowly forward.

Rising every so often from the gloom were vague shapes covered in their own spotty layer of pigeon shit. Beck realised he must be on the shop floor, or one of them. The shapes were the abandoned hulks of machines. What machines he couldn't tell, because only the bases and parts of the housings seemed to be left intact, all the working parts and valuable components presumably stripped away long ago and sold for scrap when the factory was abandoned.

The voice echoed strangely in the building. It seemed to be coming now from outside. Beck figured Old Barney – if that's who it was – must be on another floor. He began to climb the staircase.

He climbed cautiously, testing each step. Floor after floor until he reached the fifth. There he stopped, peered out over the landscape beyond. There was no rail to hold on to and no wall to separate him from a fall to the ground.

Here the voice was clear, free of all but minor echoes. This was it. He left the stairwell and moved along the short corridor. The walls were brick and tile here, beneath layers of peeling paper, damp and foul smelling. Sheets of insulation had peeled away from the ceiling and partially blocked the corridor. Beck scowled as he pushed past them, following a line of rooms through whose shattered exterior walls the sunlight shone in a blinding chiaroscuro, until the corridor opened into a huge space which must once have been a canteen for the workers.

The voice was much louder here. Beck picked his way slowly through the rubble and pigeon shit, the odd twisted table or broken chair, until he located the room, at the far end of the canteen, from which the voice seemed to come.

'Anyone home?' His voice sounded lost, dead, crushed by the cathedral vastness of the building. As he spoke the singing stopped. A pigeon cooed softly in the silence, then flapped past Beck and out into the air where the side of the building no longer existed. Beck moved towards the wall separating the canteen area from what had once been offices or kitchens behind it. A doorway loomed, narrow, dark. Beyond was silence.

No, not silence. A kind of shuffling sound. Wheezy breathing.

And a voice.

'The machines. Oh yes, the machines. Come for you they will. Come for to carry you home. The machines. Oh the machines.'

Beck stepped up to the doorway. 'Is your name Barney, sir?'

'Who wants to know?'

'Police, sir.' Beck took half a step into the room, tried to pierce the gloom. The room was thick with rubble. Holes in the ceiling let in dazzling shafts of sunlight. Glittering dust floated in the shafts. The light did nothing to dispel the gloom, only made the furthest corners of the room darker still. Beck felt like he was walking through a grainy black and white photograph of a room. Felt as flat and two-dimensional himself. The thought came close to making him lose it. He shook himself. This was crap. He was scaring himself. He'd been listening to Fitz too damn much.

The voice had resumed again. Muttering about machines and violence. It seemed to be coming from directly behind the brightest shaft of light.

Beck took another step inwards.

The voice stopped.

So did Beck.

He sucked nervously on his roll-up. This place was enough to scare a sideshow freak. 'You were standing by a cash machine on the high street last night. Is that right, sir?' Beck made a great effort and managed to keep his voice sounding fairly normal. 'Sir?' He added when there was no reply other than a wheezy breathing.

Then suddenly a shapeless bundle in a dark corner unfolded, stretching upwards until it topped Beck's height by inches. The shape was dark, flappy, covered in old clothes. Currents of air swirled the dust through the shafts of sunlight, bringing the stink of decay and meths and unwashed skin to Beck.

He took a nervous step backwards. 'The cashpoint, sir?'

'You've come from the machines, haven't you? They sent you, didn't they? Sent you to get me?' Old Barney took a step forward into a narrow shaft of sunlight. Beck recoiled. The man's face was ruddy with alcohol abuse but beyond that one side was horribly scarred, possibly burnt.

Barney swung his face to and fro in the beam of light. 'Do

they want me like this?' The scar. 'Or like this?'

Gathering his wits, Beck said, 'The high street, sir. Last night. Were you by the cash machine?'

'The machine? Oh yes. The machines. They run our lives you know. Yes they do. I can see the truth you see. And I'm not afraid to say so. It's why they've sent you to get me, isn't it?'

Beck sucked impatiently on his roll-up. 'I'm a bit pushed for time, sir.' *And I hate heights and I hate smashed-up old buildings and I really hate old pigeon shit.* 'So if you'll just help me out for a minute I'll leave you to your singing.'

Barney appeared to think about this. He swung his head to and fro in the narrow shaft of sunlight, finally presenting the scarred side of his face to Beck again. 'Falklands war. Then I came home to this.' He looked around at the dead building. 'The machines tried to pretend they were dead. But they're not. I know that now. I've found them out, you see. I thought all the machines had died in the war. But no. They're still here. Hiding. Listening. Waiting.'

'Yeah, well. I'm interested in events a bit closer to home, sir. Like last night, on the high street. The cash machine there. I was hoping you could give me a description of someone using the machine.'

'Oh, we don't use the machines, don't you see? They use us!' Barney's voice was a frightened whimper in the darkness, at odds with his hugely frightening appearance. He swayed slightly, in and out of the light, like a pendulum. There. Gone. Back again. Beck saw Barney was holding a bottle. The bottle flashed in the sunlight and Beck saw the glass was dirty. Amber liquid sloshed about inside, and some splashed onto the floor.

'The machines. Barney. The machines.' Beck muttered impatiently. 'Tell me if someone was using the –'

'I've told you, you don't use them, they use us. Do you hear me? They're using us all and we don't even know!' Barney's voice rose to a shrill screech. And then suddenly

he was moving, swinging forward, clothes and face flapping in the shaft of sunlight, feet crunching on the floor, racing towards Beck, and he was screaming, no *squealing* like a slaughtered animal as he raised the hand with the bottle to slash at Beck.

'*I'll tell you about the machines. They run us. They rule us. They make us destroy each other. I killed for the machines and others tried to kill me. All for the machines. All for the machines!*'

And the bottle swept down to strike Beck a glancing blow across the forehead. Fortunately the bottle didn't break, but the blow was still meaty enough to send him reeling back against the wall.

He had enough time to swear once and then suddenly he was moving again, downwards this time as the floor beneath him suddenly dropped about six inches.

'Christ!'

He lurched to his feet, scrambled out of the little room and into the main canteen area as the whole floor suddenly collapsed with a terrifying crack and fell into the floor below. He stared back into the room, saw Barney imprisoned for a moment like a bird in a cage of light, then he was falling, the bottle whirling away somewhere to smash into a thousand pieces, and Beck lurched back into the room to grab the old tramp a second before he would have fallen thirty feet to serious injury if not death, his body smashed against shattered concrete or impaled upon rusted half-inch metal structural members.

'Hang on, you old bastard,' Beck gasped as he grabbed Barney round the waist.

Barney screeched and struggled in Beck's grip.

'Take it easy, you silly bugger. I need a description from you and I ain't letting you go until I damn well get it!'

Beck began the slow process of easing the hysterical Barney back over the newly formed hole in the floor.

It was at that moment that the floor fell away under him

and Jimmy Beck fell, clutching Barney like a lost lover, into darkness.

He hit the pile of concrete beneath, his leg twisted underneath him and he fell again – landing this time on Barney who screamed – and rolled away across the concrete with a groan. Beck fell again. There was a sudden pain in his arm and he screamed.

He was still moaning in pain and swearing fifteen minutes later when Penhaligon found them both and called a paramedic team.

But he had the description.

TEN

While Penhaligon and Beck were out investigating the various implications of the cash machine lists, Fitz was in the Robin Hood getting, not to put too fine a point on it, thoroughly wrecked. He'd been in the pub less than two hours and had somehow managed to down more than a baker's dozen shorts and chasers. He only hesitated slightly when he was down to his last fiver – and only then because he wasn't quite drunk enough not to realise it was a goodly walk home if he couldn't pay the taxi fare. Then again, a hesitation was all it finally proved to be. His fifteenth and final short left him shaking at the front door, eyeing the mid-evening sunshine dubiously – and when Ronnie the barman wouldn't serve him another drink without cash up front, Fitz capitulated to an unfair world and called a cab.

The inside of the cab was one of those prickly spaces where there were more notices for things you couldn't do than Fitz had had drinks that evening. Notices such as:

No Cheques.

No Smoking.

No Alcohol.

No Food.

No Fouling.

No Feet On The Seats.

Do Not Eat In This Taxi.

Do Not Try To Open Door Whilst Vehicle In Motion.

Do Not Distract The Driver's Attention.

Do Not Leave Me Your Rubbish.

'Is it all right if I fart, then?' Without waiting for a reply, Fitz climbed into the cab, took a swig from a miniature bottle of Bells, stuffed the last of his peanuts into his mouth, dropped the wrapper on the floor, lit up a high tar, put his feet up on the seat, settled back, let out a healthy belch and for the next mile and a half engaged the cab driver in infuriatingly accurate gossip about the state of neurotransmitter chemicals in the brain of the average E'ed-up teenager.

Halfway home the cab stopped at a red light and the sound of church music drifted into the cab.

Fitz stared blearily out of the window. 'My mum wouldn't have gone. Reclaim the Night. She saw that for what it was. A bunch of middle-class do-gooder feminists who've never gone short in their lives trying to drive the girls off their nice gentrified streets. Trying to drive the punters off, no grasp of reality whatsoever, couldn't give a monkey's that the girls wouldn't make any money that night, that their kids wouldn't eat, that their kids wouldn't get a new pair of shoes. They as good as killed Jean McIlvanney. If there'd been no march there would've been more punters, less chance of her going off with that man.'

By now they were in the heart of the march, people jostling against the cab as it slowly forged a way through the throng.

Fitz leaned out of the window and screamed drunkenly. 'It's all your bloody fault she died! Didn't you think about her kids? It's your fault you hypocritical bas . . .' he belched loudly. 'Bastards.'

'You want to get us lynched, you old fart?' The cabbie was incensed.

By now the crowd had turned their attention to the cab and its occupant and were hurling middle-class feminist abuse at him. But the crowd had thinned now. Fitz did a fair Queen Mother, waving loftily from the cab window as it

104

accelerated away, leaving the chanting and the music and the placard-waving crowd behind.

'Oh, go on, then,' Fitz finally, and in flagrant breach of Rule Number Nine, responded to the cabbie's last irritable words. 'Tell me you don't agree with me. Tell me you think it's all right for the silly buggers to do what they're doing. They don't understand the psycho-social dynamic of a city. We need those girls. We need them more than a dog needs a tree to piss up. If they weren't there the city would explode! There'd be unrest, violence, you . . .' Another whisky-sodden belch. 'Name it.'

The cabbie muttered something to himself.

'You what?' Fitz said.

'I said, good party trick. Sitting on your arse and talking through it at the same time.'

Fitz laughed. 'Anal humour. You responded to psycho-social analysis in terms of anal humour. Have you any idea how much that tells me about you?'

The cabbie slammed on the brakes. 'Right, you, out. Now!'

'But it's another half a mile!'

'So crawl.'

Fitz practically fell out of the open door. 'Farewell cruel world.'

'Hang about! That's five fifty on the clock.'

'Five fifty! We've only gone a mile and a half.'

'Five fifty. Plus extras.'

'Plus extras?' squeaked Fitz indignantly. He scrambled to his feet and peered in through the cabbie's window. 'Take a cheque?' He giggled. 'Ha. Thass all of 'em, innit? Bust 'em all, now dinn I? All those blooming rules.'

'Five fifty,' said the cabbie. 'Plus extras.' He stared at Fitz. 'Cash.'

'Or?' Fitz leered, swaying from side to side. He looked about as threatening as a wet Wednesday afternoon.

'Or I do something you'll regret.'

The cabbie opened his door. Unfortunately it hit Fitz in the stomach. Fitz responded by throwing up promptly all over the door and, through the open window, the cabbie.

'Well. That's definitely all of 'em now,' he apologised. He clicked his teeth together stickily and grinned.

The cabbie looked at Fitz for a long time, then let fly with a thoroughly professional left jab.

Fitz sat down in the road, suddenly, his nose bleeding. The cab zoomed off in a cloud of smoke. The smoke hit Fitz right in the face and he threw up again, this time all over his own legs.

'Mmm,' he said. He dabbed his nose with his sleeve. Fresh stains of blood and vomit appeared alongside yesterday's birdshit. He studied both sleeve and stains thoughtfully. 'Picture of an artist at work.'

He held his thumb up drunkenly as if to gauge the scale of something he was going to paint. Focusing past it he realised he was looking at his own front garden gate. 'Ha. Free ride home afer all,' he said, pleased with himself. Then he refocused again. There was a face staring at him from behind the gate. Judith. And more faces. Danny. Mark. Katie.

Fitz grinned inanely, staggered to his feet and, after struggling manfully with, though failing to open, the gate catch, climbed over the gate, fell over, struggled upright a second time, brushed past his audience and headed for the downstairs bathroom, where he threw up again.

The phone was ringing as he came out of the bathroom some time later. 'Isn't anyone going to answer that?'

Evidently nobody was. They were all still staring at Fitz. All four of them. Five of them if you counted the baby. Fitz frowned. Did an eight-and-a-half-month-old foetus count as a living being? Well according to some it didn't; nobody had yet proved that a foetus was actually capable of self-awareness, but then from a purely practical viewpoint it had all the right bits in all the right places, all just waiting to be kick-started into action by exposure to this jolly old world of ours . . . In fact, now he came to think about it –

Fitz frowned again. Something was different. The phone had stopped ringing. Mark was holding the handset towards him.

'Boadicea,' Mark said humourlessly.

Panhandle.

Fitz stumbled forward and took the handset from his son. A moment later he was the only person in the hallway.

Fitz put the phone to his ear. 'Who? No. Sorry. Where are you?'

'In my car at the end of your road.'

'Why?'

'Because I can't face your wife.'

'You and me both. Give me five minutes.'

It was more like twenty minutes. Fitz had to change his clothes, gulp a couple of mugs of coffee, face down Danny and the kids, and particularly Judith, and then lurch, only marginally less unsteadily, along the road to the very end, where a reading light and an open door told him which car was Penhaligon's Volvo.

'Well,' he said. 'I knew you wouldn't be able to keep your hands off me for long.'

Penhaligon uttered a short humourless laugh. 'Beck's in hospital. Thought he might have broken his arm. You might get the same if you're not careful.'

'Oh?' Fitz found it hard to repress a grin. 'You do it, did you?'

'If I'd done it, it would have been his neck. He fell through a concrete floor while interviewing an old drunk named Barney. Beck's OK, but even so it was worth it. We got a name, a witness, a description of Jean that matches that of the body and a description of the man with her at the cash machine. Harvey. David Harvey.'

Fitz grinned.

'David. Like Chrissie said.'

Penhaligon nodded. 'Like Chrissie said. Right again. Make you feel big does it?'

Fitz nodded and grinned even wider. The rest of the journey was conducted in silence.

Maggie Harvey let them in without a fuss when Penhaligon produced her ID. They waited in the lounge while Maggie took the kids upstairs to bed. There were four kids, aged from five to nine. Two boys, two girls. Fitz grinned at them as they filed past the door of the lounge. They looked nervously at him, not knowing what to make of either him or Penhaligon.

While he was thinking this thought, David Harvey came in. Penhaligon introduced herself and Fitz. David looked uneasily from one to the other. To Fitz he was an open book. Guilty as sin. Written all over his face in Ulverscroft Large Print. He might as well have been waving a banner saying 'It's a fair cop, guv, I did it.' And there was something familiar about his face. Something . . . no. He'd lost it among the revelry of the evening.

Maggie returned then, having settled the children, interrupting Fitz's train of thought, and all four sat down.

Maggie offered them a drink. Penhaligon declined. So did Fitz when she shot a sideways glance at him.

'What can we do for you, then?' David asked eventually.

'We're investigating a murder which took place last night.'

'I was here all last night,' said David. 'Right, Maggs?'

She nodded. 'Watching telly.'

'A rerun of *London's Burning*. Bit where the chemicals explode so they evacuate the factory and all the houses. It was on before *Hill Street Blues*.'

Fitz studied David Harvey closely. 'Let it burn, that's what I say.'

'Sorry?' That was David. Why was his face so familiar?

108

'Have we met?' Fitz decided a sideways approach might bring a result.

David shook his head. 'I don't think so. You want me to go on?'

Fitz shook his head abruptly, loosening all the gummy alcoholic cobwebs inside. Something was rattling around in there, a gleam, a little glimpse of the truth. Now what was it . . . was it . . . ah! That was it! 'There's something I don't understand. Don't get me wrong by the way, I know you're totally innocent. You're describing a programme you watched between nine and ten, yeah?'

'Yeah.'

'In copious detail, right?'

'Right.'

'So . . . it's like you know she was murdered between nine and ten. Isn't it?'

A quick exchange of glances, David and Maggie. Fitz clocked the looks, slotted them into the context of the conversation. 'And that's interesting. Because the police have never released that information.'

Fitz watched them both again. David was floundering.

Maggie stepped in with, 'We didn't watch anything before nine, that's all.'

Fitz nodded, shot a little glance to Penhaligon, who added, 'So can you explain why your bank card was used when you were in here watching telly?'

'I . . .' David shut up after a glare from Maggie.

Fitz said helpfully, 'You could have given it to your son, asked him to get a few bob for you.'

'Except he's only nine years old,' added Penhaligon.

Fitz followed up with, 'And it was used more than five miles from here, half a mile from the victim's flat.'

Penhaligon produced the last bit of evidence. 'You've reported your car stolen?'

No answer.

'A blue Renault. A blue Renault was seen in the area. Jean

McIlvanney was last seen getting into a blue Renault.'

David blinked, licked his lips, looked from Maggie to Penhaligon, to Fitz and back to his wife. Maggie just sat there, silent. Fitz could see the anger building inside her. Building to explosion point as Penhaligon ended the conversation with an inarguable statement.

'Mister David Harvey I'm arresting you in connection with the murder of Jean McIlvanney.' She cautioned him. 'Do you understand your rights as I have stated them?'

And Maggie screeched, '*Of course he understands them!*'

And as Penhaligon cuffed the unresisting David Harvey and led him to the car past a line of confused, bleary-eyed kids, Maggie followed, shouting all the way. 'I'll be at the station first thing in the morning. I'll come with Michael. We'll have you out in no time. I'll get the kids off to school and I'll come straight down and we'll have you out. We'll have you back home, David, in no time at all . . .'

Fitz heard her voice, her anger, echoing in his head long after they had put David Harvey into the back seat of Penhaligon's Volvo and driven away into the night. Later, Fitz would wish he had listened more closely to the voice, responded to the anger there. But for right now he was just too pleased with himself and too drunk to really give a damn.

ELEVEN

Later, as David Harvey slept fitfully in a police cell, nightmares crowding close with the tears, Joyce Watkins checked on her eight-month-old son before posing coquettishly and singing 'How much is that doggie in the window?'

Another Reclaim the Night march had sent punters scurrying for home and brought business to an all-time low. So she had time to chat.

Joyce had her eyes closed, was giggling when the first of the many blows that eventually killed her fell.

She never saw the chisel.

The cancer that was David Harvey was spreading.

WEDNESDAY

TWELVE

Next morning Denise Fletcher was called in and positively identified David Harvey as the man she saw last with Jean McIlvanney. Fitz watched the scene from behind the one-way glass normally reserved for witnesses. Denise chose to confront the line of men, picked Harvey out, identified him and then proceeded to deliver a very professional right cross to the jaw that had Harvey on the floor and two coppers, including Beck, manhandling Denise away before she incurred a further charge of assault. All this was done in silence. Denise didn't utter a single word except to identify Harvey. Only at the end, with two policemen taking her through the door and the other nine men in the line-up grinning and chortling to themselves, did she say anything, and that was pronounced with such cold precision that it might have been a dagger for the effect it had on Harvey.

'Jean was the best friend I've had in a long time. What you've done is going to have consequences you can't even begin to imagine. I want you hung for what you did to her. No. Hanging's too good for you. I want to take that chisel of yours and ram it up your arse and watch you bleed to death, you son of a bitch. I want to –' At that point the door to the ID room had swung shut behind her.

Harvey had been cuffed and led away to a cell.

Denise had not been charged with assault. She'd been shut in a cell for twenty minutes and given some tea. Eventually she had calmed down. Now she was crying to herself, curled up on the bunk. Fitz thought the best thing for her was to sleep it off. She had gone a long way towards ridding herself of the anger she felt towards Harvey, and in that respect she was lucky. So few victims or friends of victims were able to take that most important first step on the road to healing. And let's face it, Fitz added to himself, he should know.

Now Fitz was on the way to interview room one where Maggie and Michael Harvey had been taken when they arrived at the station to demand David's release an hour ago.

Penhaligon and Bobby Skelton were with the Harveys when Fitz arrived. Skelton looked at Fitz and grinned a hello. Penhaligon barely threw a look in his direction. Contemptuous. Angry. Well, he knew what that was all about. He'd stuck his nose in and now she wanted to bite it off.

A good result here could change all that.

Fitz didn't sit. He stood behind Penhaligon. *Loomed* might have been a better word. He lit up a high tar and puffed smoke at the ceiling light. He tried for a smoke ring, failed miserably. He looked first at Michael Harvey. He'd done a lot of thinking during the night and had remembered where he'd seen David Harvey before.

'David was at the presbytery when Danny and I called round yesterday to arrange the details of Mum's funeral.'

Michael affected a puzzled look. 'He's my brother. You brought yours as I recall.'

'Actually I'd argue that point. He brought me. Dragged me more like. I don't like churches.'

'I gathered.'

Fitz sucked on his high tar. Penhaligon shuffled slightly before him. She couldn't turn to see him, see his face, and that was making her edgy. Well tough. 'He seemed nervous. Your brother David.'

'He always does.'

Fitz nodded. Decided to sneak up sideways on the situation. 'You're wearing your collar.'

116

'So what?'

'Priests like you – liberal, streetwise – they very seldom wear their collars. You're wearing it now for effect.'

Michael shrugged. 'Whatever you say. You're the psychologist.'

Fitz pursed his lips. More background needed. More seeds of doubt to sow. He looked at Maggie. She was calmer than Michael. Less obviously frightened. More obviously angry.

'Your husband,' said Fitz to Maggie, 'goes with prostitutes.'

Maggie shook her head. 'He doesn't.'

Fitz grinned. ' I know you're lying. I'm an expert in body language. He goes with prostitutes and you know it.'

'No.'

'One of them picked your husband out at an identity parade.'

'A prostitute?' Was that a hesitation in her voice? The first crack in her resolve?

Fitz pushed harder. 'Oh yes. A friend of the dead woman's. She told us she last saw Jean McIlvanney with your husband. Climbing into a car he later claimed had been stolen earlier that evening.'

Maggie blinked. 'I bet she's got a string of convictions as long as my arm. She'll make a great witness, won't she?'

Fitz put his head to one side, puffed smoke while he considered Maggie's words. And her body language as well. Her attitude, posture. The way Michael deferred to her; the way she seemed not to need any looks of reassurance from him. At length he said, 'You've obviously had time to think about this. A lot more than, what,' he checked his watch, 'the four or five hours since we arrested him.'

Maggie said nothing.

Fitz said, 'And you weren't really that angry last night were you? I've seen people lose their tempers when their loved ones were arrested for a crime they didn't do and they

117

were like wildcats. Or dazed. As if they were drugged. You were neither.'

'I was confused.'

'Well look, it's like this, Maggie. When I was at school my English teacher used to read my stories and she used to say, Edward Fitzgerald, I want you to *show, not tell*. And what you did last night was tell me you were angry. As loudly and as often as you could. You *told* me, but you didn't *show* me. You never broke a sweat. You weren't frightened, not right down in your belly, in the animal part of you that can't hide its feelings.' Fitz blew more smoke. 'You *expected* David to be arrested. Didn't you?'

Maggie said nothing.

'You planned for it, didn't you? Hoped it wouldn't happen, but planned for it if it did.'

'That's utter rubbish!'

'Then why haven't you brought a lawyer, Maggie? Your husband's in clink for a crime he didn't commit. Where's the legal eagle who's going to spring him and make me and her', a gesture towards Penhaligon that earned him an irritated glare, 'look like complete idiots?'

Maggie was silent for a long time. Eventually she said, 'I can't afford one.'

'There's legal aid.' Fitz grinned. 'Then again there's also the theory that free advice is worth exactly what you pay for it.'

Maggie shrugged. 'Yeah.'

'So.' Fitz sucked on his high tar and then stubbed out the butt. 'You don't want legal counsel and your husband doesn't go with prostitutes.'

'That's right.'

Fitz sighed. 'No it's not. It's rubbish and you know it. David Harvey, your husband, went out on the pull last night, had sex with Jean McIlvanney, murdered her, then came home to you.'

'So you say.'

118

'Did you have sex?'

Maggie stared at the floor.

'He'd just murdered someone. That can be a bit of a turn-on. Did you have sex?'

Eventually, 'No.'

'But it's happened in the past? Hmm? He's come home, got into bed with you, made love, kept his eyes tight shut, imagined he was with the prostitute he's just left. Doing the things she would let him do. Because he was paying her.'

Maggie frowned. 'I'm an attractive woman. David loves me. I've got four kids. I'm hardly frigid. Why would he have sex with anyone else?'

Fitz pursed his lips. 'I don't know. Why don't you tell me?'

Maggie said nothing.

Fitz shrugged. 'Four kids?'

'Yes.' Ah. More confidence. Thought she was on safer ground.

'You're not on the pill?'

'No.'

'No form of birth control at all?'

'No.'

'I had a patient once. Young catholic girl. I advised her to go on the pill. She said it was useless. Every time she stood up it fell out.'

'I'm not sexually naive, if that's what you're saying.'

'No?'

'No.'

'Then why does your husband visit prostitutes?'

Maggie chewed her lip. 'I've told you: he doesn't visit prostitutes. We've got a good sex life, a healthy sex life. He doesn't need to visit prostitutes.'

'Healthy?'

'That's what I said.'

Fitz nodded to himself. 'What would be unhealthy?'

Maggie said nothing.

'Doing it with a chisel?'

Maggie said nothing.

Interesting.

'I don't blame the Pope.' A glance at Michael. 'I really don't.'

Michael frowned. 'I'm sure he'll be relieved to hear that.'

'I blame Clark Gable. "Frankly my dear I don't give a damn." No-one ever told Clark they had a headache. A sly look, a fade to black, cut to waves crashing on the shore, the earth moving. That's how sex should be. Seamless. Romantic. Hi-fidelity surround sound and colour by Technicolor. No fumbling around with a condom. Trouble is, that way gets you pregnant. And to do it any other way, to stop and fumble around with things, well, that's cold, calculating. Far better not to do it at all.'

Maggie uttered a humourless laugh. 'Are you suggesting my husband's sex-starved?'

Fitz scratched his head, took his glasses out and put them on, peered at Maggie over the rims. 'Possibly.'

'He's not!'

Fitz nodded, shot a look towards Michael. 'And God of course. He's to blame as well.'

'Really?'

'Yeah. Oh come on. How many times have you thought, "If only he hadn't put the nice bits next to the smelly bits?"'

Fitz looked to Michael for an answer but, as he expected, it was Maggie who responded.

'I don't find sex disgusting.'

'I think you do.'

'I don't. We get on fine. There's nothing wrong between me and my husband.'

'In that case why didn't you bat an eyelid when I suggested he might have used a chisel during sex?'

Maggie gasped then. Fitz had her and he knew it and

120

she knew that he knew. 'Well. You were obviously being facetious.'

Fitz uttered a laugh. 'Were you aware that your husband used a chisel when he killed Jean McIlvanney?'

Maggie's face crumpled. 'That's – How could you suggest that? My husband hasn't killed anyone! He doesn't need to go with prostitutes. And he *doesn't* go with prostitutes.'

Fitz thought about this for a moment and then asked, 'Have you told the kids yet?'

A fresh flow of tears. 'Yes.'

'Catholic school?'

Maggie nodded. Michael handed her his handkerchief and she wiped her face.

'It'll be all round there soon, won't it? Not the fact that their dad's killed someone – I know catholic morality – no. The fact that their dad goes with prostitutes.'

Maggie looked down, began to weep in earnest. Fitz watched her for a moment. Quiet little sobs. Inoffensive. Unaggressive. Useless for exorcising the pain, the fear, the anger; which was what crying, after all, was all about. Was she faking it?

'They'll have to change schools.'

That brought the dam down, finally. And as Fitz moved from his position to study her more closely, he caught a glimpse of Penhaligon out of the corner of his eye for the first time during the conversation. Her face was rigid. Her eyes unblinking, glossy with unshed tears. In that moment her look told him everything.

Why do you do it, Fitz? Why torture me as well? Why make me a victim?

And Fitz knew the truth. That she made herself a victim. And that was awful because he wanted to tell her and heal her and he could do neither. All he could do was increase her pain, and, by association, his own.

Maybe that was the truth. That he needed to punish

121

himself for ignoring his mother for so long before her death; that he punished himself by hurting Penhaligon and then feeling guilty about it afterwards.

Which was all rubbish of course. Because the last thing the pain brought was absolution. It only spread the humiliation and guilt, corrupting the lives of everyone it touched until the problems became insurmountable.

Fitz had a sudden urge to get some air. Abruptly he walked to the door and left the interview room. The hell with them. He needed to get his head straight. He'd come back later and talk to the Harveys some more. Or Penhaligon could finish the job. She was more than capable.

But Penhaligon had followed him from the room. Why? To accuse him of causing more pain? To condemn his less than ethical interview techniques? To tell him there was birdshit on his suit?

Well. The only way to find out was to dig in there and get to the truth of the matter.

'What?' he asked her aggressively.

'Nothing,' she responded with equal hostility.

'You're not up to this.'

'I follow you from the room and you think I want to go to bed with you. I'd call that stroking your ego, Fitz. And anyway. I've met someone.'

'Oh yeah? What's he like?'

'The total opposite of you.'

'Looks aren't everything.'

'I didn't mean looks.'

Fitz was about to respond when Wise came along the corridor from the door to interview room two. The room where he and Beck had been talking to David Harvey. Psychologically torturing him, more like. Fitz knew the way those two operated.

Wise looked from Fitz to Penhaligon and back.

'Who's with the Harveys?'

'Bobby Skelton, sir.'

'I want you with the Harveys, Jane. Get me?'

'Sir.'

'Good. Off you trot then.'

Fitz gazed at Wise, offended on Penhaligon's behalf by his brusqueness. 'Our piles playing us up today, are they?'

'Don't project, Fitz.'

Bugger.

'You could try codeine though, if they're really bad. *After* you've got matey in here to cough, that is.'

Fitz frowned.

Leaving Penhaligon grinning outside interview room one, Fitz followed Wise back in to interview room two.

Inside the room David Harvey and Jimmy Beck were head to head across the wooden table. Harvey was looking much the worse for wear. Then again Beck wasn't looking so sharp himself.

Fitz grinned at Beck. 'By the look of the ashtray you're going to chainsmoke yourself into an early grave. If you don't fall off a building first.'

Beck sent Fitz a glance which very clearly said *Up yours*.

Fitz grinned again, turned to Harvey. 'Getting fed up with the good-cop-bad-cop routine? Never mind. I'm here now. A breath of fresh air in the psychological mire of police technique.'

Beck grunted, pushed his chair back with a squeal of rubber on linoleum.

Fitz drew up a chair. Sat down. 'Hello again.'

Harvey remained expressionless. 'Hello.'

'You said we hadn't met before.' He lit up a high tar, jammed it into his mouth and sucked deeply. 'We have.' He blew smoke, emptied Beck's ashtray all over the floor and tapped fresh ash into it.

'Have we?' Harvey's voice was neutral. Fitz wondered why. Was he pretending innocence or had he passed the emotional cut-off point, the fear threshold?

'At your brother's. He's doing my mother's funeral.'

'I don't remember.'

'It was only yesterday. What were you doing there? Death in the family?'

'He's my brother.' As if that said everything. In a way it did.

'You needed a bit of advice? What to do with the body, that sort of thing?'

'No!' Harvey licked his lips. 'I was simply visiting my brother.'

Fitz nodded, changed tack. 'I've just been speaking to your wife.'

Harvey crumpled a little then. 'How is she?'

'Alive.' Fitz waited but there was no response. 'Ecstatic. She's going to get the blame, you know that don't you? If you'd been getting it at home, you wouldn't have gone to that prostitute. She'd still be alive. That's what people will say.'

'They'll be wrong.' A sudden conviction, as if the thought of his wife had loaned Harvey some inner strength.

Again Fitz nodded. Another suck on the high tar, another tap of ash. Another plume of smoke. 'I knew you'd be catholic. Dressing like Shirley Temple, singing the doggie song – innocence, virginity, catholicism.'

Harvey sighed, thumping his elbows onto the table. 'I don't know what you're talking about.'

Fitz sighed. Wise was right. His arse was killing him. Scotch and codeine. That was the answer. It was time to finish this. Or try to.

'You do. We understand each other perfectly. Married sex. Shall I tell you about it? The kids come along so you do it quietly in case you wake them up. The kids grow up, you do it quietly in case they hear. You get used to doing it quietly. No great fuss. You go to the pictures, turn on the TV. Cataclysmic sex. They start off on the balcony, pass through the bedroom, end up in the kitchen. Screaming, groaning. And you and the missus watch, fixed grins, faint embarrassment, squirming inside . . . because it reminds you of your own pathetic, silent clinches. Yes?'

124

'My wife and I have –'

' "A healthy sex life" – that's exactly what she said. Isn't that strange?'

'It's the truth.'

Fitz studied Harvey. There were ways in. He knew it. 'Question: what do lobster thermidor and oral sex have in common?'

Harvey looked at Fitz as though he were mad. 'How should I know?'

'I would have thought it was obvious: you never get either at home. You get the point I'm making?'

'No.' Puzzled. Vague amusement.

Fitz sighed. Brought it down to earth for him. 'The things you'd like to do to women. The things you'd like them to do to you. Not the wife, of course, you've got to see her the next morning. And we're talking real filth here, aren't we, David? I mean, you're catholic. There are two ways to do it and anything else is filth. That's true isn't it, David? Because you're a catholic? And you don't want the wife to know you're capable of even thinking those things. So what's the answer? A prostitute, a tart.'

Harvey blinked rapidly. His face was still carefully blank, but on the table, his hands were shaking, the tendons standing out. Fitz grinned. He was getting to the man. Good. Time for another salvo.

'I'm not blaming you for it. What have you done? You've put your wife on a pedestal, that's all. I've seen that picture on the wall. Madonna and Child. But you're a man. You need somewhere to dump all that filth, all that lust, and you can't dump it on a woman you worship. So you dump it on a tart. I can understand that. We all can. I mean, let's get it straight here, for God's sake: we're talking about a prostitute, a woman who sells herself, who –'

'– does it for money.' Harvey's voice was shaking now, like his hands. His face was cracking, showing the first hint of emotion, the first smidgeon of fear.

'And what do you think of a woman like that? Slut?'

'Yes.'

'Slag?'

'Yes.'

'Bitch?'

'Yes!'

'Scheming, grasping, crafty whore?'

'Yes, yes, yes!'

It was a barrage, and Harvey was crumbling. Fitz was on a huge buzz. He was going to have him. David Harvey was going to fall.

'Your alibi is in bits. The cash card. A prostitute picking you out of a line-up. Your car, which you reported missing, having been seen by neighbours outside your house the night you claim it was stolen. A witness who puts you in the car that picked up Jean McIlvanney. Perry Mason couldn't get you off.'

'I know.' His voice was tiny, a crushed thing, cowering beneath the barrage of Fitz's words.

'She wants you to plead not guilty. The other scheming, grasping, filthy whore. A trial you see. Publicity. She can sell her story, tell the world everything you did to her. What'll that do to your wife and kids, David? I mean, that's why you killed her in the first place, isn't it? To avoid a scene?'

Harvey tried to speak but all that came out was a kind of grunting sound. He was crouched forward now, staring at the table, hands shaking, face screwed up against the truth of Fitz's words.

'A busy road. People passing. She's making a scene, yeah? A common slut like that making a show of you? A family man like you?'

'Yes.'

'Is that why you killed her? For God's sake, you only have to take one look at her and you'd know. A slag. A prostitute, screaming about money, insulting people, you; people passing, looking at you.'

'She said she wanted to come into my house.'

In his head Fitz was leaping and screaming. Harvey was toast. He'd gone for it. He was going to cough.

'To your wife and kids?'

'If I couldn't get the money from somewhere else.'

'She was going to stand there in front of your wife and kids and demand money?'

'Yes.'

'And that's why you killed her?'

Harvey looked up at Fitz then. His face held the answer but it wasn't enough. Had to be verbal. Had to be for the record.

'Why the chisel? Hitting her with it, fine, I can understand that. But sticking it in her, inside her? Why do that?'

Harvey was stuttering a reply. It was nonsense.

'I know why. It helps, doesn't it? To know someone understands. You've killed her. She's dead, lying there, legs apart. And that thing between her legs. It's not part of her. Nothing to do with her. It's just that thing between her legs and it's brought you to this, to murder.'

A pause. Harvey was with him, Fitz was dragging him by the scruff of his neck to a confession.

'Remember going to confession? Getting those black marks off your soul? How good it felt afterwards? Tell me you did it, David. You killed Jean McIlvanney. You raped her and put a chisel in her and killed her. You did it. Tell me you did it. Tell me you did it.'

And Harvey looked up then, tears cutting tracks through the sweat running down his face, tendons on his neck standing out like guy wires, and Fitz still had him. He could see his throat working, getting the words ready, ready to spit out. Ready to confess, confess that he did it, that he, David Harvey killed Jean McIlvanney.

Fitz waited.

Harvey said, 'I –'

And the door burst open and DC Temple burst in and to

Fitz his excited voice was the executioner's blade. 'Fitz! Wise said to tell you there's been another one. Last night. Another girl was killed last night. Same method. Chisel and everything.'

And Fitz saw the expression die in Harvey's eyes. He saw his face assume its former blank neutrality and he knew that he'd get nothing out of Harvey now. Not if he tried for a month of Sundays.

THIRTEEN

Penhaligon studied the duty sergeant's report containing the brief details of Joyce Watkins's death as told to him by her neighbour, Sandra Burley, the woman who had found her body. By all accounts, Sandra had been kept awake by the noise of singing and then that of a record stuck on the phase 'Doggie-doggie-doggie-doggie'. When Sandra had gone next door to bang on the door and complain about the noise, she'd found the door open and a trail of blood leading past her own door, down the common stairs of the flats where she lived to the huddled shape of Joyce Watkins, barely alive, at the bottom. She'd managed to crawl that far to find help before collapsing.

Putting down the report, Penhaligon entered the interview room. Sandra Burley had come to make a full statement. She was a mess. Hair in disarray through rubbing her head, no makeup, eyes bleary with tears. A carrycot sat on a chair beside her. A baby gurgled quietly inside the cot.

She looked up as Penhaligon entered and almost broke down then and there. 'It could have been me,' she whispered. 'It could have been me. Joyce had a kid. A little baby. I heard him crying in the flat. I didn't go in because of all the blood. It could have been me. It could have been my baby. It could have been me.'

Penhaligon nodded. 'I know, Sandra. I know.' She looked around the interview room, noted the lack of any comforts. She directed her gaze at DC Skelton who was standing stock still beside the door as if on guard. 'Bobby, get us a couple of cups of tea, will you?'

Skelton nodded and left.

Penhaligon sat at the table, opposite Sandra, and switched on the evidence recorder.

Sandra's eyes flickered towards the machine; Penhaligon smiled reassuringly. 'It's OK, you're not under suspicion. I just have to record what you say so I can write it up as evidence for when we catch whoever did this.'

Sandra nodded blearily. She rubbed her eyes.

Penhaligon rummaged in her purse and offered the other woman a small box of Freshets.

Sandra tore the foil and wiped her face with the napkin. 'Thanks. That's better. I hate it when your face is all sticky.'

Penhaligon nodded.

Skelton returned with the tea at that point. A tray, two mugs and a steaming pot. Penhaligon poured two mugs of tea. She offered one to Sandra, who took it and sipped gratefully. With her hands cupped tightly around the mug, she seemed to Penhaligon to be more interested in taking comfort from its warmth than drinking the tea.

'Was there no-one to come in with you today? Not married or anything? Boyfriend?'

Sandra shook her head. 'The flats where I live. They're emergency housing. Lots of single mothers and kids. Joyce had a kid.'

Penhaligon nodded sympathetically. The sympathy was real but not as pronounced as it could be. Penhaligon had never really seen the need for kids. Then again thirty-four wasn't old, was it? There was still time.

'Did you know Joyce well?'

'We were neighbours. There are only two flats to each floor in any one block. They built them door to door with a common staircase going down to street level. There's a street door every second flat.'

'So you must have known each other quite well then?'

'Well, you know. Joyce was OK, I suppose. She loaned me her vacuum cleaner sometimes. But she played her music so loudly. And I was always getting men accidentally buzzing my number from the street and asking for her. And for all different names too.' Sandra sipped her tea and looked straight at Penhaligon. 'She was . . . she was doing it wasn't she? On the game?'

Penhaligon nodded. 'Yes she was.'

Sandra frowned. 'You'd think there would be a better way for her to earn a living. She was only a kid. Years younger than me. Good looking too, if you took off all that rubbish she put on her face.' Sandra suddenly giggled. There was no humour in the sound at all. 'Then again, I suppose she needed it in her line of work.'

Penhaligon let Sandra drink some more tea. Her own mug stood untouched on the table. Steam drifted quietly upwards. The tape whirred in its wooden box.

'Tell me how you found the body.'

Sandra gripped the mug tightly. Her knuckles whitened until they matched the china itself.

'I know how upsetting this must be for you, but it's very important.'

'I know.' Sandra nodded, put the mug down slightly too hard. A few drops of tea slopped onto the table. 'Well. Joyce had been playing her music all afternoon. The walls are like paper in the flats so the sound travels really easily. I can stand it in the day time. That's fair enough. I had to go out to do some shopping, sign on and stuff. But I always put Ben – that's my boy – to bed about six o'clock. He's only eight months old.' Sandra's face crumpled a little bit then. 'Only a bit older than Joyce's kid. Anyway. I put him to bed and watched telly, but the music was loud and I couldn't concentrate. I couldn't go out because of Ben. In the end I put my headphones on and tried to read.'

'What about Ben? What if he cried and you couldn't hear him?'

'Oh, I brought his carrycot into the living room.'

Penhaligon nodded. 'What then?'

'The music stopped for a while about ten or so and I went to bed. It started again an hour later and woke me up. Only it wasn't the radio. It was Joyce. She was singing.'

'What was she singing?'

' "How much is that doggie in the window?" '

'How long did this go on for?'

'Ten minutes or so. Then the record started. It jammed almost immediately, played over and over again. It woke Ben up. Drove me mad. I thumped on the wall but it didn't do any good.'

'Did you hear any other voices?'

'I didn't listen, really. There might have been conversation when the record went on, but I couldn't tell. I thought I heard someone swearing at one point.'

'Man or woman?'

'Couldn't tell. Joyce has got – Joyce had a low voice. I think she sang in a choir somewhere.'

'And what time did you hear this?'

'About . . . about three I think. Three or four a.m. I'm not sure.'

'And then?'

'And then I heard a front door slam. I thought Joyce had gone out and left it going. I put my headphones on and tried to get some sleep. I couldn't sleep. An hour later it was still going.'

'And that's when you went to investigate.'

'Well, yeah. I was worried by then. You know. A record sticks all night. You hear sounds. You don't know what to think.'

'And what did you find in the flat?'

'I didn't get that far. Joyce and I, we're on the top floor of these flats. There're only three floors. The doors face one another across a landing which opens directly onto the staircase. When I opened my door I saw the blood straight away.' Sandra licked her lips, took a gulp from her mug. 'I saw the blood and . . . there was so much! It was all over the

132

landing. Like someone had dragged a dead animal out of Joyce's flat and chucked it down the stairs.'

'So you saw that it came from the flat then?'

Sandra nodded. 'I don't have a phone. I got Ben dressed and started to go out to the phone across the street – and that's when I found her. Huddled at the bottom of the stairs halfway to the second floor. That's as far as she got.' Sandra blinked. Tears threatened to come again. 'Her eyes were open. She looked up at me. Oh God, the blood. It was all over her. All over her nightie, the stairs. She just looked up at me and it was like she didn't even have the strength to close her eyes. The pain in them.'

'Did she say anything?'

Sandra was crying again now. She pulled another Freshet from its sachet and wiped her eyes. 'No. She tried to but there was just more blood. It was coming out of her mouth. Everywhere. And I heard her baby crying then. Missed his feed, I expect. And I stepped over her, and went downstairs to the phone and I called the police and an ambulance.'

Sandra dried her eyes.

Penhaligon allowed her a few minutes to catch her breath. 'Would you like some more tea?'

'Oh yes please.'

By now the tea was lukewarm and stewed, but Sandra guzzled another mugful down without hesitation. She was shaking. Penhaligon knew exactly what she was going through. After all hadn't she and Jimmy Beck found DCI Bilborough's body under almost identical circumstances only a year ago? Stomach ripped open, blood everywhere. Bilborough had dragged himself out of the house where he'd been attacked to die jack-knifed into the gutter, body open to the world, steaming in the pale afternoon sunlight.

Penhaligon shook herself mentally. Bilborough's death. Her rape. Jimmy Beck. They were all connected. A grand circle of cosmic karma coming back for another shot at revenge or redemption.

Oh cut the crap, Jane.

With a tremendous effort Penhaligon cut the maudlin thoughts dead, looked back at Sandra.

'Can you tell me anything else? Did anyone buzz for Joyce the day before?'

'Now you mention it, yes. A couple of blokes. They got her name right. And a woman. She sounded like she was canvassing. Got the name wrong and everything.'

'Would you recognise the men's voices?'

Sandra shrugged. 'Those intercoms, you know. They're crap really. Whoever's on the other end sounds like they're phoning from Mars.' The joke wasn't funny but Penhaligon could see Sandra needed to make it, needed the release of tension. Christ, she was wound as tight as a clockspring herself.

Penhaligon nodded her thanks. 'We'll be in touch if there's anything more we need. If there's anything more you remember, you can reach me on this number.' She handed Sandra a card.

Sandra nodded, tucked the card into her purse. She rose to leave and then stopped. She looked back at Penhaligon and her question was as obvious as the nose on her face.

'I'm sorry, Sandra. Joyce died in hospital early this morning. She just lost too much blood. Nothing you could've done would've made a difference. I really am very sorry.'

Sandra nodded and it was obvious that was the answer she had expected.

Penhaligon had Skelton give Sandra and her son a ride home. After they had gone she sat for a long time in the interview room, trying to get her thoughts in order. This was no good. She was a professional, damn it. She was a bloody good copper. Why was this case getting to her so much?

The answer was obvious.

The rape.

134

Bilborough's murder.

Jimmy Beck.

And Fitz poking his nose into the whole sodding mess.

Penhaligon retied her hair, tightly, as if the pain of her stretched scalp would drive away the bad thoughts, the memories of that day.

All that happened was that she got a headache that had her reaching into her purse for the Nurofen.

Wise had the pathology report when Penhaligon got back to the duty room. He was reading a summary from it as she passed through the crowded room and sat at her desk.

'Joyce Watkins. Prostitute. Twenty-two. Fractures to the skull. Bruising to the vagina. She'd had intercourse. Murder weapon was a chisel. It was inserted prior to death. Copeley thinks she was killed by the same man who killed Jean McIlvanney.'

Beck sucked on his roll-up and said, 'That's impossible.' He shot a glance towards Penhaligon. 'Batman and Robin brought him in last night. He's been in a cell all night. He was in a cell when this assault was committed.'

Penhaligon felt her hatred of Beck growing. Her headache too.

Wise nodded thoughtfully to the roomful of officers. 'So. Two identical murders. But we've got the killer banged up when the second one takes place. How do we explain that?'

Beck had what he obviously thought was the answer. 'The second one's a copycat.'

Penhaligon sighed. 'No-one knew about the chisel, Jimmy.'

Wise backed her up. 'It didn't go out on the news broadcast, nor to the papers. But all the same we're going to have to read every issue of yesterday's papers just in case some pillock *did* get wind of the chisel and mentioned it somewhere.'

From a plastic Marks and Sparks bag Wise took several

135

double handfuls of yesterday's newspapers. He spread them on the desk in front of him. 'Don't all rush, will you? Here Jimmy. You can start. The *Sun*.'

Penhaligon grabbed herself a copy of the *Independent* and began to read. The phone on her desk rang. She picked it up idly. 'Duty room.'

'Can I speak to Doctor Fitzgerald, please?'

'He's interviewing someone at the moment.' Something about the voice was familiar. Who was she kidding? The voice was as familiar as Fitz's was. 'Is that Judith?'

'Yes. Is that . . . is that Jane? Jane Penhaligon?'

'Yes.'

Long silence.

'Hello.'

'Hello.'

Another long silence. Penhaligon realised she was shaking. It was his wife. His bloody wife. A woman she hated, despised, could cheerfully have strangled. The woman she thought was strangling Fitz's life. She tried to put the phone back on the cradle, break the connection. Her arm wouldn't work.

Judith said, 'Can we talk some time?'

Penhaligon licked her lips. Was Judith playing games with her? Did she hate her that much? Well, Fitz married her and loved her, so the games part of it was reasonable. And let's face it, she hated Judith without reservation for the way she'd screwed up her own relationship with Fitz. 'Fitz has got my number.'

The answer came after a moment. 'Face to face.'

'I'm not ready for that just yet.' Again Penhaligon tried to put down the phone. Again something stopped her. This time it was Judith's words.

'We've made love once since I came back. Early hours of the morning. He was pissed. Half asleep when he started. He woke up. I saw the disappointment in his eyes when he realised it was me. He'd thought it was you.'

136

Penhaligon made a tremendous effort to keep her voice from cracking. 'He said that?'

'He didn't have to.'

Right. Like you don't have to torture me with these head games!

'You hate me.'

No hesitation this time. And Penhaligon found herself wishing she could see Judith's face this once. 'Part of me does, yes. I'm the wronged wife. Every weapon at my disposal. But they're all useless.' And Penhaligon knew what was coming then. Sympathy; and she needed that like she needed a hole in the head. She got it anyway, from the person from whom it meant the least. 'You've been raped.'

Her voice hardened. 'I wouldn't let a little thing like that stop you.'

Another pause. Judith weighing up the anger in Penhaligon's voice, wondering how much of it was due to herself, how much was due to Fitz.

'You know who did it.'

Penhaligon shot a glance at Jimmy Beck, flipping through the personal ads in the *Sun*. 'Yeah.'

'Does Fitz know?'

'Yeah.'

'I'm sorry, Jane. For what it's worth. Really. Please. Let's talk soon, yes?'

'Maybe. I'll tell Fitz you phoned. Goodbye.'

This time Penhaligon found the phone almost hurled itself out of her hand and back onto the cradle.

Jimmy Beck looked over at her and lifted one corner of his mouth in a lopsided grin. He sucked on his roll-up and blew smoke. God she hated him.

The doors to the duty room burst open then and Fitz strolled in like a wild west marshall into a saloon. A rather careworn and down-at-heel marshall with a crumpled suit two sizes too small and battered ego still several sizes too large.

Wise looked up as he entered. 'How do you kill a woman when you're behind bars?'

'Voodoo.' Fitz snapped back the answer with a tired smile. He picked up the set of forensics photographs and shuffled through them as if they were a deck of cards. Penhaligon didn't need to see them to imagine what they showed. Joyce Watkins, half-naked, crumpled in a heap, blood everywhere.

Wise filled Fitz in. 'She dragged herself to the stairs. Fell down the lot of them.'

'The chisel?'

'Found it lying on the stairs.'

Fitz nodded, selected more photos. 'These shots of the flat. She'd had tea. Two cups. Two sets of prints?'

'One set only. The victim's. And none on the chisel. Like Jean.' Wise sighed. 'How did you get on?'

Fitz put down the photographs, began to leaf idly through the pages of yesterday's *Sporting Times*. 'David Harvey did it. He definitely killed Jean McIlvanney.'

That got everyone's attention. 'He coughed?'

Fitz shot a look at Temple, who blushed sheepishly. 'Nearly. But I'm sure he did it. The profile's right. His state of mind is fragile. Very fragile. He's drawing on strength. Maggie's strength. She's all that's keeping him going.'

'Jimmy thought the second murder was a copycat.'

Fitz laughed outright. 'You still asleep, Jimmy?' Fitz nodded towards the photographs. 'Whoever killed Joyce Watkins has to be someone David Harvey confided in.'

'Bollocks.' That was Beck, defending his reputation, his ego. 'You've just killed someone. Murdered them. Shoved a chisel up their skirt. Would you tell anyone what you'd done?'

'Well. I'm not David Harvey. And I don't carry around the catholic guilt that David Harvey does. And I've seen him since the murder of Jean McIlvanney with at least one person other than his wife.'

138

Beck scowled.

Everyone else looked interested.

'Go ahead, lad,' said Wise gruffly.

'You're a rapist and killer. You're catholic. You're guilty as sin.' Fitz stared directly at Beck. 'Who would you confide in?'

Beck folded the *Sun*, blew smoke, said nothing.

'Your priest. Your brother.' He paused for effect. 'Michael Harvey is both David's brother and a priest.'

And he grinned. Because he was right and he knew it. And Penhaligon grinned along with him because, try as he might, even Jimmy Beck couldn't argue with the truth of Fitz's words.

Fitz moved closer to Wise and began to talk details. She was about to join them when Beck sidled up to her and sat on the edge of her desk.

She stared up at him, willing him to slip off the desk and give himself a hernia.

He returned her gaze moment for moment.

Evenually she sighed. 'It's very common, Jimmy: the rapist blaming the victim.'

Beck grinned. 'Do you know what day it is?'

Penhaligon held her temper in check with a tremendous effort. When she spoke her voice was a tense whisper. 'I'm going to get promotion, Jimmy. DI. And when I do, I'll have you running round this station like a PC again. I'll make your life a misery.'

And Beck grinned even wider. He produced a paper envelope. 'It's Bilborough's birthday.' He placed the card in front of a dumbfounded Penhaligon. 'If you sign that I'll pretend you remembered. It might cheer Catriona up.'

Damn.

She signed the card. Jimmy took it and strolled back to his desk. The grin never faltered.

FOURTEEN

Maggie and Michael Harvey had been released about an hour previously. Fitz asked Wise for a police driver to take him out to the Harveys' house. His feelings were mixed when Wise gave the job to Penhaligon. On the one hand he was glad to have her with him. Professionally speaking she was sharp as a new pin. On the other hand, however, things between them were rather evidently strained. Oh, he tried to lighten the mood a bit, cracked a few crap jokes while they drove. Penhaligon responded to neither his humour nor his growing frustration. She simply ignored him altogether.

When they arrived at the Harveys' house Maggie answered the door wearing an apron. 'Dinner,' she explained brusquely. 'Someone's got to make it.'

Penhaligon smiled understandingly. 'Have you got a minute, Mrs Harvey?'

Maggie sighed, led them inside, pointedly did not take off the apron.

Without preamble, Fitz said, 'We've come here to ask you a few questions, Maggie.'

'Well, you better ask away, then, hadn't you?'

'D'you get on well with Father Michael?'

'Yes. I do actually.'

'And your husband. David. He gets on with him?'

'They're brothers.'

'So were Cain and Abel.' Fitz was acutely aware of the allusion he'd used and how it related to his own relationship with Danny. Still. Any weapon at his disposal . . .

'What's your point?'

Fitz shook his head, deliberately missed her point. 'They trust each other? David and Michael?'

'Yes.' Utter conviction. Some irritation. Was the dinner burning? Did Maggie know something she shouldn't?

'They wouldn't hide anything from each other?'

'Of course not!' Exasperation now. And impatience.

'You must resent that.'

Maggie rolled her eyes. 'What is this about, Doctor Fitzgerald? These questions are a load of –'

'I'm afraid they're police business,' Penhaligon interrupted politely. 'You must answer them.'

Maggie huffed impatiently. 'Oh very well. Yes. Sometimes I resented their closeness.'

Fitz nodded. Pursed his lips. Pulled his glasses from a pocket and placed them on the end of his nose. 'Does Michael visit prostitutes?'

'What?!'

'Does Michael visit prostitutes?'

'He's a *priest*!'

'He's human.'

And Maggie was firing back. 'I know you. And people like you. One or two priests make a mistake, you seize on it. This is what they're all like. Well, they're not.'

Fitz frowned. Studied Maggie through his spectacles. She was lying. He knew it. Every bone and muscle in her body was calling her a liar. Every glance. Every twitch.

'Make a mistake? You'd call murder making a mistake?'

'Murder?'

'Yes.'

'You think Michael could kill someone?'

'Yes.'

A moment of silence, then, 'You bastard. It's not enough for you to condemn my husband, now you've got to go after his brother. You bastard.' She looked at Penhaligon. 'Can I make a complaint about this man?'

Penhaligon shook her head. 'No. Please answer the questions, Mrs Harvey.'

'Does Michael visit prostitutes? No!'

Fitz sniffed. Lit up a high tar without asking permission. He puffed smoke. 'You think you owe Michael anything? I don't. Your husband went with prostitutes for years. He told me this morning. Had sex with them. Spent all that money on them. You think he wouldn't tell his priest? His brother? They trusted one another. Confided in one another. You said that. They wouldn't hide anything from each other. Father Michael's known for years, Maggie. He just hasn't bothered to tell you.'

Maggie ran into the kitchen then, drew a glass of water and gulped it down. Fitz cruised after her, pushing, unwilling to give up the advantage.

'All those years of marriage. All that trust. And he told Michael. Not you. Michael.'

Maggie banged the glass down on the sink. Turned angrily. 'What do you want? Why don't you just tell me what you want!'

'Does Father Michael use prostitutes?'

Maggie was shaking. 'Yes.'

'David told you?'

'Yes. Once. Years ago. He was drunk. He's probably forgotten he ever said anything.' Maggie threw the apron onto the kitchen table, began to adjust dials on the cooker. 'I have to . . .' she mumbled, 'I have to . . .'

'Quite.' Fitz smiled his thanks. Then he and Penhaligon left Maggie to her cooking.

In the car Penhaligon spoke the first words she'd said to him all day. 'Where to?'

'St Catherine's. I have to talk to Michael.'

Penhaligon drove him there. But when she made to leave the car and follow him into the church, he stopped her. 'It's personal. This guy's going to bury my mum. Sorry.'

143

She nodded. 'I'll wait in the car.'

The church was as he remembered it. Old, a quaint tilt, sunlight from the canal glimmering across the grey stone walls. Inside was different. It had been refurbished in the last two years. Gone were the ancient stained pews, the echoing stone. Instead neat wooden panelling lined the walls and pulpit; new pews gleamed and new flagstones held the dust of less than a year's worth of parishioners.

The confessional was different too. It was well lit. A table. Chairs facing one another. Fitz was disappointed. He felt like he had walked back into the interview room at Anson Road.

Michael was seated at the table. He looked up at Fitz, gauged his reaction to his surroundings. 'Surprised?'

Fitz nodded, somewhat taken aback. 'It used to be dark. Just the grille. The priest running his hand through his hair; dandruff spinning in a shaft of light.'

'Things have changed. Vatican Two. Head and Shoulders.' Michael grinned. 'What can I do for you, Fitz?'

Fitz sat, feeling the chair creak unsteadily beneath his not inconsiderable weight. Modern workmanship for you.

'I'm going to take communion at my mother's funeral.'

'She'd have liked that.'

'So I've got to get all the mucky bits off my soul. And that's not two minutes with a wet sponge. It's more like two weeks sandblasting.'

Michael nodded. 'I thought communion meant nothing to you?'

'It doesn't.'

'So why bother with this? Just take it.'

Fitz laughed aloud at the impossibility of Michael's suggestion. 'Your lot did too good a job on me when I was a kid.'

Michael grinned again, slightly.

And then Fitz was into it. 'Bless me Father for I have sinned. It's thirty odd years since my last confession.'

'May the Lord help you to confess your sins with true sorrow.'

Fitz pursed his lips. 'Sorrow? That's the problem. The first one's adultery and I'm not sorry at all. What do you get for it these days, a novena? She was worth it.' He uttered a humourless laugh. 'She's sitting in a car outside.'

'Does your wife know?'

Fitz felt the pain of guilt. 'I'm sorry about that, yes. That I hurt my wife.'

'Anything else?'

'I drink too much. I smoke too much. I gamble too much.' Fitz thought for a moment, added, 'I *am* too much.'

Michael nodded. 'I know. Your mother used to worry about you.'

And that hit Fitz right where it was supposed to. And it stuck. And it hurt. There was a long moment of silence. Then Fitz said, quietly, 'Suppose the priest isn't worthy of being a priest? Am I still absolved?'

'Yes.' Simple. Direct.

Fitz laughed inwardly. 'And tomorrow, that bit of bread's going to turn into the body of Christ, yeah?'

'Yes.'

'Even if . . . what? The priest's involved in murder?'

Now Fitz looked at Michael. He hadn't even broken a sweat. Fitz wondered briefly how many philosophical conversations he took at confessional.

Michael said, 'Yes. Because God wouldn't punish you for the sins of your priest.'

Fitz reached into his pocket and touched the photographs tucked away there. The pictures of Joyce Watkins, half naked, smeared with blood, barely alive, crumpled at the foot of a concrete staircase.

'You don't like prostitutes?'

'Prostitution.' The correction was automatic.

'You despise them?'

'I despise what they do. They sell sex. They sell something that's sacred.'

Fitz grinned. 'So you've got a lot in common.' Without waiting for the reaction he knew his remark would provoke, Fitz continued, 'Mind you, prostitutes sell it cheap. Twenty, thirty quid a time. You traded yours in for a house, a car, a job for life. Food in your belly, clothes on your back.'

Michael held Fitz's gaze steadily, showed no outward reaction to this deconstruction of his faith. 'You have got a romantic notion of prostitutes, haven't you, Eddie?'

'Fitz.'

Michael shrugged. 'They're only going out to put shoes on the kids' feet, food in their bellies, yeah?'

Fitz nodded. The pictures of Joyce Watkins were burning a hole in his brain. 'Yes.'

'But how do their punters get the money? By seeing their own wives go short. Their own kids go hungry. Prostitutes take money off other women, not men.'

Fitz laughed. Short, irritable. 'Is that what you told David? Did it make him feel better about killing Jean McIlvanney?'

Michael studied Fitz. Ignored his question, instead asked one of his own. 'Why do you drink so much?'

'I'm easily bored.'

Michael smiled. 'Lots of drunks say that. It's bullshit. You drink because you despise yourself. Or the people around you. Or you've got a sexual problem. Or a psychological problem.'

Fitz frowned. 'I think you're a murderer.'

Michael's smile widened. 'Now you're trying to convince me it's psychological.'

'I'm serious.'

Michael laughed then. 'I couldn't murder a pint. I certainly couldn't do what that man did.'

Interesting.

'And what did he do?'

Michael hesitated, as if recognising he'd made an

146

assumption he ought not to have. 'He murdered someone.'

'You implied something more.'

'I didn't.'

' "I certainly couldn't do what that man did." Those words. That tone of voice. Self-righteous. That implies a lot more, that he defiled the body in some way.'

'Did he?'

'Yes. But the question is: how did you know that?'

'I didn't. The police described it as a brutal murder. It's that that implies things.'

'All murders are brutal.'

Michael licked his lips. 'Do you think you were a good son?'

Fitz recognised the attempt for what it was: a desperate change of subject designed to put Fitz off his stride. No way. 'This is what he did.' Fitz pulled the photographs from his pocket and laid them on the table. He spread them out for Michael to see.

Joyce covered in blood, crumpled on the stairs. 'And this.'

Blood smeared across the steps, a chisel in shot, slick with blood. 'And this.'

A shot of her child in his crib in the living room, squealing, hand outstretched for food. 'And this.'

And another of Joyce. A different angle. More blood. The slashed legs and stomach. And another, another.

A shot of her face.

And Fitz nearly yelled with delight. Despite the fact that he looked ready to throw up, Michael's eyes had narrowed at the shot of Joyce's face. *He recognised her.*

Michael shook his head slowly. 'You think I'm capable of that?'

Fitz nodded.

'But you'll let me bury your mother?'

'My mother's dead. You're putting her in a hole in the ground, that's all.'

Fitz lowered his head for a moment, closed his eyes. 'You know how I know it's you? Shall I tell you your first big mistake?'

'Why do you despise the church, Fitz?'

Fitz steamrollered over Michael's question. 'You had a cup of tea. Two sugars according to forensics. And you do take two sugars because I've seen you do it. At the time I put it down to celibacy. Oral gratification. You see, Joyce wouldn't give a punter a cup of tea. She got rid of them as quickly as possible. But you'd only come for a chat. And how did she know you'd come for a chat? You were wearing your dog collar. You want to know your second big mistake?'

Michael said, 'I never worry about people who despise the church. People who are simply bored with it, yes, but those who despise it – well it must really matter to them.'

Fitz grinned. Michael wanted to play games. Word games. Well. It had been a long time. But word games were Fitz's stock in trade.

'You left no prints on the cup. Or saucer. Or spoon. You wore gloves. Big mistake.'

Michael seemed to be speaking to avoid thinking, to avoid listening to what Fitz was saying. 'You'll come back to us. When your body can't take the booze any more. When you can't get rid of a cough. When there's a lump that won't go away.'

And Fitz heard the words, cutting, the truth. But he ignored them. 'A prostitute down the road's been murdered but she sits there with a man wearing gloves. Joyce must've felt really safe with that man. She did. He was wearing a dog collar.'

'Joyce?' Surprise.

'Yes.'

'Not Jean? A different woman?'

Don't give me that. You know her. You've used her. You've paid her.

'When my brother was behind bars?'

'Yes.'

'Excuse me.' And Michael left the confessional. Grinning, Fitz scooped up the photographs and followed him to the church sacristy. He had picked up the phone there and was dialling. He turned as Fitz entered. 'Will you wait outside please?' His voice was cracked, stressed, almost a screech.

Fitz turned to go, saw a bottle of altar wine on a nearby table, scanned the label. 'Fifteen per cent proof. I feel a vocation coming on.'

'Will you *leave* please?'

Fitz smiled, put down the wine and left. But not before he heard Michael say, 'Maggie? Wait a minute will you?' And then the priest turned and stared at Fitz until he closed the door and wandered back to Penhaligon, waiting in the Volvo in the car park.

He told her what had happened. Who Michael had phoned.

She nodded. 'All right. I'll call in. Have someone watch the Harveys' house.' She thought for a moment. 'By the way, Judith phoned earlier.'

Fitz affected nonchalance. 'Oh really? What did she want?'

'Well, she said she wanted to speak to you, but we had a nice long chat in the end.'

Fitz shook his head. 'Beam me up, Scotty.'

Penhaligon said nothing, started the car, drove Fitz home.

'Cuppa?' Fitzed asked as she parked the car outside his house. 'You and Judith could have a nice heart-to-heart about me.'

Penhaligon grinned then. 'Oh? What makes you think we were talking about you?'

And Fitz was out of the car, halfway up the garden path before Penhaligon let in the clutch and roared away.

● ● ●

Mark was sitting on the porch, smoking what looked suspiciously like a joint. Fitz stared pointedly. Mark stared back.

'Is that a joint?'

'I see you cleaned the shit off your suit.'

Fitz sighed.

'Mum in?'

'Living room. Flat on her back. Not feeling so good.'

Fitz stepped over his son, found Judith exactly as Mark had described her, resting her back on a row of cushions on the floor.

Puffing with effort, Fitz lowered himself to the floor beside her. She looked at him. He took her hand. She let him.

'You called the station today.'

'I don't want to talk about it.'

'You spoke to her.'

'To Jane? Yes, we had words. Fitz, I don't want to talk about it.'

Fitz nodded.

'Screams, hysteria, that sort of thing?'

Judith took her hand back. 'Why do you persist in assuming we talked about you?'

'I'm a bloody psychologist, Judith. I know about these things. I've had an affair. The great green jealousy monster. You're angry with me. She's angry with me.'

'Come off it, Fitz. *You're* angry with you. That's what it is and you know it.'

It was the truth and Fitz knew it.

Judith grinned. 'See. Twenty-three years married to a psychologist and you can't help but pick up some of the lingua franca.'

Fitz had to grin then.

Judith gave him her hand back. 'I've got a bad back.'

He rubbed the hand. 'Celtic have got four.'

Judith's smile faded. She adjusted her position slightly. Fascinated, Fitz watched her belly ripple with the movement.

'You're an engine, do you know that? A biological engine. Inside your body something is happening that fundamentally defines the whole human race.'

Judith huffed softly. 'I love it when you talk dirty.'

A moment passed.

Judith said, 'Can I have a whinge?'

'Of course.'

'A long one.'

'Long as you like.'

Judith sighed. 'The hospital phoned. They're going to induce me. My blood pressure's up. And they keep going on about my age. Well, I don't want to be induced. I want to be a seed pod. I want to be a biological engine that fundamentally defines the human race. I want to go "pop" like I did with Katie. And post-natal exercises "suitable to a woman my age". I know what they mean. They mean I'm never going to get my figure back. I'm never going to be thin again. And then I think of you and Jane, that bloody stick insect, and it hurts, Fitz, it damn well hurts.'

Fitz licked his lips, stared at the floor. 'That's over.'

'Your choice or hers?'

Actually – yours. 'Either way. It's over.'

'I know, but it still hurts. And I'm not missed in work. I thought the phone would ring nineteen to the dozen since I began maternity leave but it hasn't rung once. I am utterly dispensable. And if I have a boy I don't want him called Charles Laughton Fitzgerald. I'm not naming a son of mine after the man who played the hunchback of Notre Dame. And I know how selfish, how wimpish, how pathetic all this sounds when you're grieving about your mother and that just makes me feel even worse.' Judith was silent a moment, considering, then added, 'Whinge over.'

'That was a long one.'

'Can't say I didn't warn you.'

Fitz considered. 'Not Charles Laughton?'

'No.'

'What about . . .' Fitz grinned suddenly. 'Boris?'

Suddenly the moment broke and Judith was laughing, and he was laughing too, because it felt so good just to share the laughter, except that it wasn't laughter, it was tears, and they were laughing and crying all at once and he couldn't tell where one ended and the other began. He only knew how good it was to hold her, to have her here, where she belonged, where *they* belonged.

Together.

For however long it might be.

FIFTEEN

For Jimmy Beck the nightmare had begun about a year ago. It had begun with a moment of compassion which had gone against every gut instinct he had. The compassion had been a mistake, one which had resulted in a psychotic headcase walking free, which had resulted in the death of his boss and closest friend DCI David Bilborough.

Since that day Beck had been a man walking a tightrope. Some days it was as much as he could do to maintain the balance in his life between what was real and what wasn't. Now as he got out of his car and approached David Bilborough's house he clutched a bouquet of flowers hard enough to bruise the stems. The card he'd had everyone sign was tucked into the bouquet. He was going to see Catriona. David's wife. David's widow. And baby Ryan. David's son. A boy who would never know the love of a father, never be taken to the footey or pictures, out for a burger or bowling. Who would never have that inevitable man-to-man chat about girls, who would never blag the use of the car to take that special girl out, who would never argue what time he had to be back in, who would never –

The sound of a door bell broke the stream of tortured thoughts. Beck realised his finger was white-knuckled on the bell push.

He straightened his tie while he waited for her to answer.

And the latch clicked and the door opened and there she was, with baby Ryan, now over a year old.

Catriona.

Her hair had grown since his death. Her smile was radiant

as ever it had been. Her eyes ... he'd expected them to be haunted, pain-filled, pining, but, God, they seemed so happy. She seemed so happy.

So normal.

The smile widened when Catriona saw who it was.

'Jimmy. It's been a while.' And she bounced Ryan a little until he began to giggle. 'Look who it is, pesky one. It's your Uncle Jimbo.'

She ushered Beck in and shut the door with her hip. 'You know where the living room is, Jimmy. Fix yourself a drink while I ditch trouble here.' She waggled Ryan and he giggled again.

Beck walked through to the living room. A moment later Catriona was back without Ryan. Beck turned as she entered. 'Get you anything?'

'I'm OK, thanks.'

And indeed he was already heading towards the glasses and bottles on the low coffee table which was the centre-piece of the room.

Beck poured himself a drink. Scotch. Neat. Sucked it down. Felt the slide, the slow burn, lost in memories for a moment. Himself and David shooting the breeze over a video of United's latest disaster. Himself and David and Catriona making short work of a Sunday roast. The three of them cheerfully arguing over soon-to-be baby Bilborough's name.

David never lived to see his son's christening.

Beck studied the photos on the mantelpiece. The wedding photos. The christening. Himself and Catriona, surrounded by guests in the church grounds. Baby Ryan, little more than a wriggling bundle with a fluff of damp hair and a squealing face poking out of a blanket being held by a tearful Catriona.

'How have you been, Jimmy?'

Her words startled him back to the present. 'I was going to ask you that. You know. With today being his birthday and all.'

154

Catriona shrugged. 'I've been getting through it. People have been around.'

Jimmy looked back at the table full of glasses. That was true enough.

'Are those for me?'

Beck was suddenly aware that he was still holding the flowers and card he'd brought for her.

'Yeah. Miles away. Sorry.'

She nodded. 'I get like that sometimes.'

'I miss him.'

She nodded again, more thoughtfully this time. 'It gets better with time.'

Beck studied her closely as she took the flowers from him. 'Does it?'

'Oh yes. All things heal with time, Jimmy. You should know that.'

Startled, Beck said, overloudly, 'What do you mean?'

'You know. Your parents. The accident.'

'Oh. Yeah. That was a long time ago.'

'Like I said. Time's a great healer.'

Bloody platitudes. How can she believe that line?

'Sure.'

'I'll be back in a sec'. Just go and pop these in some water.'

'Sure.'

Catriona went into the kitchen and Jimmy wandered over to the French windows. Beyond was the garden. Someone had installed a swing there. And a baby slide. And –

Beck jerked as if slapped.

David Bilborough was cradling his son on his lap as he rocked backwards and forwards slowly on the garden swing.

Beck was aware of a noise. An animal noise, coming from his own throat.

David rocked his son backwards and forwards.

Ryan gurgled happily.

David grinned, the picture of fatherhood.

Beck choked, felt bile rise in his throat.

David, it was David Bilborough, his best mate, his dead buddy rocking his son on the garden swing; a dead guy wrapped in a cliché of domestic bliss –

And Jimmy Beck felt the room whirling around him. The telly, the christening pictures, the table, the sofa, his drink, *his stomach ripped open and steaming in the pale afternoon sunlight –*

And suddenly little Ryan was covered in blood because David was *dead*, he was *dead* and his stomach was *ripped open* and there was *blood and intestines* oozing slowly over his son as they swung together through wisps of steam, and then Jimmy Beck was swaying with them and the blood was dripping into the grass, and little ropes of intestines were flapping back and forth beneath the swing because he was *dead*, David was *dead* and –

'You remember John, Jimmy. David's brother.'

Catriona's words jerked Beck back to the present again as if he'd been slapped.

'Yes. John. Uh. John. Yes. Uh. Startled me for a moment that's all. Saw the movement out of the corner of my eye.'

Catriona smiled, quite unaware that Beck was avoiding throwing up only by a monumental effort.

'Once a copper always a copper, eh, Jimmy?'

Beck managed a grunted affirmative.

'Nice to know we've got someone so smart looking out for us.'

Beck nodded. Bad move. The room spun again. 'Catriona. Excuse me for a moment –' And he lurched out of the room, feeling sure he must look like some shambling madman, stumbled up the stairs to the bathroom, splashed cold water on his face again and again, while David's voice echoed from every dark space in the room and it told him, *this is evidence; the statement of a dying man; I want you to get this man Jimmy, get him for me and Catriona –*

156

And Beck closed his eyes, squeezed them tightly shut against the voice, against David's voice, but he couldn't escape in the darkness, because he was in there himself, and it was too much to confront himself, so he stayed quite still for a moment, hands on the edges of the basin, cold water dripping into the sink, *plop, plop, plop*, eyes blinking slowly, hair standing on end and his balls shrinking somewhere into his gut with the fear and then . . . and then . . .

. . . slowly . . .

. . . so slowly . . .

. . . he started to get control.

It felt like an hour before he could open his eyes. When he did the whole process started right over again.

Two. There were *two*.

On the sink, in the holder.

Two *toothbrushes*.

Beck reeled again, stumbled away from the sink, nearly fell, reached out for the bathroom cabinet to steady himself. And the door popped open, *clink!* and there they were, staring at him like grinning gargoyles, all in a row, neat as soldiers, monsters from Jimmy Beck's ID, his and hers cliché of the century. Aftershave. Shaving foam. A razor.

Beck made it to the toilet pan just in time.

He squeezed toothpaste onto a finger and rinsed his mouth.

When he got back to the living room Catriona looked at him with some concern. 'You OK, Jimmy?'

Beck thought about nodding, stopped himself just in time. 'Yes. Are you living with someone?'

Catriona looked surprised. She nodded. 'John.'

'His brother?'

Again she nodded. Something in her expression said, *Don't judge me, Jimmy Beck. We're friends, but don't you dare judge me!*

'He moved in last month.'

Beck saw her study him, felt her gaze rake across him.

157

'He won't replace him, Jimmy. He can't. But life goes on. Nothing's changed. We can still be friends.'

'Yeah. Sure. Fine.'

Hey ho, Johnnie, let's watch some footey on the vid, eh? Take Ryan to the park, devour a Sunday roast, discuss her second child's name. And while we're at it let's try not to talk about him or even think of him, of David, my best mate, your brother, her husband. Let's try that shall we?

Christ he needed a roll-up. And a drink. Several drinks.

'Look, Catriona. I've gotta go. I'll drop in again in a week or so, OK?'

She nodded 'OK, Jimmy. Take it easy, all right?'

'Sure.'

And then he was out into the night, driving, with no idea of how he got behind the wheel, no recollection of how he got from the house to the car, just the words of a dead man pounding in his brain like the mother of all hangovers, pounding like thunder, like guns, like fists thudding against –

'What do you want?'

The voice. Female. Aggressive. Recognition.

Where was he?

Beck looked around. A hallway. A block of flats. Broken lights. Graffiti on the walls.

'Well?'

He focused on the owner of the voice. 'Denise. Denise Fletcher.'

She shook her head. 'You coppers are sharp as new pins, ain't ya?'

Beck sucked instinctively on a roll-up he hadn't made yet. 'Can I stay here? Sleep here? Spend the night?'

Denise sighed. 'It's my busy time, Jimmy. You know that.'

'I'll pay.'

She stared narrowly at him. 'Have you been at the bottle?'

'What?'

'Shooting up? You look well spaced.'

'I'm . . . I'll be . . . I just don't want to be alone tonight. That's all.'

Denise sniffed. 'There's a maniac on the loose, so don't take this personally.' And leaving the door on the chain she picked up the hall phone and dialled. Beck heard her voice as if from a great distance. 'Paula? I'm letting Jimmy Beck in. Sure I will. You too. Bye.'

She came back to the door, closed it long enough to take the chain off. Beck entered. The door closed.

'We're phoning each other, looking after each other.'

Beck nodded. 'Sure. Whatever.'

Denise led him through to the bedroom. Beck was aware of a weight in his left hand. He looked down. A carrier bag. Valubuys. Where had that come from? He took the bottle of Bells that was weighing the bag down and unscrewed the cap. He drank from the bottle. He took his wallet from his pocket, threw it on the bed.

Denise studied him for a moment, then picked up the wallet. 'God, Jimmy. There's at least a hundred in here.'

That sounded vaguely right. 'Take as much as you want.' He looked at the room. Dim light. Nice rug. Nice bedspread. A few prints. A dresser with makeup and perfume. A mirror. Candles. It was nice. Homey. Warm. Comforting. Perhaps he'd be able to lay some demons here. Or at the very least to get some kip.

'Fitz says you sell it too cheap. You remember Fitz?'

'Yeah. Seemed OK to me.'

'He's right. I know a woman. Married to a copper. He died. The body's still warm but she's already screwing his brother. Why not? He's got a good job. He brings home the bacon. Week after week.'

Beck sat down on the bed.

'That's my bed, Jimmy. Punters go in the spare room.'

'Sure. Whatever.' Beck drifted to his feet, stumbled

numbly into the next room. It was bare. A cheap rug, boring wallpaper, no prints. The bed was standard, nothing special. Sheets. Blankets. All bog standard. A work room. That's what it was. A place of work.

Beck sank onto the bed. Denise followed him into the room. He sensed her standing over him, even with his eyes shut.

'Jimmy. This is a lot of lolly. Do you want me to . . .'

'If you like.'

'Better get undressed then. Or do you want me to do that for you?'

'I don't care.'

And he didn't care. Or respond. Even when she gave him the full hundred quid's worth. Even later, as he surrendered to orgasm, the only thought in his head was a picture, and the picture was that of a dead man, stomach split and steaming, rocking his son on a garden swing and smiling sweetly as he fell apart before Beck's tortured eyes.

SIXTEEN

When Maggie let him in Michael went straight to the living room. Ordinarily neat, the room was covered with paper. Pay slips. Hundreds of them. Years' worth. Maggie was distraught, her eyes shining with rage, paper clutched in one hand, a calculator in the other. David had put something in Maggie, some bit of himself, and it had grown, like a cancer, grown and spread.

'Maggie. Slow down. Where are the kids? Are you all right?'

'They're in bed. Found all this stuff in a box in his wardrobe. Had to break it open. Pay slips. He's lied to me. For years he's lied to me. He's earned fifty, sixty, seventy pounds more than he ever told me. Money. Whenever we rowed, we rowed about money. Never enough money. And sex. Always with a condom. I never wanted it that way. But any other way means a baby on its way and a baby costs money and we didn't have it, did we?'

Michael studied her face, shining with tears, the grief replaced by anger, both mixing to twist her into a screeching caricature of herself.

'So I went along with it. 'Cos I love him. I went along with it. And now I find out he's been doing it with prostitutes. Filthy prostitutes. And he's come home stinking of those women.'

'Did you kill Joyce Watkins?'

Michael's words halted Maggie for a moment. She stared at him, tears gleaming in her eyes, running down her face.

'Not one speck of dust. I keep this house shining for him.

161

Sparkling. And he comes in and treads their filth through my house. Through my house, Michael!'

'You're not even surprised by the question, are you?'

'I hate them all. Filthy. Selling it. Pitying me. Pitying women like me for living with men like him. Pitying *me*! And there's the guilt. If I hadn't taken money out of his wallet he'd've paid the filthy bitch. She'd still be alive. I wouldn't've got to know anything about it. But no. He told me. He had to tell me. He had to get his guilt out. I've learned to live with the guilt. You do that. If you can learn to live with the death of a child, you can learn to live with anything.'

'Did you kill Joyce Watkins?'

'Thousands of pounds. Thousands. I'd stand for an hour in the supermarket, waiting for them to mark down the food, food past its sell-by date, and they'd look at me and know what I was waiting for. And he's spending thousands on –'

'Did you –'

'– prostitutes he's spending thousands –'

'– kill that woman, did you –'

'– while his kids go hungry and –'

'– kill Joyce Watkins?'

'– and do you know what else? I phoned Wise today, that copper at Anson Road. I phoned him and asked him how he could keep David in jail when a second identical murder had taken place? He said he could! He said it was an ongoing investigation into a serious matter. He said he was in charge and he could keep David locked up as long as he wanted. Locked up away from his kids and his wife. I told him, I said, I'm not a lawyer but I'd get one, because he had a lot of explaining to do, but he just said I should stop wasting police time if I wanted it to go easier with David, and I told him, I said to him, you're putting all women in danger, I said, it's not just one man being unfairly treated, being falsely accused, it's the women in danger that I was thinking of, and he just told me to stop wasting police time.' She caught her breath on a sob. 'Me! Stop wasting police time! What about the time he's taking from David? Time he should be at home with his kids and me?'

And there was silence then. And Maggie stared at Michael and he could see that whatever sickness David had put into her had blinded her to everything except her guilt and her rage. And the awful thing – the awful *truth* – was that it was his fault David had done that, told her, created that rage. If Maggie was responsible for the death of Joyce Watkins then they were all three of them equally to blame.

Michael felt his head reeling at the thought. How fast things get out of control. How fast the disease, the cancer, spreads. David, himself, Maggie. Jean. Joyce. Who next?

Who next?

SEVENTEEN

And long after Michael Harvey left Maggie to wander guilt-stricken through the pale, starlit streets of Manchester, long after Maggie Harvey had given in once more to her guilt and anger, a woman named Paula Devereau sat in conversation in her flat with someone she thought had been a punter but had turned out not to be after all.

Over a pot of tea she warmed to her visitor, as that person put her at ease. When the questions came she was more than willing to answer. She even thought for a while the visitor must be attached to the police force. A psychologist or a social worker. They were that sort of questions.

'This room. Looks a bit like a church.'

'Got me nun's outfit in here.' Paula giggled. 'Sister Concepta. You want to see it?'

'You're serious?'

'I'd do it on the altar if they paid enough; the marble's a bit cold.' Paula giggled again. Girlish. Trusting.

'What did he want from you? Shirley Temple?'

'I'd sing the doggie song. He'd give me a load of grief. Swear. Lots of "fuck yous" and "bitches", "sluts", that sort of thing. He liked to bully me. Sick really. Then he'd start.' She reached into the wardrobe. 'I've got the wig here.'

Paula turned, holding the wig, and that was when she realised her visitor was neither trustworthy nor a police officer.

Of course it was too late by then.

Even when she screamed she knew that.

THURSDAY

EIGHTEEN

Fitz woke up the next morning with another hangover, only to realise it was the day – if not nearly the hour – of his mother's funeral. Danny turned up at eleven thirty with twenty or so people in tow; Mum's friends from the old neighbourhood. Fitz gawped as they strolled up the path and filtered into the kitchen and living room of his house. Who on earth were they all? Surely Mum hadn't had so many friends? It was like something out of the bloody *Hobbit*. Dwalin and Balin, Kili and Fili, Dori, Nori, Ori, Oin and Gloin, Bifur, Bofur, Bombur and Thorin Oakenshield. And *Mrs* Dwalin, Balin, Kili, Fili, Dori, Nori, Ori, Oin, Gloin, Bifur, Bofur, Bombur and Thorin Oakenshield. And all their offspring as well; by the look of it, most of Middle Earth and the Lands to the West.

Fitz sighed. Coffee. That's what he needed. Hot, strong, black. And lots of it. The problem was the kitchen was full of black-dressed people making over-polite conversation and eating Judith's seed cake and drinking tea.

Fitz suddenly felt a huge desire for scotch. He headed for the dining room. Danny was holding court there while waiting for the hearse. Fitz couldn't see the other side of the room for milling funeral-goers.

Desperation increasing, Fitz considered his options for escape. With the kitchen and dining room occupied by the enemy that only left the toilet or the kids' bedrooms. Mark and Katie would presumably have taken refuge in their own rooms, Judith would find him in a second in their bedroom; that only left the downstairs bathroom.

It was occupied.

Fitz turned to find himself face to face with four black-dressed women whose total ages might have rivalled Methuselah himself.

The horsewomen of the apocalypse.

He grinned. Partly nerves, partly terror.

They smiled back.

'Oh *look*!'

'It *can't* be!'

'It *is*!'

'It's *little Eddie*!'

'*Hasn't* he put on *weight*!'

It was going to be one *bitch* of a day.

The bathroom door opened then to allow a grandfatherly type to emerge. Fitz didn't know this character, but fortunately the women did, and Fitz was able to take refuge in the bathroom while they discussed Mum, himself and Danny.

How much time could he waste?

He bolted the door. Flushed the toilet. Ran some water into the basin. Splashed it about.

With any luck he could hide here until the cavalcade had vanished off to Gettysburg.

If only he had a book.

He was considering the risk involved in making a quick dash for Chatwin's *Songlines*, located upstairs on the dresser, when a sharp knock on the bathroom door confirmed the enemy had better intelligence than he did.

'Fitz. The cars are here.'

Fitz muttered, 'Better spy satellites than the Americans.'

'What?'

'Nothing, dear. Just coming.'

'Good. Danny wants you to help carry the coffin.'

Wouldn't he just?

That was every bit the nightmare Fitz knew it would be. There were six pallbearers. All about the size of Hobbits.

Danny was a bit taller at five-eight. At six-four Fitz topped all of them by a head and Danny by eight inches.

The coffin tipped dangerously.

Fitz felt a giggle bubbling inside.

Balin, Dwalin, Kili, Fili, Dori, Nori, Ori, Oin, Gloin, Bifur, Bofur, Bombur, Thorin Oakenshield and their respective spouses and offspring watched with bemusement as the coffin wobbled.

Danny hissed, 'Stoop, you pillock.'

'I'm stooping, you bloody dwarf,' Fitz huffed back over-loudly.

A child giggled.

Fitz felt like joining in.

Then they were at the cars.

'Only two?' hissed Fitz.

Danny grunted, 'She wanted it done on the Social. Get as much as you can out of the tight sods.'

'How's everyone getting to the church then?'

'You and me are paying for taxis.'

Fitz managed a sort of strangled yelp. The coffin wobbled dangerously. The Hobbits shuffled underneath, just managed to stop it falling onto the rhododendrons.

'You all right?' hissed Danny.

'Just get her into the bloody car before I give myself a hernia, will you?'

And it was the same story at St Catherine's. The coffin tilting, kids giggling, Danny blaming Fitz and Fitz finding himself giggling louder than the kids.

Then the wobbling coffin was ensconced in the nave. Fitz and the other pallbearers filed back into the pews.

Fitz caught Katie's eye as he sat beside her. 'Cheer up. At least she didn't die of anything serious,' he whispered. Katie grinned. Fitz got an elbow in his ribs from Judith for his trouble.

The rest of the ceremony passed in a blur of vaguely bad

taste at which Fitz felt sure his mother would have taken great delight if she had been alive to witness it.

Danny spoke first; the usual religious guff. There were some psalms. A hymn or two. Fitz used this interval to check out the congregation. He found to his surprise a few faces he had not expected. DCI Wise. Jimmy Beck. Temple. Penhaligon. That was sweet of them. Then he saw Maggie Harvey with her kids and realised why the police officers were there.

Danny had finished droning on by then; and the fun stuff started.

Fitz took the stand. He studied the Bible laid out before him. The prayer books. Then he picked them up, one by one and flung them into the congregation. 'John. Mark. Luke. Peter. Paul. And Uncle Tom Cobley and all,' he sang at the top of his voice. The congregation were stunned.

He grinned.

Oh yes. This was it. Her life. Her death. Her moment. He was taking it for her but it was her moment.

Aware that Michael Harvey was staring at him as if he were mad, Fitz said loudly, 'Me old Mum's dead. She had her life and now she's gone. And you lot out there. Bugger all point in you being here really. She knew what you thought of her and I don't care what you think of me.' He sighed. 'Yep. She's dead. Still,' a quick scan of the audience. Did he have them? He did. 'You've never lived till you've died. Right?'

There were vague mutterings from the six rows occupied by friends of the family.

Fitz grinned. 'But I know you didn't come here for a lecture on philosophy. You came here to watch an old friend take the first step towards becoming worm-food. Celebrate that fact that it's not you while simultaneously acknowledging that one day it will be. But that's sad, right? And she wasn't sad, me old Mum. Many things but never sad. And so, in the glorious tradition of the family Fitzgerald, I ask you to join me now in a short silence followed by ... a thumping good game of bingo! Cards are on the pews. Eyes down, look in!'

The congregation moved as one being. Never had so many moved with but a single thought. Cards flapped. Biros clicked. One fountain pen unscrewed. Fitz stared at Danny: hatred. Judith: despair. Katie: amusement. Mark: contempt. Michael ... Well, what was that on Michael's face? Contempt? Fear?

Oh bugger the lot of 'em. It was his mum wasn't it?

And he produced a little bag full of scribbled bits of paper.

'First prize is a bottle of communion wine and the stuff they use here is fifteen per cent proof. First number! Five and six, fifty six!'

One of the four horsewomen of the apocalypse 'Ooh!'-ed excitedly and crossed out a number on her card.

Fitz's grin widened to biblical proportions. They were his. He was Moses, leading them out of the bondage of a rigidly structured society and into a new life of indulgence, and plenty of it.

'Top of the shop, ninety. Two and three, twenty-three. Two little ducks, twenty-two.'

And there was the moment. That bright, shining, *glittering* moment when it all made sense. When the whole congregation, with one voice, quacked like a duck.

Even Judith.

And they were smiling and laughing and crying all at once. And Fitz knew they were exorcising more emotional demons than any priest or religion was capable of removing for them. It was an emotional catharsis of biblical proportions and it was all, every last sob and giggle, down to him, to Edward Fitzgerald; his mother's son and through whom she would live on. Through him and after him Katie and Mark, and their children, and grandchildren, and with the luck of aces and kings she would *never ever die.*

Fitz himself was crying as he pulled more numbers from the bag.

'Thank you quackers. Seven and eight, seventy-eight. On its own, number six. Major's den, number ten.'

A pause then, *'Get him out!'* from the entire congregation.

And more tears from Fitz.

And more numbers. 'On its own, one. Five and seven, fifty-seven. Eight and three, eighty-three.'

And more numbers. And tears. And laughter. And numbers. And –

'House!' squealed an ancient voice unable to contain its excitement.

Wouldn't you know it? One of the four horsewomen of the apocalypse. Ah well. Destiny takes a hand in these things. I expect the old bat had a one-to-one chatline with God.

Fitz said, 'Thank you ladies and gentlemen. A round of applause please for our lucky winner. See Father Michael Harvey afterwards with your completed card to claim your prize. I will now continue the proceedings with a few humble words of my own.'

A pause and then, from the back, a shuffling of feet. Maggie Harvey, leaving, dragging her kids with her. One giggled and she slapped him. Her face said it all. How dare Fitz profane this holy place with his contempt? She would have no part of it. A church was a place of worship, not sarcasm.

Fitz waved. 'Don't forget your free wafers!'

Maggie Harvey shot Fitz a dangerous look and left. Fitz noticed Wise and Penhaligon watched her go, exchanged looks. Wise pulled out his R/T and whispered into it.

Fitz said, 'A serious moment, if you please. I'm gonna kick off with Dad. Every other week he'd work nights. Twelve-hour nights, seven days a week. As a kid I looked forward to this. He'd be back home before we got up, you see, and the fire would be lit and the light would be on and all the cockroaches would've disappeared. I used to watch

174

him going to work, coming home from work, turning up the money. I used to think – why does he do it? Why doesn't he leave us and spend all his hard-earned money on himself? I never thought that about Mum. She was part of us. Me and Danny. A love so strong you could take it for granted.'

Fitz paused for a moment, aware of the eyes of the congregation on him. Judith. Danny. Particularly Danny. He continued. 'One example. There was a fight on the telly. I can't remember who. Me and Danny stood outside in the hall and watched through a crack in the door. But it was freezing in the lobby and I could see Mum and Dad watching the fight in comfort with the fire blazing and I knew, I just knew that if I pushed open that door Mum would see us and realise how much we wanted to watch that fight. So I pushed it open. Dad started to shout at us. Danny was giving me daggers, and then Mum said, "OK, but straight to bed as soon as it's over." Like that. I knew she'd say it. Just took it for granted. She wasn't one for rational analyses. She preferred a row.'

Another pause. This time to exorcise a few mental demons of his own before continuing. 'One in particular sticks in my mind. She woke up after a night out, couldn't find her false teeth. Accused Dad of hiding them out of spite. They didn't speak for two days. Then she found them tucked down beside the headboard.'

Even Danny was smiling now. 'At times like this you wish you believed in heaven. I don't. But if it does exist, she's up there now, her glasses on, her tongue sticking out, the *Racing Post* open in front of her, picking out the winners. And –'

And that was as far as Fitz got before the hyperbole ran out and grief hit him. The real, solid, no mucking about kind of grief that feels like you've been punched in the balls by a guy who bench presses bulldozers for a living. And Fitz leaned against the pulpit and heaved a sigh that turned into a sob that turned into a flood of tears.

Michael stepped up beside him then.

Fitz stared at him. *Look at me. Fitz the walking cliché.*

Michael said quietly, 'There's no shame in grief.'

Fitz struggled for a reply, wasn't really surprised when he found none. There was a silence as he took his place back in the pews beside his family.

Michael spoke a eulogy then, and they sang a few more hymns. Even Fitz joined in.

And later, after the coffin was lowered into the ground, Michael picked up a handful of dirt and scattered it over the lid.

Fitz followed suit with a betting slip.

The four horsewomen of the apocalypse let fly with bingo cards.

As if that was the signal a storm of paper flew into the hole. Bingo cards, betting slips, used lottery tickets, playing cards, a domino, a pair of jacks, half a dozen dice, a dungeons and dragons spinner.

Fitz capped it all with a copy of the day's *Racing Post*.

When they got in the funeral car, Judith took Fitz by the hand. 'Home?'

He looked at her with eyes filled with tears. 'I need a drink. Driver. Take us to the Blarney Castle.'

As the car accelerated smoothly away from the graveyard, something made Fitz look back. Some lingering thought, a nagging feeling, *something* . . . and he was just in time to see Michael Harvey hurrying into his car and driving away by another exit to the churchyard, closely followed by Penhaligon in her Volvo. He couldn't help wondering where Michael was going in such a hurry.

He balanced the need to worry against the need for alcohol; the drink won hands down.

The Blarney Castle was a tiny working-class pub. The Fitzgerald party absolutely rammed it to the limit. Fitz slapped fifty quid on the bar and ordered the first round.

Five shorts and chasers later, Fitz found himself joining in the chorus of 'I'll take the high road', before collapsing in a fit of drunken laughter into an empty chair beside Judith, Danny, Katie and Mark.

The chair creaked alarmingly. 'Truly, human furniture is not made for one with a stature such as I.'

Katie and Mark were looking very bored. Neither laughed at the joke. Judith looked disapprovingly on as Fitz drowned the punch line in yet another whisky.

'Don't you think that's enough, Fitz? We've got to pay for the taxis home yet.'

Fitz belched. 'If God had wanted me to pay for them to be driven home he'd have given them meters.' He sniffed. That actually wasn't that funny. Hm. He'd have to watch it. Didn't want to get drunk. Not today. No respect, see. Have to watch it. Maybe just one more whisky . . .

Judith's expression seemed to indicate she agreed with his train of thought.

Oh she did did she? Well tough. If he wanted a drink he'd damn well have one. Right? Right.

Fitz staggered to the bar and bought another round.

He managed to get it back to the table with the glasses half full. An improvement on the last time when a drunken belch had caught him halfway and precipitated the entire round, nuts and all, into the inner workings of the *Star Trek: Next Generation* pinball machine.

He managed to get this round to the table more or less intact.

Katie and Mark weren't there.

Judith said, 'I've asked them to wait in the car. We're going. Come with us, Fitz. You've had enough. Come home and sleep it off, have a cuddle, eh?'

'No. Having too much fun.'

'Fitz, please. We've been here an hour and a half. Everyone's drunk, no-one will miss us. And I'm not sure this is the right place. You know. The baby. All this smoke.

Specially after what they said about inducing me . . .'

Fitz studied Judith closely. Her face seemed to be pulsing ever so slightly, as if it were painted onto a balloon which someone was alternately blowing up and then letting the air out of.

'Thinking of yourself again. It's my mum's funeral. It's just me mum, but I loved her. You hated her.'

'Fitz, you're drunk. Of course I didn't hate her.'

But Fitz was off. 'You sneered at her. The way she used to get things on the cheap. On the old Freemans Catalogue. You found it amusing. You found it quaint.'

And that was too much for Judith. 'Fitz, you never went to see her for five months. You know why? 'Cos I wasn't there to remind you. To make you go. You can't blame me for anything. I know it's hard. Grief's hard enough at the best of times, but when you're feeling guilty as sin, well it must be unbearable.' And Judith got up, waved a goodbye to Danny and walked out while Fitz was still formulating a shattering response.

Fitz tried to get up to follow her. It took him a moment. Ah yes. The old sea legs not what they used to be, Cap'n. Still. Avast there and belay the gunwales. Or whatever.

By the time he got to the door of the pub Judith was already driving out of the car park.

Damn.

He turned, found himself collared by the old geezer who had been ensconced in the loo that morning when Fitz had needed to hide there. 'The thing about Scousers is this: they're all descended from the feckless Irish, innit? The ones who got off the boat at Liverpool and said, "Sod this for a game of soldiers, I'm stopping here." The ones with any bottle carried on. London at least. America. So it's in the genes, you know what I mean . . .'

Fitz stared at the old man, then pushed rudely past. He felt a bad case of the dry heaves coming on. Only they wouldn't be dry in his case. Far from it. He needed a seat. Now. Fast.

He managed to get to the table. Danny was there. He'd watched the whole palaver. Judith. The old bloke. The lot.

'Fitz. You know what. You're a bloody snob.'

Danny was more than somewhat pissed himself and Fitz could see that slanted things for him just a wee bit. But there was still no call for that tone of voice.

'Fuck off.'

''s true. You're a snob. Do you recognise that bloke who was just talking to you? Albert Quince. Friend of Mum's. Used to be a fireman.'

'What – until they made buggering the horses illegal?'

'You're a bloody snob. Do you recognise *any* of these people?'

Fitz pointed in rapid succession to the four horsewomen of the apocalypse, cackling to themselves in a little gaggle a bit like the crows in *Dumbo*. 'Fire. Famine. Plague. Pestilence.' He shot the words out fast as bullets, quite proud that he didn't slur any. Pestilence could have been a particular problem, but no, he managed to keep things nicely together there, thank you very much.

Danny stared at him. 'You snob.'

'Your record's stuck. "The old neighbourhood" bit. Pathetic.' Fitz dolloped a minimal amount of dry ginger into a glass full of Bells and downed the lot in one hit.

Danny took a swallow from his own glass. Guinness. Hm. That was suspect straight away. 'You grew up with these people and you don't even recognise them.'

'Danny, for heaven's sake, it was forty years ago! I'm surprised any of them are still alive!'

'You've hardly spoken to any of them.'

'I don't *know* any of them!'

'That's exactly my point!'

'So we agree then?'

'Yes. No. Oh sod it. You want a drink?'

Fitz stared at the table. It was absolutely groaning with drinks.

179

'Yeah. And it's your round. And before you go I want to tell you something.'

'Yeah?'

'Yeah. You stayed. That's the point you're trying to make. You're a fine upstanding pillar of the local community. But I'll tell you why you stayed. You stayed because you didn't have the money to get out. That's the only reason you stayed, you bloody hypocrite! Now get those drinks in, bro'. Mine's a whisky and ginger. And hold the ginger.'

Danny's eyes widened in drunken outrage. 'Dad's birthday. You said you'd phone. She sat in all morning waiting for you to phone. It broke her heart. She went out. When she came back I said you'd phoned. I used to say you'd come round while she was out and you were really sorry to miss her. I'd have to make things up 'cos she'd ask me how you were getting on and what you were up to these days. I was always doing it.' Danny sniffed, reached for his drink, seemed to decide a few tears would be in order instead. 'And that time in the hall. I know why you pushed the door. You haven't got a monopoly on feelings. I know why you pushed it. But I was enjoying it there. Just watching Mum and Dad and them not knowing we were there. That's why I gave you daggers. It wasn't about the fight. I wasn't even watching the fight. I was watching Mum and Dad!'

And Danny finished then, unable to go on for crying. And Fitz became aware the whole pub had gone silent. Every eye fixed on himself and Danny.

He looked around. 'Roll up! Roll up! See the amazing Pissed Brothers. They're brothers. They're pissed. They hate each other really! Come on folks, don't be shy. It's double discount day today!'

And then Fitz collapsed into tears himself for the third time in as many hours, as the pub resumed its normal level of activity.

Fitz stumbled to his feet then. Grabbed Danny by the scruff of the neck and dragged him out of the pub.

'What now?'

'Let's put the betting shop window through again.'

Danny half laughed at the memory.

'It's reinforced glass.'

'So we'll use reinforced bricks.'

Danny laughed then.

Ten minutes later they were on the number thirty-nine bus to the high street singing Rolf Harris's classic *Two Little Boys*. Neither of them knew the words but the other passengers helped. All except one old fart who showed Fitz his mobile phone and threatened to call the police. Fitz and Danny kept singing.

They were still singing when they jumped off the bus at the corner of the high street, grabbed a couple of bricks from a nearby building site, and lobbed them as hard as they could at the plate glass window fronting the betting shop.

Fitz was still singing when his brick rebounded from the window without damaging it and hit him directly on the forehead.

From then on things got a bit confused. He remembered falling. At least he thought he remembered falling. And he remembered Danny laughing. And he remembered throwing up. And he remembered blood. And he remembered complaining to the ambulance driver about the noise of the sirens. Then he remembered the hospital. They asked him his name, stitched him up, gave him a jab for something or other in the arse. Seemed to take great delight in administering the injection as close as possible to his piles. Ooh the injustice of it. What had he ever done? Oh yeah. And they pumped his stomach. They actually pumped his stomach. He remembered protesting. 'That's mine that is,' he said, nodding at the bottle of goo they'd got out of him. 'I want a receipt for that, OK?'

They ignored him of course.

'I'm not pissed you know. You've taken it all away! I paid

181

good money for that and now you've sodding well taken it away!'

They ignored that too.

What else did he remember? Oh yeah. He remembered demanding his clothes back. Slipping as he dressed and splitting his forehead open again. He remembered the same nurse coming back to restitch him up. And he remembered something else. As he was finally dressing to leave. A voice in the corridor. Mark. And Katie. What were they doing here? Carrying Judith's overnight case?

So he asked them.

'Mum's in labour,' said Katie. 'It started in the car. She's going to have a baby!'

And Mark said: 'You've thrown up on your suit. Makes a change from birdshit, I suppose.'

NINETEEN

Defying the irritable look from Mister Geoffrey Denholm, the man whose flat they had commandeered, Jimmy Beck put his feet up on the pouffe and shoved the listening device deeper into his ear. The earphone was connected to a recorder which in turn was fed from a couple of microphones fastened with gaffer tape to the living room wall. Beside Beck were DCI Wise, Penhaligon and the irate Denholm. In the master bedroom at the top of the stairs, Temple and Skelton were repeating the bugging process. Denholm's flat was next door to that of Denise Fletcher. And that was where Michael Harvey had driven when he'd left the service for Fitz's mother an hour or so previously.

He'd been in there about twenty minutes, now. So far nothing. Denise had made a pot of tea. They had drunk it. Made vaguely irritated crosstalk. Was Michael after some? Was Denise not selling today? Beck pressed the earphone harder into his ear and listened more intently than ever.

'What you got, lad?' That was Wise, crowding in to get an earful himself.

'They're just talking. I think they know each other. Perhaps he's a regular.' Then, 'Wait a minute. We're on. He's offering her money. He says it's for Jean McIlvanney's kids.' A startled laugh. 'He's just offered her five hundred quid!'

'Yeah?' Wise leant closer. So did Denholm. Wise shot him a look. 'Police business, sir. If you wouldn't mind.' He gestured to the sofa where Penhaligon was sipping her tea. Reluctantly, Denholm sat.

Beck went on, 'She's asking why he's giving his money away. He's telling her they could do with it. We could all do with it, if you ask me.' And he grinned at Wise.

And that's when the scream came.

Beck sat up as though electrocuted, ripping the earphones from his ear. Penhaligon and Wise were up too; Temple and Skelton barrelling down from the upstiars bedroom. You didn't need a microphone to hear the terror in her voice.

'All right, lads, we're in there,' said Wise firmly. 'And no messing about, right?'

Followed by Beck and Penhaligon he left the flat at a run. Behind the police officers Geoffrey Denholm said, 'Here, that tape you used to stick your microphones up. I hope it won't tear the wallpaper.'

He was ignored in the general exodus.

Beck hit the door of Denise Fletcher's flat with his shoulder, broke the lock and chain, ran into the living room. He stopped for a moment, utterly lost. It was like a scene out of some horror flick. Denise was standing in the middle of the room, screaming, her clothes drenched with blood. On the other side of the living room table Michael Harvey was standing motionless, equally shocked. There was blood on the table. It had splashed across the cloth, the china, his clothes.

Without further thought, Beck closed the gap, grabbed hold of Michael, spun him around and cuffed him. 'Got you, you murdering bastard. No wonder they let you in. Offering the dead women's kids money. No wonder they trusted you. You bastard. I'm going to do you. You're going to hang for this. You and your brother.' And Beck slammed Michael against the wall, and despite his training thought seriously about clipping him one round the face for good measure.

But Denise was still screaming. 'What are you doing? It's coming from upstairs. *It's coming from Paula's upstairs!*'

And then Penhaligon reached past him to uncuff Michael.

Beck almost ripped her hands away from the cuffs. 'What do you think you're doing?'

Penhaligon pointed up at the ceiling. Beck looked up. There was blood there. Spreading around the light fixture and running down the flex, staining the bulb a deep crimson.

Dripping onto the table. Onto Denise.

Penhaligon's voice was tightly controlled. 'Use your eyes will you, Jimmy? The blood isn't hers. It's coming through the ceiling. It's coming from upstairs.'

Beck looked wildly around. She was right. There was nothing out of place in the room. No weapon. Denise wasn't hurt, just shocked by the blood. Penhaligon was right. Wise was already leaving the flat, Temple and Skelton in tow. Penhaligon handed Beck his cuffs back and followed them. Beck left Michael and the still screaming Denise to follow Wise himself.

There was no reply from the flat directly overhead. Wise took the door down this time, to the delight of a gaggle of interested onlookers from other flats.

Inside Beck could hear the sound of running water. A bath. Trickling. The water had flooded everywhere.

Paula Devereau was in the living room. She had managed to crawl there from the bedroom by the look of it. She was a mess. Water from the bathroom was dripping through the ceiling, flooding the living room, soaking Paula's body and carrying the blood through to Denise's flat underneath.

Jesus.

Beck felt himself go cold. There was blood everywhere. The carpet was soaked with it. Splashes all over the show. A trail led to the stairs and presumably to the bathroom.

'Get the tap, will you, Jimmy,' That was Wise. But Beck didn't move. Then he did move, lurched from the room into the hallway. Fresh air. Gotta get some fresh air. Penhaligon was in the hallway. She was looking at the telephone pad. Beck closed the distance between them. He saw there was a name on the pad.

The name was his own.

Jimmy Beck.

Her handwriting. Paula's. Neat. A little squiggle on the 'J'.

Jimmy Beck. *Jimmy* Beck. Jimmy *Beck*.

He pushed past Penhaligon, got himself onto the landing and leaned over the balcony. Air. He had to have air. He couldn't *breathe*. He couldn't *think*. And he had to think. He *had* to. He'd come face to face with himself on a dead woman's notepad and the experience drove him closer to the edge than ever before.

Beck felt someone grab his shoulder, spin him round. Wise. He was holding the pad. He showed it to Beck. As if he hadn't already got the words floating like neon signs behind his eyes already.

'What's all this then, Jimmy?'

Beck struggled for words.

Wise pushed again. 'Did you know her?'

Beck moaned inwardly. 'I might've nicked her once or twice.'

Beck felt Wise study him. Felt like collapsing in a heap, just pouring it all out. *I hurt. I hurt that woman. I hurt her badly. But I was hurt too. Oh God it's so confused. I'm so confused. I just want to die, to crawl into a hole and die.*

'Have you been here recently?'

'No sir.'

'Then what's your name doing on this pad?'

'I don't know.'

'That's a bunch of BS lad and you know it. Now I'll have the truth of the matter out of you or my name's not Charlie Wise!'

'I'm –' Beck grabbed hold of the balcony for support. Beyond Wise a bunch of faces swam in and out of focus. They were muttering to themselves. About him, he was sure of it. Muttering, mumbling, pointing him out to their friends, giggling at his plight, laughing at him. 'I'm –' And

186

again words just wouldn't come.

At that moment the crowd opened to let through the forensics team.

Wise said, 'I'll see you down the station, lad. Meantime, go back to Denholm's flat and pack up the gear.' And he shoved the pad into his pocket and pushed his way back into Paula Devereau's flat, leaving Beck shivering on the balcony, alone with his conscience.

And that, along with the staring faces, Beck couldn't stand for very long.

He trudged back downstairs and began to pack up the surveillance equipment as Wise had told him. He felt stupid. Flushed. Embarrassed. What an idiot. What a complete idiot. Why had he done it? Why had he come here last night? That business with Catriona and John. Idiot!

Denholm fussed around him as he took down the microphones, packed them into their cases. 'Don't you tear my wallpaper with that tape of yours,' he warned in somewhat less than frightening tones.

Eventually Beck finished the packing up. He sighed. Did he want to go back upstairs? Not just yet. Wise would only give him another stupid job to do. Idiot. He was still a copper wasn't he? All right his name might appear on a prostitute's phone pad but he was still a copper. Right? Right.

He collared Denholm. 'You hear anything last night? A ruckus? Screaming? Anything like that? From upstairs?'

Denholm nodded. 'Some shouting, I think.'

'Why didn't you mention it earlier?'

'Didn't ask, did you? Didn't ask if you could stick microphones to my wall either, for that matter.'

Beck sighed, somehow managed to stop himself from decking the old sod. 'What time was this?'

'Latish. About eleven, I think. Yeah. Eleven thirty.'

'That's very precise.'

'They were playing *Thought for the Night*. They always do that just before closedown.'

'Why didn't you do something about it?'

'I did. I taped it.'

'The shouting. Why didn't you do something about that?'

'It stopped, didn't it? Besides. Someone's always screaming or shouting or playing music around here. Working girls. You don't know what I have to put up with around here. Music. Thumping. Shouting. All hours of the day and night. Should all get the Queen's Award for Industry if you ask me.'

Beck shook his head, clicked his notebook shut. He packed the recording equipment and microphones into the boot of his car and then headed up to Paula's flat, where he was just in time to catch the tail end of the pathologist's preliminary report.

'Damage to the skull ... heavy instrument ... a pan or maybe a china jug, something like that. Chisel inserted into the vagina. Internal haemorrhage. Same M/O as the others. Same man, I'd reckon.'

'Time of death?' That was Penhaligon, sharp as ever.

'Well, she's been dead a good few hours. How fast was the bath running? Just a trickle? I'd say she died some time last night. Running the bath was probably the last thing she did. Perhaps she was interrupted by a visitor or a phone call. Didn't quite turn the taps off.'

Wise nodded.

Beck hovered at the edge of the room. 'That doesn't clear the priest.'

Wise turned to look at Beck. He said nothing but then again, he didn't need to.

Doesn't clear you either, Jimmy.

And Beck could do nothing to alter the truth of that.

Wise told him to hold Michael Harvey for questioning.

For once Beck did exactly as he was told.

TWENTY

Fitz wanted to see Judith. The nurse pointed out that he couldn't see her with his clothes covered in vomit, so he had to change again into a hospital gown. That was faintly ridiculous but he suffered it because there was no other choice.

Then they took him into the theatre.

Fitz looked around. The last time he had been in a delivery room was eleven years ago. There were monitors. Tubes. Wires. Needles. Big metal boxes. Small metal boxes. Glass screens with little glowing tracks on them. Things that produced a variety of sounds which were all basically one variation or another on the good old-fashioned *bleep*.

There were doctors. Nurses. A gynaecological registrar. Two midwives. A young chap dressed as a doctor whose only job seemed to be running round with a notebook writing everything down very quickly in shorthand.

And in the middle of this maze of technological nonsense and doodadery: Judith.

The human heart in the machine.

Sweating, moaning, flushed, determined, utterly exhausted, utterly beautiful.

She gritted her teeth as Fitz watched. He took her hand at the nurse's gesture. She gripped it fit to crush bones. Fitz glared at the nurse, who smiled sweetly, either oblivious to Fitz's pain or pleased that he had so readily fallen for her little trick.

Judith squeezed a couple of words out with the gasps of pain as the contractions came faster and faster.

189

Fitz bent closer to hear the words.

'I am a seed pod!' Judith suddenly screamed right in his left ear.

Fitz stood back, tried to reach his ear to massage it with the hand that wasn't being crushed by his wife.

'I am a seed pod. I am a seed pod. *Tell me I'm a bloody seed pod!'*

Fitz said obligingly, 'You're a seed pod. And I love you.'

His words were swamped in another cry from Judith and further contractions.

'Like shelling peas. Mother Earth. I. Am. Moth-aaahh! Earth!'

'Gas and air?' Fitz felt it was a helpful suggestion. It might also stop his hand being reduced to a pulp.

'Just breathe on me. That'll do. You were pissed when Mark was born, pissed when Katie was born. Why break the habit of a lifetime?' And Judith screamed again. 'Nurse. I believe I'll have that epidural now.'

After the epidural things went a lot more easily.

When the baby was born it was a very healthy seven pounds twelve ounces. They did the usual slapping and dabbing routine, then handed the baby to Judith.

'Lovely baby boy,' said one midwife.

'Gorgeous, isn't he?' said the other.

'Christ save us, it's Morecambe and Wise,' Fitz muttered.

Judith took the baby and held him, and nuzzled against Fitz, who was manfully trying to resist the temptation to massage his crushed hand.

And then Judith looked at him, utterly exhausted, utterly beautiful, like one who has been in a war and won through to victory – and he supposed there was no reason why you shouldn't look on the whole process like that – and she looked at him and smiled and there were tears all over her and blood all over the child and little fluffy hair and a willy the size of Italy and she was right, the midwives were right, he was completely and utterly beautiful.

190

Fitz stood like that for ages. Then the nurse suggested with a gesture that he might want to go and tell the rest of the family the good news.

Danny, Mark and Katie all crowded round, eager for news, as he left the delivery room.

'A boy. Everything in working order. A willy this big.'

He held his hands about as far apart as the length of the average baby.

Danny grinned, still drunk. Mark sighed. Katie giggled.

Fitz smiled cheekily. 'Actually it's *this* big.' He opened his hands a bit.

Danny grinned. 'Swollen. They get swollen during birth.'

Fitz mugged a look of great disappointment and that made them all laugh again.

An hour later Judith had been moved to a ward and the family were gathered round. Fitz had bought a use-it-once-and-throw-it-away camera from the hospital gift shop and was busy snapping pictures. Then he handed the camera to Danny, gathered in the family and picked up the baby.

'Say cheese,' said Danny.

Fitz mugged a less than useless Churchill. 'We will fight them on the beaches. We shall fight them in the fields.'

'He doesn't look anything like Winston Churchill,' said Judith in outraged tones.

Fitz wasn't going to be stopped. 'We shall fight them . . . well, when I say "we" I mean "you", of course. I shall be in America.'

Everyone smiled and the camera flashed.

Fitz began to reorganise.

'Another shot!'

'My turn to hold him!'

'What are you going to call him?'

And then he saw her. Penhaligon. Standing by the ward sister's desk.

He looked at Judith. Her expression told Fitz she'd seen Penhaligon too.

'Go on, Fitz,' Judith said.

Fitz looked at her. 'No. They can do without me this once.'

Judith licked her lips. 'Look. I'm tired anyway. Just go, will you, it's probably important.'

'If you're sure.'

'Yeah. Go, Fitz. Just make sure you come back again this time.'

And that hurt more than he could say.

Fitz allowed Penhaligon to lead him from the ward. Outside she turned. The first time she had spoken to him with anything other than enmity. 'He's beautiful.'

Fitz nodded. 'He's got a fair-sized willy.'

Penhaligon sighed. 'Well never mind, Fitz. He's got your eyes.'

'Seven pounds twelve ounces. That's the whole baby of course, not just the willy.' A thought struck Fitz. 'How could you see his eyes from where you were standing?'

Penhaligon laughed. 'They all have nice eyes, Fitz.'

She filled him in on what they knew of Paula Devereau's death as they drove back to Anson Road. At the station they walked together into the duty room to find a pall of silence surrounding a heated discussion between Wise and Beck in Wise's office. They joined the crowd and listened in. You certainly didn't need surveillance equipment to hear the ins and outs of this conversation. Fitz was immediately, intensely interested.

'You'd better come up with something, Jimmy. Y'know what –'

'I can't, all right? I can't come up with anything because –'

'– I mean? A woman's been murdered and your name's on her pad.'

'– there's just no explanation I can think of, sir . . .'

At that point Beck stared out of the glass divide between Wise's office and the duty room. He saw Fitz. Swore. Fitz gave him a little wave.

Beck seemed to reach a decision. Turned back to Wise. His voice was lower now but still audible. 'The girls are looking after each other. If they get someone in they phone a mate. Tell them the geezer's name.'

'So what?'

'I went to see Denise Fletcher last night.'

'What for?'

'I had some questions for her. She phoned up her mate. It must have been this Paula. You can check it, get a list of the calls she made.'

'How long were you there?'

Beck hesitated. Another glance at Fitz. Face screwed up in despair. 'A couple of hours.'

Wise glared narrowly at Beck. 'A couple of hours, Jimmy? That's not ten minutes and a cuppa with your notebook open. We're talking about a couple of hours. She have a bad stutter or something?'

'I had a lot of questions, sir.'

'What was the first one? "How about it?" '

'It was strictly professional, sir.'

Wise said nothing for a long moment then, abruptly, 'Off y'trot. And mind I'll be thinking on this, Jimmy. So be on your best behaviour, right? I haven't made a decision yet . . .'

Beck came out of the office. He glared around the duty room, his eyes coming to rest on Fitz. 'Sell tickets to your own mother's funeral, you, wouldn't you?'

Fitz said nothing. Felt like butting Beck a good one, but managed to hold it in. After a moment the anger passed and he smiled. 'Well, I'd certainly consider a good game of bingo, anyway.'

That got a titter from those who'd been to the funeral.

And a grin from Penhaligon that was worth all the heart-ache.

Wise came out of his office then, acquired Fitz with a look, led him to the interview room.

Michael Harvey was there already. Temple was standing guard.

Fitz watched Wise sit down. Watched him watching Michael. Fitz lit up a high tar. Blew smoke. He knew what was required of him here.

Wise said, 'Five hundred.'

Michael nodded. 'Yes.'

'You were gonna give five hundred quid to two kids?'

Michael nodded. He was sweating. 'Their mother's been murdered. They've got no-one.'

'They've got Helen McIlvanney.'

'You know what I mean.'

'Saint Michael.'

Anger then. Wise wasn't half bad at this.

'Feeling guilty, eh?'

'Hardly.'

'No, because you put a bit of business their way. Don't you?'

Puzzled now. 'I'm not with you.'

And Wise spelled it out for him. 'You go with pros-titutes.'

Michael gawped. 'For God's sake!' Fitz was almost convinced.

'Maggie told us.'

'And you believed her?'

'Why should she lie to us?'

Fitz nodded to himself at that. Good question.

Michael licked his lips. 'Look. She didn't even know her husband was going with prostitutes. How could she possibly know what I do in my spare time?'

Wise pounced. 'So you're confirming that David Harvey did go with prostitutes?'

'I didn't say that!'

'Yes you did, Mister Harvey. It's been established before but it's always good to have confirmation from the horse's mouth as it were.'

Michael collapsed then. Seemed to fold in on himself. He put his head on his hands and began to shake.

'All right. All right. She couldn't have known. But she's right. I have . . . gone with . . . prostitutes.'

And Wise glanced quickly at Fitz as if to say, *That was easy then*, before looking back at Michael and saying, 'Michael Harvey I'm arresting you in connection with the murders of Paula Devereau and Joyce Watkins.'

'No!' Michael was on his feet. 'What are you talking about! I didn't –'

'That's enough!' Wise snapped. 'We'll get you a brief if you haven't got one of your own.'

Fitz had added it all up and got a different answer from Wise. He said bluntly: 'You haven't asked Michael if he has an alibi for last night.'

Wise stared at Fitz. *Butt out!*

No way.

And eventually Wise had to acknowledge that Fitz was right. He turned to Michael. 'Where were you between the hours of ten and eleven last night?'

Michael licked his lips.

Fitz said, 'Come on, Michael. You've already admitted going with prostitutes.'

Michael nodded, sat again. 'I was with a woman. Her name is Debra. That's all I know. I'll give you her address. She'll tell you it's the truth.'

Wise turned abruptly to leave, stared daggers at Fitz as he swept out of the room. Fitz cast a final look at Michael as he turned to leave himself.

The priest was weeping openly. He looked up at Fitz. 'Will you tell anyone?'

Fitz stared at him for a moment. 'It's a lot of guilt to carry around, isn't it? Guilt for this. Guilt for that. Guilt for living a normal life, enjoying normal pleasures. A life and pleasures that any normal man would take for granted. But then you're not an ordinary man, are you, Michael? You're ordained. By God. And you love him and worship him and he denies you everything that you need to be a normal man. And being normal is hard to give up. It's wired into our hearts and heads, into our very chromosomes. So there's a conflict. That conflict is why I left the faith.'

And Fitz had to admit that was the best answer Michael would get out of him, because it was the best answer he had for himself.

At Wise's request, Fitz moved directly to interview room number two where David Harvey was sitting at an identical table. Bobby Skelton was the policeman standing watch.

Fitz had Skelton start the tape recorder and ident the tape.

'Someone else has been killed.' Start off with the big guns; shake him – see if he rattles. 'Same method. Chisel. Crushed skull. There's two now. Two more. I know you didn't do them but I do hold you responsible.'

Nothing from Harvey. Hands on the table, motionless.

'Don't you feel sorry for her?'

'Yeah.'

'Well?'

'I feel sorry for me too. I've been banged up in here. I've got the perfect alibi. You gave it to me.'

Fitz sighed. OK. So it wasn't going to be that easy. When was it ever? 'You didn't kill Joyce Watkins or Paula Devereau. But I know you killed Jean McIlvanney.'

'I didn't.'

Interesting. That was the first time he'd ever come right out and denied it. Up to now he'd simply avoided the question. Fitz thought for a moment. 'Why, Shirley Temple?'

'What do you mean?'

196

'Oh don't come the coy, David. We all know what you want when you go to these women. They've all said as much. You like them to sing. Pretend to be little kids. You like to swear at them, give them a hard time. Why? Do you hate them that much?'

David said nothing.

'If you do, why use them? Why pay all that money to them when it could go to your kids?'

More nothing. A bucketload of nothing. Fitz lit up a high tar, puffed distractedly on it. Another tack was called for. 'What about Maggie? How old were you when you met?'

'Eighteen. She was sixteen.'

'Virgin?'

'Me? No.'

'Maggie?'

'I don't know.'

'You never asked?'

'No.'

'You're lying.' Fitz pronounced the words with a confident grin he knew would maximise David's annoyance. He stared at David, who looked away. 'Did she say she was?'

'Yes.'

'Did you believe her?'

'Yes.' David licked his lips. Fitz grinned. Sometimes the lies were so easy to spot they might have been neon signs.

'You didn't, though, did you? Believe her.'

Nothing.

It didn't matter. Not to Fitz. Not now. 'Low self-esteem. If *you* can screw her, she can't be choosy. Lots of men have been there before you, hm?'

Nothing.

'Did you hate her immediately afterwards? Slut. Letting you do that to her. You can tell me. I'm a good catholic boy.'

Nothing.

Fitz waited.

197

Nothing.

Then . . . 'Yes.' That one word the first crack in the dam.

Fitz nodded. 'And that's why Shirley Temple turns you on.'

David sighed. 'I don't know what you're talking about.'

'To be the first. The very first. That's good . . . But even better; first and last. Screw a virgin. Then slaughter her. First and last.'

David stared at Fitz, then looked away unable to meet his eyes. 'You're sick.'

'I might think about it, David. You did it.'

David just shook his head tiredly.

Fitz continued the conversation for another hour but he knew it would make no difference. David was saying nothing.

Fitz nodded to Skelton, left the interview room.

Arriving back at the duty room to make his report to Wise, Fitz was unsurprised to see a number of police women dressed as prostitutes. So that was the next move in the game. Entrapment. Obvious really when you thought about it. He wondered whose idea it was. Not Wise's that was for sure.

The DCI was currently into the last bit of his pep talk. 'Rule number one, don't take any chances. You don't put yourselves at risk. You don't go off with anyone no matter what they say. You're there to observe only. Nothing else. Observe and report. The first punter to say anything about Shirley Temple, about schoolies, anything like that, you call in, right? There'll be cars all over, you'll never be alone.' His serious expression lightened. 'Rule number two: if you do make a few bob, I'm on halves, right?'

That got a titter from the blokes and a belly laugh from Debbie Chandra.

'Right then, where's Penhaligon?'

'Arming herself for the night, guv,' Chandra hit Wise

with the dirtiest wink Fitz had ever seen. 'From the machine in the loo, if you know what I mean.'

Wise shook his head. 'Daft sod. This is serious.'

Chandra was about to reply, but anything she might have said was swallowed up by the silence when Penhaligon walked back into the room.

Fitz had to admit, she'd done a job and a half on herself. The clothes didn't hide any of it either. Fitz suddenly shivered with desire. *And she'd undone her hair.*

There was a chorus of catcalls and whistles. Someone yelled, 'Give us a twirl, Anthea!'

Penhaligon just grinned. She shook her head.

Fitz saw Beck, staring, staring. Penhaligon saw him too. Beck caught himself suddenly and grinned. Fitz saw a lot in that grin. He saw a man suddenly devoid of doubt. A man proved right. A man who suddenly realised he had found the excuse he needed to blame another for his actions. No. To blame his *victim* for his actions against her.

Beck grinned and sucked on his roll-up. 'You ought to be doing this professionally.'

As a joke it fell utterly flat, but Beck didn't care.

Fitz strolled up to him. 'She'd be too expensive for you, Jimmy,' he said in a loud stage whisper. Beck whirled angrily, but the duty room was laughing by then, tension released. Beck's comment had been so obvious, Fitz's defusing of it so effortless.

Beck turned away, to find himself face to face with Penhaligon. She sauntered casually towards him, rested her hip on his desk. Stared at him. Fitz grinned. Beck couldn't look away. She had him, hook, line and sinker.

'Fancy a bit do you, Jimmy?' Only the context of her clothes and manner had changed. Penhaligon's voice was exactly the same. The officers in the duty room howled with laughter but Fitz could see the subtext. They saw someone pretending to seduce, a temptress, a tease. Someone playing a joke on a colleague. Fitz saw an angry woman determined to get even with a man she hated. He knew Penhaligon. Knew what she was capable of. Beck didn't. Not yet. He was just beginning to find out. Nothing was beyond her.

'Hey, baby, not nervous are you? Little lady at home miss you, will she? Mummy want you back by nine o'clock?'

Beck was shaking.

The whole duty room was in an uproar by now. Wise was yelling, 'Knock it off, that's enough, the both of you,' but no-one took a blind bit of notice.

Beck was mesmerised by Penhaligon's performance. She leaned over him. Breathed on him. 'Mmmmm. I love your aftershave.' Fitz winced. It was his aftershave that had revealed to Penhaligon that Beck was the man who had raped her. 'Are you dominant? Tell me how you like it. You want it on a swing? A kid's playground? Do you want to wear a mask? A leather mask? Do you want me to wear one?'

Beck was shaking now. Hands gripping the desk. And the officers in the duty room were beginning to falter in their laughter. Something was going on here. They'd sussed out that much, but couldn't work out what it was.

Fitz knew, felt his stomach clench. She had just described the rape; the place where it had happened and the rapist himself. She was playing a dangerous game. He had to love her for that, at least.

Wise said, 'Here, you two, will you knock it off like I said?'

But Penhaligon was too far gone to stop now. 'Why was your name on Paula Devereau's pad, Jimmy?'

The room fell silent.

Beck blinked. It seemed the only movement he could manage.

Fitz watched, fascinated.

'I talked to Denise afterwards. She said you'd come to her the night before. Why didn't you give her one?'

Beck struggled to speak. 'I went there to ask her some questions.'

'You slept with her. Gave her one. You wanted some company.'

'I don't need company.'

'She thinks you're a sad bastard, Jimmy. And do you know what? So do I.'

Beck stood then, as the room fell into a deathly hush. 'All right. I'll admit it. I gave her one. Not company. I went there to ask a few questions and I gave her one! I gave her several! OK?'

His face was inches from Penhaligon. He was totally hyper, a mixture of rage and guilt, confusion and bitterness. Penhaligon didn't move. She merely smiled.

Unable to hold her gaze for longer than a moment, Beck was left no alternative than to storm out of the duty room and slam the door behind him.

Penhaligon rose too. The clothes and hair and makeup – all these said *for sale* in letters a mile high – but the woman inside was still Penhaligon through and through. Her own spirit, her own woman. Nothing had changed. Fitz just shook his head and tried to work out whether the feeling he now felt was love or hate. Either would be a projection of his own expectations, and if he was truthful with himself, whatever he felt would be entirely due to the fact that she had played this little scene out as much for his benefit as for Jimmy Beck's.

And he had fallen for it, all the way. Because in showing Beck what he could never have, she was showing Fitz what she had freely offered to him, and he had rejected. He'd had her. On a plate. Love, sex, commitment, pink fluffy toilet cover, the whole package. And he'd blown it. And she knew it.

And Fitz knew, love or hate, it didn't matter. Because some days he simply stood in awe of this woman. Totally and completely in awe.

And the truth was she knew that too.

● ● ●

Fitz waited a few moments until the tension in the duty room had reached a less explosive level and then collared Wise to make his report.

'David is not going to say anything. This entrapment idea is good so far as it goes. It might get the murderer. But it won't get us any closer to making David admit that he killed Jean McIlvanney.'

Wise sighed. 'Do you ever feel like saying "Some days it'd be better just to stay in bed"?'

Fitz glanced sideways at Penhaligon. 'Absolutely.'

'All we can do is hope we can keep this entrapment thing up 'til we catch him and then, I dunno, confront them with each other or something. Make the killer admit he didn't kill Jean. Maybe that'll get us somewhere with David.'

Fitz nodded. 'It's good enough for me.'

At that moment one of the duty room phones rang. Penhaligon picked it up, listened a moment, offered the handset to Fitz. 'It's your brother.'

Fitz nodded his thanks. 'Danny?'

'I need to see you.'

Fitz felt a momentary fear.

'Don't worry, Judith's fine. So's the baby. I just need to see you. It's about Mum.'

'What's it about?'

'Well, it's good news actually.'

'I see. We buried Mum today and you're telling me it's good news. Aliens cloned her, have they?'

Danny sighed. 'You might want to buy me a drink, Fitz.'

'Well that at least sounds half reasonable.' Fitz looked around. They could manage without him here for a while. 'I'll meet you in the Robin Hood. Half an hour OK?'

When Fitz got to the Robin Hood some ten minutes later he found Beck propping up the bar, one hand massaging a temple, the other wrapped around a double whisky. Joining Beck, to the detective's obvious dismay but to his own great amusement, Fitz ordered a whisky and dry ginger. He tipped the glass to Beck when it arrived.

'Scunthorpe.'

Beck said nothing. At least not with words. But his body was telling Fitz in no uncertain terms to get out of Beck's space.

Fitz ignored the signals. He nodded in a friendly manner to Beck. 'You all right?'

Beck sighed. 'I can feel a bit of a pain in my arse but that might be something to do with you.'

Fitz smiled, waited a moment, then hit back. 'That what passes for wit in Belfast?'

Nothing from Beck. Nothing except a smouldering silence.

'I only ask because you don't look so good.'

'At least I haven't got puke on my suit.'

'Have you looked in the mirror lately, Jimmy?'

'Have you?'

Fitz guzzled his whisky.

'You're blue around the lips, Jimmy.'

Jimmy slammed back his whisky and ordered another.

'You'll be OK. As long as there's no tingling in your left arm.'

Beck sighed, turned away from Fitz. Walked over to the jukebox. Shoved in a coin and hit some random numbers.

Tammy Wynette, *Stand By Your Man.*

Beck sat at a table near the jukebox. Fitz picked up his drink and followed. 'I haven't said the wrong thing have I? You don't feel any tingling do you?'

Beck began to sing along with the music. Fitz smiled. He had him on the run. And, childish though it was, Fitz was enjoying the game.

'Tingling could mean an impending heart attack, Jimmy. A stroke. Like the one you almost had back in the station. With Penhaligon. She's a bit of all right, though isn't she? Bit of a wind-up, though, right? Leads you on? Bet you'd like to though, eh Jimmy? Especially dressed like that. Like a tart. Bit of a fantasy of yours, yeah? Saw it in your eyes. Like Shirley Temple. Young. Innocent.'

'I didn't kill them Fitz! You hear me? I killed no-one!'

'You think I give a toss what you did with your filthy friends?' Fitz cocked his head to one side and studied Beck, allowed the deliberate anger to drain from his voice. 'I've got you a tad worried, haven't I? Your heart rate's up. Your blood pressure's up. Only a bit but you can feel it. Like she felt it. On the swing. In the mud underneath. Heart thudding like a trip hammer, blood pressure like fire hydrant. And you, in the mask. Giving her one. Giving her one like there's no tomorrow. Again. Again.'

'Fitz, piss off, will you! I just want a drink, a quiet drink, so why don't you –'

But Fitz was in there again, relentless, implacable. 'Oxygen required, Jimmy. Take a gasp. Another. Like she did. But you can't get enough. Something's wrong. Something in your mouth now. He's holding you down and something's in your mouth. Can't breathe! Oxygen required! There's a message flashing round your body. Something wrong. Violation. Oxygen required. Adrenalin required. More. More.'

And Beck's glass slammed back to the table spilling whisky everywhere, and he was hyperventilating, breathing along with the tempo of Fitz's words. And Fitz knew the game had turned serious, dangerous, but he didn't care, was pushing it all the way. Making Beck see the rape through the eyes of his victim.

'You can feel that adrenalin, yeah? From the fear. The chemical buzz. What are you going to do? Flight or fight. Flight's out, he's holding you down. What you going to do? There's nothing you can do. Not a thing. But all that adrenalin. Got to go somewhere, do something, or you'll explode. Not enough room inside for it all. But he's still holding you down. Still inside you. Pushing, pushing, pushing. And you can't run. You can't hide. Down in the mud. Under the swing. Chains clinking, a dog barking somewhere, the smell of whisky and aftershave and the mask and your arteries are narrowing, heart rate's way up, blood pressure's through the roof and he's still holding you down and doing it to you, penetrating you, again and again and *again* and *again*!'

And Beck was gasping, wheezing, caught in the throes of a terrible panic attack. And he was up, muttering words indistinguishable from moans of pain, up and running for the toilet as the whisky glass tumbled to the floor in a golden rain.

And Fitz was up too, following him, pushing through the same door, pushing him through a barrier, back to that day. 'More oxygen required. But you can't get any more, Jimmy. Your lungs've ceased to function. It's called hyperventilation, Jimmy. Every nerve in your body's screaming out the same message. Something wrong, life and death, more adrenalin required! Stop him doing this to me, stop him, I'm going to die, stop him stop him oh please stop him now!'

And Beck was into a stall, bent up over the bowl and throwing up again and again, words slipping out past the vomit. 'No, Daddy, stop it, stop it, stop it!'

And Fitz was flushed, his heart singing with the same adrenalin buzz as Beck's, only for him it was an unparalleled high. 'And the adrenalin just flows on and on. Your arteries get even narrower, the heart's pumping away, blood pressure's through the roof, head's exploding, you're gonna die, Jimmy, you can't take any more of this abuse, you're going to die, he's going to kill you and you're going to die!'

Beck sagged against the toilet bowl, dry heaving, gasping for breath, choking on his own vomit. And Fitz watched. And did nothing.

'Get it off your chest, Jimmy. Why that expression? Because guilt suffocates. You need to get it off your chest. Just to me. No-one else. And I'll help you. I promise.'

Beck looked up then and Fitz felt like howling in triumph. He'd got the bastard, got him in the palm of his hand.

Dragged the truth kicking and screaming from him, out into the light of day, out into the light of God's brand new day.

'Just do it.'

Fitz smiled. Produced a crisp packet. Gave it to Beck.

'Blow into this.'

Beck did.

'Breathe from it. Deep. Slow. Carbon dioxide. That's what you need. Breathe your own waste products. It will help you. That's it. Deep breaths. Slow, deep breaths . . .'

The toilet opened and Danny came in. 'Hey, Fitz, thought I might find you in . . .' He stopped. Looked down at Beck. At Fitz bending over him.

Without straightening, Fitz said, 'Piss off, Danny, all right? Just do one.'

Danny about faced and left without so much as a word.

And Fitz looked back at Beck, wondering if he'd lost him.

He needn't have worried. Beck had cracked. Like Judith he was a seed pod from which words flowed like new life. 'Bilborough died because I showed a villain a bit of compassion. And I wanted a bit of compassion back. From her. A bit of understanding. But I got none. She despised me for it.'

'You think she loved him?'

'I did. She can turn it on and off like a tap. They all can. Bloody compassion.'

'Women?'

And Beck put the crisp bag down, breathing easier now, and it all came out. 'I came over here when I was fourteen. I took stick. Mick. Paddy. Get back to the bog. Irish runt. I knew what I had to do. Throw a few punches, take a few punches, earn a bit of respect. I didn't. I hung around with the girls. They showed a bit of compassion, you see. And I fell for it. A month passes, I'm not a fresh face any more, they're bored with me, they dump me. I've got to take the punches now, only they're worse now, harder to take, because I've been hanging around with the girls.'

Beck licked his lips. Fitz waited. Beck said, 'Women need rape.'

Fitz said nothing.

'It's their weapon. A woman goes up to the heavyweight champion of the world. Hotel bedroom. Early hours of the morning. He gives her one, gets done for rape, ends up in nick. The heavyweight champion, one of the bravest men in the world, if it can happen to him it can happen to any one of us. And that's what they want, it's their weapon, it keeps us on our toes.'

Another pause. Another few breaths from the crisp bag. Little bits of smokey bacon clinging to his moustache.

'Penhaligon needs rape.'

'Needs *raping*.'

'No. Needs rape. Her department. Her little empire. She can treat me like muck when it's rape 'cos she's a woman and women know and we don't. Well, that's bollocks, she knows nothing about rape. Rape is about loving your parents and being abused by your father again and again, and running to your mother and begging her to do something and her not believing you and just letting it happen again and again and again ... That's what rape is. It's not just physical. It's not just getting fucked. It's getting head-fucked.'

'I understand. So you decided to teach her something about it?'

'This is in confidence?'

Fitz nodded. 'Doctor–patient.'

'Total confidence?'

'Yeah.'

'I don't believe you.'

Fitz pushed a little. 'Total confidence Jimmy.' *Hold him with your eyes, don't let him walk now!*

'Swear!'

'Bloody, bloody, bloody!'

207

'On the life of your wife and kids.'

'I swear on the life of my wife and kids that I won't repeat anything you tell me.'

It wasn't enough for Beck. 'Swear on the life of your new-born baby.'

And it all twisted then, a game no longer, suddenly it was for real and Fitz knew it was for real and knew that Beck did too.

'You're sick.'

Beck laughed. 'Swear.'

'I swear on the life of my new-born child I won't repeat anything you tell me.'

Beck sighed. The decision was already made. It was only a matter of timing. And the time was now. Right here and now. Fitz could see that and wasn't going to spoil the moment.

'I never intended to rape her. As God is my judge I never intended to. I just wanted to . . . terrify her. I was gonna pull the mask off at the last moment and laugh in her face. But something happened. She looked so . . . so . . .'

'Vulnerable.'

'Vulnerable. Frightened. Weak. And I felt so . . . strong, so powerful and . . . you want the truth? I'll tell you the truth. I'd never had such a hard-on in my whole life. And I realised . . . well, that I could get away with it. I could rape her and get away with it. Just walk away from it. And that's why I did it. Because . . . just because. I could.'

And Fitz felt the floor slide away from underneath him and he sat down beside Beck.

Beck looked at him. 'Don't you dare despise me. You'd have done it. Every man I know would have done it.'

And Fitz sat there, in the dregs of Jimmy Beck's vomit, both of them like twins worshipping at a china altar, and despite the fear, the anger, the terror, the irony of the situation didn't escape him. In Beck's mind they were the same. Who was he to say they weren't?

208

They sat in silence for a while and then Beck said, 'When are you going to tell her?'

And after an even longer pause Fitz said, 'I swore, remember. On the life of my new-born child.'

And Beck smiled then. 'Then, all this. You were doing all this for yourself. Not for her. We are the same.'

And he pulled himself upright and left the toilet.

Fitz remained a moment longer, then washed up as best he could. As he left the toilet himself he reached out for the flush.

Danny was waiting for him as he came out.

Fitz sighed. Of all the things he needed now, his brother was last on his list. Avoiding Danny for as long as he could, he bought another drink. He sidled over to the fruit machine, dropped some coins in, began to play.

Danny joined him ten minutes later. He'd won two quid and lost a fiver.

He ignored Danny. His head was whirling faster than the little neon fruit in front of him. Beck. Penhaligon. Two lemons and a cherry. Lost opportunities. Judith. The baby. An orange, a grapefruit, another orange. Mum. Penhaligon. Beck. The rape. Any way he looked at the situation he lost.

When Fitz had finally blown all his change on the machine he turned to Danny. He rubbed his face with a sleeve that was grimy and stank of booze. 'All right. You're here. I won't pretend that I like you. I won't pretend that I've had a splendid day. But you are my brother, so I suppose I have to listen to what you have to say. So go on. Give me the perfect end to a perfect day.'

Danny stared contemptuously at Fitz. He slapped an envelope down on the fruit machine in front of him. 'Mum had an endowment policy on her mortgage. Thirty grand. Fifteen is yours. I thought you'd want it in cash.' He stared at the whisky glass Fitz had perched on top of the fruit machine. 'There's lipstick on your glass, Fitz. Get a clean one for God's sake.'

He left then, and Fitz stared at the package. He stared at the package for a long time.

Somehow it only made things worse.

TWENTY-ONE

Memories. A shower. Hot water then cold. Out of the bathroom and towel dry. Rub colour into the skin. Foundation. Rouge. Lipstick. Mascara.

Who will it be tonight?

The feather touch of a makeup brush against her lashes. Another at her cheeks. Fake silver clasped at her throat.

What will he want me to do?

Stockings and shoes. That dress. No bra.

Will he want to talk?

Would he look at me afterwards?

Her short jacket, the denim one that showed off her arse.

What will he think of me?

What will he say to me?

How much will he pay?

No. Stop that. Stop that right now. Ask yourself questions like that and you just empower them. Let them use you. It's my choice to work this way. It's my body. I am in control.

Jane Penhaligon walked slowly along City Road. It wasn't late. Pubs were still open. But there was still some business about. Some girls, hovering, the odd kerb-crawler.

So far no-one had approached her.

She walked.

Her feet were killing her. The shoes, right? How did they do it, night after night?

She looked around as a car sped past, cloud of fumes, a rude gesture from the boy racer at the wheel.

Somewhere in the evening stillness a police siren blared. Ahead of her a woman looked up. Rozzers. Were they after

211

her? Were they going to arrest her? How would she pay the fine? It was all there. All there in the body language.

Another car, then quiet. Shoes clicking on the pavement. Stockings hissing between her legs. Feeling the night against her bare arms, her face. Feeling vulnerable. More alone than ever before in her life. Oh she was no blushing virgin. But for her, sex had never been the Errol Flynn variety. That was OK. Penhaligon knew the realism of sex. Of love. She was no victim. She was capable of offering love and taking it, and she would hurt as much as anyone when that which she offered was refused. Exactly the same as anyone else. No more, no less.

That was the truth, wasn't it?

Then why did she sigh? Why did she think of him so often? Of Fitz. And Beck. Lover friend. Colleague and rapist. Between the two of them they must have encompassed just about every kind of relationship if was possible to have.

Why was she so confused then?

Answer: she wasn't confused. She was angry. No. She was outraged. They'd both violated her. No. Not outraged. *En*raged. Furious. Boiling.

She thought of what she'd done to Jimmy Beck in the duty room. How she'd teased him, tortured him. That wasn't fair. That was using her power. No. Actually it was using his own inadequacies against him. Her power was not sexual. Her power was in seeing his weakness. Her power was not linked to her femininity but her *mind*. That was why she was such a bloody good copper. That's why Fitz fell in love with her. If he had.

She tried to remember if he had ever said he loved her. She couldn't remember. With Fitz you just never knew. Everything he did and said was couched in half truths and double meanings she felt sure he didn't understand himself half the time. And when it wasn't double meanings it was double entendres. One was as bad as the other.

212

She hated him. Loved him. All at once. That was what the truth was. Hated him because he was a man and a man had raped her. Loved him because he was, well, lovable. Hated him because he had betrayed her friendship and trust. Had gone back to his wife. Had not been there to help her when she so desperately needed his help.

Loved him because of the head games he played.

Hated him because of the head games he played.

'Hi there.'

Penhaligon jumped half out of her skin. She turned. A car had pulled up alongside her. Gold Mondeo. She memorised the licence number.

She looked at the driver. What did he want her to say? 'All right?' She didn't move.

He opened the Mondeo's passenger door, an invitation. She blinked.

He said, 'D'you do French?'

'I got an O level at school.' The response was automatic. The guy seemed perfectly friendly. It wasn't what he looked like, though. It was his actions. He wanted to buy her. Buy her body. Rent it cheap more like.

'I can pay you forty.'

She curled a lip; half thoughtful, half contempt. 'Just French?'

'Yeah.'

'Nothing else?'

'No.'

Nothing doing here.

'I'm waiting for someone.' She turned to walk along the road.

The car edged forward, drew level with her. The driver said, 'Who you waiting for?'

'A well known popular novelist.'

'I can go to fifty.' Hopeful? Desperate!

'You can go to hell.'

'You name it then.' The poor bastard was serious.

213

'I've told you. I'm waiting for someone.'

'Sixty. That's as far as I'm going.'

Penhaligon sighed. She had visions of Wise and Beck in Beck's car listening to the wire she wore and killing themselves. They'd probably be cracking jokes about her working under them and taking bets on how high Mister Mondeo would go.

'It won't take long. I'll bring you back. Look. I'll go to sixty-five.'

She reached into her purse, showed him her ID. 'I'm a copper. Now piss off, OK?'

The Mondeo pulled away fast and she was hit by a cloud of hot fumes.

She closed her eyes and choked. When she opened them another car was pulling past her, further up the road. She couldn't see the driver. The car pulled in beside a woman who was standing in a pool of light cast by a neon cross mounted on the side of the Salvation Army building.

Penhaligon's eyes narrowed. There was something about that car. She spoke into the microphone concealed in her necklace. 'Boss. Penhaligon here. What type of car does Michael Harvey drive?'

'*Dark green Alfasud.*' The answer rattled in the earphone whose wire was concealed by a dangling set of earrings.

'A dark green Alfasud just pulled up in front of me.'

'*Jesus! Check it out. But be careful.*'

'OK.'

Penhaligon walked closer to the car. She still couldn't see in; light from the cross reflected in a white bar off the rear windscreen. Closer then. Keep it casual. You're just looking for work, right? For some sad punter with slightly more money than sense. Right? Right.

Closer. Closer.

She could hear voices now. Snatches of words.

'. . . you following me?'

A murmur from inside the Alfa.

214

'. . . ain't a careers officer.'

Penhaligon got closer.

The woman turned. A quick look at Penhaligon and then back to her conversation. Penhaligon didn't recognise the woman. She kept on walking. Slow, slow. Look around for cars, you're out for business.

She heard the woman say, 'You're thinking of going on the game?'

Penhaligon began to tingle. That wasn't the kind of thing you'd ask a punter.

A murmur from inside the car.

The woman said, 'Like I said. I ain't a careers officer. But if you're dead set on it . . .' She leaned into the car window and her words became inaudible.

And then Penhaligon had it. In a blinding flash of revelation, there under the neon cross, she had it. And she was running forward, heart pounding, eyes probing the glaze of light shrouding the car, and she was pulling at the door, pushing the woman aside as she protested, and the door flew open and –

– she was staring at a familiar face.

The driver was a woman.

Maggie Harvey.

And then everything seemed to happen really fast. She was calling information into her R/T, as Maggie saw her and recognised her, shoved the Alfa into gear and floored the accelerator.

The Alfa shot away and Penhaligon had to jump clear to avoid being flattened by the still open door. As it was the door caught her jacket, knocking her into the wall with enough force to bruise her left leg and hip and elbow. Penhaligon hit the wall, rolled, fell to the ground. The Alfa weaved onto and then off the pavement, roared up City Road, ran a red light and turned out of sight on to the high street.

Penhaligon scrambled to her feet, grinning triumphantly,

unaware that her left side was smeared with blood from a graze running from her left shoulder to her elbow. Beside her the prostitute stared open-mouthed, as if Penhaligon were some insane creature who had just emerged in a flash of light from a sewer grating.

Penhaligon didn't care. Not about the woman. Not about her bruised hip. Not about her bloody arm.

That was how the killer got in to see Joyce and Paula. That was why the girls trusted their visitor. Fitz thought that they'd trusted him because he was a priest. No way. They'd trusted him because he wasn't a him, he was a her.

Maggie Harvey.

They'd found their killer and it was *Maggie bloody Harvey*!

TWENTY-TWO

Getting hold of the keys to Michael's car had been easy. A trip to Valubuys. Food for the kids. Easy as pie. He even offered to drive.

Now look at the shopping trip it had turned into.

Maggie drove fast, pedal to the metal. So they knew. Well good. It didn't change anything. Didn't change the fact that David was in jail and her kids were going to be short of food, short of clothes. Henry, Robert, Jane, Jerry. And Peter. *Oh Peter*. And that psychologist Fitz was right. The other kids would laugh at them. They'd have to move. How could they do that with no money? With David in jail?

It was simple. A simple choice. David didn't do it. He didn't go with prostitutes and he didn't commit murder.

Something in Maggie screamed out then. Demanded acknowledgement.

If David hadn't killed Jean McIlvanney, then who did?

Maggie knew the answer to that one.

The same person who killed Paula Devereau and Joyce Watkins.

Ahead there was a red light. Maggie slowed the car. Go easy. Don't make them suspicious. One more item on the shopping list. One more item and then we can go home. Just a little shopping. And then we can go.

The light turned from red to green. Maggie pulled away. First to second. Third. A corner. The address the prostitute had given her burning a hole in her head. That address. That woman. The woman who had identified her David. The one who had picked him out of the parade. Denise. Denise bloody Fletcher. That was her name. Of all of them, all the filthy stinking whores she was the worst. If she'd gone with David Jean wouldn't be dead and none of this would have happened. Except that David hadn't killed Jean, had he? Hadn't killed that filthy, child-robbing bitch. No. Not her David. Not the man she loved.

Shifting down, Maggie took another corner, overtook some lunatic with L plates doing fifteen miles an hour. Bloody maniac. Shouldn't be allowed on the road. Anything could happen. Someone could die. Someone could get killed.

Like Denise. She could have got killed. Not by David, no, but by someone. This killer of Joyce and Paula for example. Yes, that was logical. It was Denise that should have died. She was the one who had refused him. Paula had refused him. Joyce had refused him, Denise had refused him. Now Paula and Joyce were dead and only one name, one item, remained on the shopping list.

It had taken her two days to find out Denise's address. And the irony was it was exactly beneath the flat where she'd been just the previous night.

Maggie smiled.

Irony. Fate. Destiny. Logic. All gone. Flying away now. Only love was left. Only love. For her kids. For Henry, Robert, Jane, Jerry.

And Peter.

She pulled over to the kerb, parked. Got out of the car. Walked through the main entrance to the flats and into the

church, between the pews over to the tiny altar where the candles were lit in remembrance of the dead, and the children were with her, and they were giggling, they were only young, they didn't understand, and Henry, the eldest, said, 'Aw Mum, have I got to do this again?' and she smacked him, she smacked Henry hard on the back of the leg because he didn't understand yet and had to be taught, had to be taught to light a candle in remembrance of the dead, to light a candle for Peter –

'I beg your pardon, love?'

The voice was unfamiliar.

Maggie blinked. She was on the third floor. Red brick. Peeling paint on the windowsills. Graffiti on every exposed surface. Birdshit on the balcony handrail.

'Are you Denise Fletcher?'

'What if I am?'

'Can I come in?'

'Why?'

'I need your advice.'

'I've got to work.'

'I've got to work too. I've got four kids and *Peter!*

I need to make a bit of money. I'm desperate.'

Maggie felt Denise's gaze on her. Judging her.

'Have you ever been on the game before?'

'No.'

'Then I've got something to show you.'

She opened the door and Maggie followed her into the living room. Denise turned to face her. 'You know what you get when you go on the game? Murdered.' And she pointed to the ceiling where an ochre stain had spread around the light fixture and dyed the light cord brown. 'See that? That's blood, love. Now go home and forget all about it.'

Maggie stared at the blood. Paula's blood. It had come out from inside her. From inside Paula. Her life's blood paid for by who knew how many men with more money than sense?

And David. Had David gone with Paula?

No. David didn't go with prostitutes.

David didn't kill prostitutes.

That was down to whoever had killed Paula. Joyce. Jean McIlvanney.

Maggie wondered what kind of person could kill a woman so savagely that all that remained was that huge lake of blood.

She moved closer, sat at the table. Now the blood was directly overhead. A murky halo.

'How do you stay safe?'

Denise shrugged. 'We phone each other up.'

'There's nothing else you can do?'

Denise laughed humourlessly. 'You can pick and choose your partners but most of them are weirdos anyway.'

Maggie nodded. The truth was self-evident. 'Did you ever come across him?'

'Who? Shirley? Yeah.'

'What did you do? What . . . did he want you to do?'

'He'd get you to dress up like a kid and sing. "How much is that doggie in the window?" Pervert.'

Maggie tilted her head to one side. Now she could see the blood again, right in the corner of her eye. It was overlaid on the image of Denise, standing in front of her, arms crossed as if with cold, pacing the living room like a nervous animal.

'How much did you charge him?'

'Shirley? Forty quid. I'd ask fifty, he'd knock me down.'

Maggie nodded again.

'How many times did you . . . did you see him?'

'Every couple of months. I dunno. Twenty times altogether. I'm not sure.'

'What did you do?'

'Straight sex. I'd have to go all coy. He'd start screaming. Slut, slag, all of that. Then he'd strip me. Straight sex, me on top.' Denise seemed to catch a hint of Maggie's tension then. 'Why are you interested in him? Like pervs do you?' A thought seemed to strike her. 'Here. You're not a reporter, are you? 'Cos if you are you can bugger off or cough up. This is my working time. No-one gets a free story from me.'

Maggie smiled. 'Fancy a cuppa?'

Denise frowned. Then grinned. 'Oh the hell with it, why not?'

A few minutes later the kettle had boiled and the tea was brewing.

'Have you got names for them all?'

'You are a bloody reporter.'

'Do you?'

'Just the pervs. Who do you work for?'

'Do you think it's right to take all that money off a man and call him a perv behind his back?'

'Who are you, love? Mother Teresa?'

'I mean. You let him do those things to you. Doesn't that make you worse?'

Denise put a pot of tea and two mugs on the table. 'One thing's for sure, you aren't working for *Woman's Own*.'

Maggie studied Denise closely. She did not seem to want an answer to her question. 'Shall I be mother?' Maggie poured two mugs of tea. She sipped her own, watched the steam rise, let it guide her eyes back to the bloodstained ceiling. 'You even advertise it. You advertise filth for sale. And then you've got the cheek to criticise the men who buy it.'

Maggie saw the change in Denise. The change she was looking for. From indulgence to anger. 'Get out! Sod your story. Go on. Sod off!'

And Maggie stood then, as if to leave, but at the last moment swept the teapot into her hand and brought it crashing down on Denise's head.

Denise fell with a groan.

Maggie studied her thoughtfully as she wriggled on the floor. 'I'm his wife. You called him a pervert. What does that make me?'

Tea dripped from the table, from Denise's face and hair. It puddled on the carpet, soaked the broken pieces of china.

Maggie stood quite still, the broken handle clutched in her hand, with a shred or two of teapot still attached.

'What do you imagine he does to me? What do you imagine, you dirty filthy bitch?'

Denise groaned. Stirred. Blinked tea out of her eyes.

'Eight hundred pounds.'

221

Denise began to crawl. Maggie watched her go, inch by pain filled inch. Her eyes blinded by scalding tea, her fingers scrabbling across the carpet for a way out.

'Twenty times. Forty pounds a time. That's eight hundred pounds you took off him.'

Denise groaned, more loudly this time. Her head had started to bleed. The blood mixed with the tea still in her hair and laid a trail across the carpet.

'He's got four kids. Henry, Robert, Jane, Jerry. Peter. Four kids. You've been taking the food out of the mouths of four kids.'

Denise coughed. 'You bitch. I'll kill you. I earned that money. I earned that –'

Maggie moved again. Opened her hand. The handle fell and landed with a soft thump. Denise let out a little scream of fear. Began to crawl faster.

Maggie took the chisel out of her handbag.

'He would come home after being with you. A filthy stinking slut. He'd get into my bed, sheets I'd just washed. He touched me. Held me. Held me after being with a filthy, stinking whore like you.'

Maggie closed the distance between herself and Denise with a single stride. Denise screamed. The chisel descended again. A crack. Bone breaking. Denise's nose. More blood. New blood, red, not brown like that on the ceiling. That was interesting. Now they both had haloes. Haloes of blood.

Denise tried to scream, only managed a low, bubbling moan. She tried once more to crawl away. Maggie hammered her hand with the chisel. Denise screamed. She cradled the shattered hand to her breast. More blood bubbled from her mouth as she tried to speak. To swear. No chance.

Denise collapsed, exhausted. Her chest heaved with pain.

Maggie studied the damage to Denise's face. The torn skin, lacerations, the splinter of bone protruding from the cheek. The broken nose. The blood. The tea burns.

How could anyone do that to a woman? Kill her, smash in

her head like that? Puncture her with a chisel, let out the life inside like an old balloon? Maggie was appalled. Such a terrible crime. Thank God it wasn't her David that did it. But then David didn't go with prostitutes, did he? Not with dirty, stinking, filthy, whoremongering prostitutes. Not her David. And he didn't kill women either, did he? Of course not! David couldn't be the killer. It was obvious when you thought about it. He was in jail. And she was here with Denise. She was here and David wasn't. He couldn't be the killer.

That was the moment when Maggie understood for the first time, really understood, with a surprise and pleasure akin to religious ecstasy, that her husband wasn't the killer; couldn't be, for the simple reason that she herself was.

She explained it calmly to Denise. 'Taking money off my kids. Taking food out of the mouths of my kids. Filthy bitch. Scheming bitch. Stinking cow. Grabbing bitch. You should hang. You all should hang. Letting my kids starve.' Keep it calm. Make sure she understands. It's very simple really. A child could get it.

Denise was shaking.

Maggie raised the chisel.

Last time.

She grabbed hold of Denise's ankle.

Pulled her legs apart.

Last time.

Last time.

Last –

There was a noise. The front door. She turned. Why was the front door on the floor? That wasn't right. Doors are for walking through not walking on. Like that man was walking on it. Running actually. Coming towards her. She recognised him. The policeman. Beck. Behind Beck others crowded into the room. Two more men. A woman. Slim. Red hair. The policewoman. Penhaligon. Dressed like Denise. Dressed like a thieving whore.

She explained it to them.

'Filthy bitch. Whore. Kids. Money. Food. Slut. Thief. Killer. Kids.'

There. They'd understand that surely?

Beck was close now. She looked for understanding in his eyes.

He punched her in the face.

She sat down suddenly. Dropped the chisel. Under her hands the carpet was slippery with blood and tea. This was no good. No good at all. Now she wouldn't be able to finish her shopping, the last item on the list. She wondered if he would listen if she tried to explain again. She thought he might. She was shopping for the children after all.

'Victim.' She said the word slowly, for maximum clarity. Above her the blood halo impressed into the ceiling wobbled dangerously, threatened to fall and drench her.

'I'm a victim too.'

And she saw the light in his eyes then. The recognition. The familiarity. The understanding. The truth. The horror.

He understood her. He'd used those words. He understood her.

She reached for the chisel.

He hit her again.

TWENTY-THREE

Fitz studied Maggie Harvey across the interview room table. Black eye. Contusions. A bruise the size of a lemon across her left cheek.

Beck.

Was he justified?

He obviously thought he was. He was standing in the interview room, a little to one side. A place by the wall where he could observe both Fitz and Maggie.

Penhaligon had made her statement. She was getting changed now.

And Fitz was here for the usual job. Fishing for the truth. Dragging it kicking and screaming out of the psychotic mire that was Maggie Harvey's tortured personality.

'You hate Denise Fletcher.'

Maggie looked at him. Fitz expected aggression. He got vague bemusement. 'Isn't that obvious?'

'A broken nose, lacerations to the throat, hairline fracture of the skull, shattered cheekbone . . .' Fitz shrugged. 'You tell me.'

Maggie sighed. She smiled too. Patience. Forbearance. As if Fitz were *her* patient. 'She's lucky to be alive. Lucky *you* turned up.' A look at Beck here. Then back to Fitz. A little shake of the head. 'Beck understood. I explained it to him and he understood.' A little sideways tilt of the head. Maggie was studying Fitz. Was he capable of understanding, as Beck had done?

Fitz sucked on his high tar. Patience. Wait for the moment.

225

Maggie seemed to come to a decision. She nodded slightly to herself. Worried the bruise on her cheek.

'Is it sore?' Fitz asked kindly.

'I've been hurt worse than this.'

'Oh?'

And she smiled a little then, a tearful smile, head obviously bound up in some memory she was not prepared to share. Yet. Then the moment passed and she was back here, with Fitz. And she really was here. He could tell that. As lucid as anyone he'd ever met. He sighed. 'Maggie. Don't you think it's time to tell the truth?'

Maggie nodded. 'Oh yes. The truth. That's important. That's what I explained to Detective Beck. He understood.'

Fitz smiled reassuringly. 'I'll understand too. That's my job. I know how important it is to you, Maggie. And I think it's time. Don't you?'

'All right.' Calm. Open. Confident. 'I killed Joyce Watkins. And I killed Paula Devereau. You already know I tried to kill Denise Fletcher.'

'And Jean McIlvanney?'

Maggie blinked. 'Sorry. Forgot about her for a moment. Yes. I killed Jean McIlvanney as well.'

'That's a load of grade-A bollocks!' Beck took a step forward, eyes glaring.

Fitz knocked him back with a look. He turned back to Maggie. 'I know that's a lie.' Keep it calm. The truth is in there somewhere. Don't frighten it off.

Maggie nodded. Her smile was that of a teacher who has seen a pupil muff a bit of homework. 'Oh no. You're wrong. I killed Jean. Just like all the others. Blows to the skull. Chisel. Same method of operation. It was me all right.'

Fitz narrowed his eyes thoughtfully. Carefully now. One badly judged sentence and it was all over. 'Your husband killed Jean McIlvanney. David killed her. You killed Joyce and Paula. Why did you do that? Did you think you could free your husband by going on killing? If others died when

226

David was imprisoned then he would have to be released. Right? I know you killed the others. But David killed Jean.'

Maggie was shaking her head again. 'Look you've got it all wrong,' she said mildly. 'David doesn't use prostitutes. He doesn't. Honestly. He wouldn't waste the money. The kids need the money. He wouldn't use prostitutes. They're dirty. They carry diseases. You know that. They're thieves and they take money from wives and children.'

Fitz blew out his cheeks. 'Jean McIlvanney was a mother you know. She had two children.'

Maggie looked down at the table. A hint of sadness crept into her voice. 'That's awful. Who'll look after them? Is there anyone to look after them?'

Fitz sucked once again on his high tar, blew smoke thoughtfully. Maggie was interesting. He knew she was a cruel and savage killer, yet she presented the aspect of a benign schoolteacher with absolute confidence. It was as if for her the importance lay not in admitting her crimes but explaining them. Explaining herself. That in itself was not so unusual. But to have so bizarre a set of circumstances presented with such . . . thoughtfulness. Such consideration. Fitz had to admit he found it somewhat unnerving. Fascinating but unnerving.

He said, 'You're worried about your own kids.'

'Who wouldn't be? Those women taking food out of their mouths. No. I can't really call them women. Those sluts. Tarts. Whoremongering thieves. Those –'

'– mothers?'

Maggie stared at him then and Fitz found himself reminded of a day when as a child, he'd been sent to bed by his mother for being facetious. He didn't even know what the word meant then. He thought he was just cracking a fairly cool joke. Danny had laughed anyway. Maggie's look now reminded him of his mother's of that day. More sad than angry. But Fitz was sharper now. He'd seen the logical flaw in Maggie's argument. It was time to burst the bubble.

'Tell me, Maggie. If David didn't use prostitutes, as you say, what reason would you have for killing them?'

'That's easy, I –' Maggie paused then. Just locked up like a hung computer. Face blank. Eyes fixed in a thoughtful, almost puzzled expression.

'Maggie?' Fitz leaned forward. 'Maggie?' He studied her. She was motionless. Some kind of withdrawal? He took her hand in order to take her pulse. 'Beck. I think we may need to call a –'

Then movement. Explosive movement. And noise. Screaming.

'No you bastard don't you touch me get your filthy hands off me get out of my bed you've been with her I can smell her so don't lie to me just get out of my bed you filthy whoremongering son of a bitch!'

And Maggie wrenched her arm away from Fitz, the movement tipping her back, the chair toppling, and she was on the floor, scrabbling away from Fitz, crawling away, sobbing, screaming, backing into a corner of the room where she plastered herself against the tiles and cast her eyes around urgently like some cornered animal looking for escape from the predator that was about to take its life.

Fitz crouched down, followed slowly. 'It's all right, Maggie. You're back. I'm here. I can help you.'

Maggie looked wildly around, finally fixed on Fitz as the nearest object. 'I followed him. I saw him pick up Jean. I saw them go to her place. I saw them go to the cash machine. It all happened like you said.'

'And David killed her.'

'No. I've told you. I did that.'

All right. Time for a push. Fitz leaned closer. 'It's a bit daft you both going down for a stretch. And you've got no chance. Caught red-handed. So confess to all three murders and David gets out to look after the kids. Yes?'

Maggie was shaking now. Tense with ... what? Anger? Fear?

228

For the first time Fitz had an inkling of how she could have committed such brutal crimes. 'Two victims. Three victims. You think it makes no difference. But it does. It will. Not now but in ten, fifteen years time. A parole board likes a good motive, you see. "Here's a woman who killed twice to get her husband out of prison, well, that's something we can understand." But killing three times. Out of anger. Out of spite. You'll rot.'

'I killed Jean McIlvanney.' Jaw clenched. Words squeezed out syllable by syllable. Maggie was fighting against herself now.

'You know how you got away with it for so long?' Fitz pushed again. 'The chisel. It had to be a man. No woman could do that to another woman. But you had to do it. Had to force yourself. Because that's what David did to Jean McIlvanney.'

Maggie made a choking noise. More words trying to get out, jammed together in her throat, caged by tendons like guy ropes.

Fitz said, 'Did you think about him when you stuck it in them? Did you think about him penetrating them when you penetrated them? You didn't think about them, obviously. Joyce or Paula. You had to despise them, think of them as somehow not human. Yes?'

Maggie pushed herself into the corner, trying to get away. Beck came closer, curious, but Fitz waved him away. He'd served his purpose.

'Did you think about your daughters? Of course not. Because Joyce and Paula were someone's daughters, weren't they? There'd be some mother sobbing somewhere. What *did* you think about them, Maggie? What could drive you, madden you enough to do something like that?'

Maggie scrunched further back into the corner of the room. She mumbled something Fitz couldn't hear.

He leaned closer. 'Pardon, Maggie?'

And she screamed, 'Light a candle for him, light a candle

for my son, for Peter, *light a candle for Peter*!'

And suddenly Fitz had the whole picture, right there, in the palm of his hand; Maggie's heart and soul, her motivation, like a bright jewel in the palm of his hand.

It was nothing to do with David. Nothing at all. She hated David.

Peter. It was about a child called *Peter*.

And Fitz said, 'When did he die, Maggie?'

'I killed him.'

'Before he was born?'

Maggie nodded.

'Abortion?'

'Michael said I should do what I thought best. He said the choice was mine. But it never was mine. Not that choice. It was God's choice. Wasn't it?'

Fitz said nothing, allowed his silence to prompt her.

'But that's not a crime is it? The murder of an innocent? The murder of a guilt-ridden, pox-ridden prostitute is.' And Fitz didn't need to ask Maggie to continue, she explained it all to him in terms even Jimmy Beck could understand. 'I got pregnant again. Another mouth to feed. No money to spare. David wanted me to get rid of it. I said no but he kept on and on. I said we'd talk to Michael. I knew Michael would say, "No. Abortion's wrong." He's a priest for God's sake. He'd say no and David would stop. But Michael didn't say no. He said, we must do what we must do. We'd always be welcome in his church. And there was no way I could refuse any more so I had the abortion. And then I found ... then I found we had enough money after all but he was spending it on those bloody women. You ask me how I could put a chisel into another woman? It was easy when I thought of my baby. Whatever mess I made of them, it was nothing to what they did to my baby.'

And then Fitz felt a whirling sensation in his stomach, a premonition if you like. He knew what she was going to say next.

'I killed them all. Joyce Watkins, Paula Devereau, Jean McIlvanney. David is innocent. Please. Please let him go home and look after my children. Please. Please let him do that. For my children. Please.'

And Fitz knew in that moment that Maggie Harvey would never say anything different. Because as far as she was concerned she had killed Jean McIlvanney. And all the conflict in her story, all the psychosis, the confusion, none of it would boil down to anything worth an ounce of salt. Because she had admitted voluntarily to killing Jean McIlvanney and on that she was as clear as day. And that was how the system would judge her.

Fitz climbed tiredly to his feet, studied Maggie Harvey as she continued to press herself into the corner of the interview room. A woman. A mother. A killer. What made her so different from the women she had so brutally murdered? A set of values? A moral code? And who imposed that on her? Fitz knew the answer to that one.

And murder? Who was responsible for that? The prostitutes weren't to blame. Maggie herself wasn't to blame; they were the same after all. So who – or what – was left to carry the blame?

Fitz knew the answer to that question too.

The implications of it terrified him.

TWENTY-FOUR

Beck sucked on his roll-up as Fitz left the interview room, leaving him alone with Maggie Harvey. Had Fitz done that deliberately? He knew Maggie was lying. Fitz knew it and he knew it too. The question was, what should he do about it? How could he get her to admit the truth? She'd confessed to a crime she didn't commit. But she had committed two other murders and that did complicate things.

Beck's first inclination was to jolly her along a bit. The old, good cop bad cop routine that had always worked so well for him in the past. There were no witnesses. A bit of . . . what shall we say? A bit of *cajoling* and she would probably change her tune quickly enough.

Beck studied Maggie thoughtfully. She was still crouched in the corner of the room. She was trembling. He thought she might begin to cry again. He thought what a waste it was that such an attractive woman could be so screwed up inside.

He took a step towards her. Held out his hand to help her rise.

The door to the interview room opened and Penhaligon entered. 'They want us in the duty room –' She stopped.

Beck turned, aware of how the situation must look to her. 'It's not what you think –'

Penhaligon stared contemptuously at him, crossed the room as Beck lowered his hand, crouched beside Maggie as Beck watched helplessly.

'Did he hurt you? Are you all right?'

Maggie stared at Penhaligon, eyes bright with anger.

'Slut! Filthy whore! It was you! On the street! It was you that told them where I was going! Slut! Whoremongering, thieving slut!'

Penhaligon recoiled from the utter hatred in Maggie's voice.

'Told you so.' Beck was unable to keep the pleasure from his voice.

Penhaligon stared at him with almost as much hatred as Maggie had stared at her. 'I'll get her back to a cell. Wise and the chief super want you now.'

All women together then. Fine. Frankly I can do without the grief.

Beck blew smoke, dumped the butt into an ashtray already overflowing with Fitz's dog-ends and left the interview room.

Beck felt the tension as soon as he entered the duty room. A conversation was already in progress between Wise and Chief Superintendent Allen. Allen, a cuddly sort of bloke who looked as if he wouldn't be capable of hurting a fly, was currently displaying a temper roughly matching the wrath of God. A temper which at this moment was directed at Wise and, by extension, at everyone in the duty room.

'It's no bloody good, Charlie, and you know it! We've nothing. What the hell is this? Amateur week?'

Then Allen caught sight of Beck through the glass office divide and beckoned.

Beck entered the office. 'I was told you wanted to see me, sir.'

Wise deferred to Allen, who said, 'I understand you witnessed the attack by Maggie Harvey on this Denise what's her name.'

'Fletcher, sir.'

'Yes. On Denise Fletcher.'

'That's partly correct, sir, yes. I caught the end of it.'

'Describe it to me.'

Beck shrugged. 'Thoroughly vicious. Fractured her skull with a teapot. Broke her nose too. Laid open her cheek with a chisel. Broke her nose. I thought she was going to kill her.' A hesitation. 'I had to hit her to stop her.'

Allen turned to Wise. 'You see what we're dealing with here?'

Beck also turned to Wise. 'Sir?'

Wise sighed. 'Thanks, Jimmy. Off you trot.'

'But –'

'That's *all*, Jimmy.'

'Sir.' Beck left the office, sat at his desk, listened closely to the rest of the conversation as it filtered through the office wall.

Wise was saying, 'But we *know* he did it! We've got an ID that puts him with Jean McIlvanney an hour and a half before she died.'

Allen fumed. 'The ID's bloody useless. The press has got wind of it. We've already held him longer than we've a right to.'

'But he had sex with her –'

'I'm not denying that he had sex with her, Charlie! That's not the point here and you know it. All right he had sex with her. So have half a hundred men this week; God knows how many she had the same night as David Harvey!' Allen hesitated then, and Beck saw him struggle to maintain a more even temperament. 'Just because he's had sex with her that doesn't make him a killer. You know it. I know it. More importantly Maggie Harvey knows it. And according to Mister Blobby out there –' Beck smiled humourlessly as Allen gestured through the glass office divide to where Fitz was perched on the edge of Penhaligon's desk. '– there's no way on God's green earth we'll get Maggie Harvey to change her story. And you know what that means.'

Beck suddenly understood what his conversation with Allen had been about. Ammunition. He began to get a bad feeling in his stomach. An acid feeling. This wasn't looking good. He shot a glance round the duty room. Everyone's face told the same story. Fitz's said it loudest of all. *They're going to let him go*.

Wise said, 'He was the last man to see her alive, for God's sake!'

'No-one's denying that either. But he wasn't the last *person* to see her alive. The last person to see her alive was his own bloody wife.'

'She's lying.' Wise was getting desperate now. And Beck could identify with that. How many times had a killer walked from this station? Even once was one time too many.

Allen turned away. 'I'm not convinced.'

'Look.' Wise sighed. 'It's not our problem, you know what I mean. We pass everything to the Crown Prosecution Service and leave it to them to decide.'

Allen rounded on Wise again. 'But we haven't got a case! No forensic. No fingerprints. No tyre marks or footprints because the ground where she was killed was too hard. We've nothing! Nothing to link him with the crime.'

'But –'

'– on the other hand, she has confessed. His wife has confessed. We've got that on tape. A confession by his wife. We've got to do it, Charlie. Got to let him go. If we don't we'll be a laughing stock and that won't exactly do wonders for your career, you know.'

Beck felt his insides churning violently. He wanted to be sick. Harvey was going to walk. That murdering bastard was going to walk and it was all down to his lying bitch of a wife. Jesus. Didn't anyone have any values anymore? Innocent until proven guilty. Bollocks. Grade-A bollocks. David Harvey was as guilty as sin. You only had to look at him to see that. Guilty as sin. As –

Behind Beck the door opened and Penhaligon walked in. She took in the scene in a glance. Allen. Wise. The expressions on the faces of all the officers on duty. It didn't take a genius to put it together.

Beck stared at her for a moment. She met his eyes and he found himself unable to maintain eye contact. She walked over to Fitz. That tub of lard. It was all his fault. If he hadn't scared the shit out of Maggie Harvey she'd have coughed. At least she might have if he, Beck, had been able to talk to her, chivvy her along a bit. Then both of them would be on the way down and he might have scored a few brownie points to boot. Not that he really cared about brownie points. What did he want Wise's job for? Or Allen's? A load of grief. That's all that was. A bunch of bleeding hearts in a job softer than a caramel cream.

Allen opened the door to Wise's office, nodded politely to the watching officers and left the duty room. A moment later Wise also came out of the office. His face was less calm. Thunderous might have been a better word to describe it. 'We're letting David Harvey go.'

Beck thought he had prepared himself for those words. He was wrong.

The desire to throw up returned. The room spun around him. Wise's voice echoed, became that of David Bilborough. *Get this man for me, Jimmy. Get this man for me and Catriona.*

He swayed. Reached for a desk. Found himself eyeball to eyeball with Penhaligon. She wore a contemptuous smile. 'He's not the first man to get off scot free.' The smile widened. 'Is he, Jimmy?'

Get this man for me, Jimmy.

Beck grabbed the edge of his desk to stop himself reeling. A moment. Deep breaths. Control. 'D'you want him punished?' Beck asked the question of David Bilborough, but it was Penhaligon who answered.

'You're a bloody hypocrite, Jimmy.'

For me and Catriona. Get this man, Jimmy.

'D'you want him punished?' And now Beck was talking to Bilborough and Penhaligon. And he couldn't tell where

237

one ended and the other began. 'He's guilty, right? You think he's guilty so you must want him punished, right?'

And Fitz was pushing foward then, sticking his oar in, but before he could say a word, Penhaligon lost it, just for a second, but it was enough.

'Yes, I want him punished! All right? I want the bastard punished! Is that all right for you, Jimmy? I want you punished!'

Beck smiled. Because her voice was David Bilborough's and his was hers and the two were one, and at last all the voices in his head were saying the same thing, and the peace it brought him, the relief from torment, was akin to orgasm; the best he'd ever had, which had also been the first, sitting on his father's knee all those years ago in Belfast . . .

Beck suddenly rose to his feet. He couldn't stay here another minute. Not here with the compassionate bastards, the do-gooders, the love-thy-neighbours, the innocent-until-proven-guiltys. He had to get out. Now. Right now. Out and away. Home.

He didn't need to be here. Not here. Oh no. Not with her. Not with any of them. What he needed was to be home.

Home with Mother. Home with Dad.

Ignoring the startled looks, the gestures of surprise, Jimmy Beck stiffened his back and walked out of the duty room. He was vaguely aware that Wise called out after him, but he ignored that too.

He got into the car and drove to the flat.

What he needed was a drink. A double.

What he needed was a writing pad and a pen and an envelope labelled *dear sis*.

What he needed was the gun.

He needed to caress it, press the barrel against his cheek, to kiss it, to taste for a second time the cold steel with its patina of gun oil and ancient cordite.

His father's gun. The gun from the war. The gun which had saved his father's life so he could come home and make

238

love with his wife and have a child which would grow up to become Jimmy Beck.

The last thing he did before leaving the flat was to load the gun with six bullets from a dusty cardboard box.

Last time it had been used the gun had been empty.

No mistakes this time.

TWENTY-FIVE

Fitz stared at the roulette wheel, the table laid out before it, and almost laughed. He had been making a mistake all these years and he now realised what it was. Life wasn't shades of grey. It was stark. Monochrome. Black and white. Or rather, red. Black and red. All those choices, the fuzzy, indistinct moments, all the confusion, the women, the patients, the books, the guilt. All boiled down to a simple choice. The whole of life boiled down to a simple choice. Black or red. That simple. Black. Or red.

Fitz studied the roulette wheel. Was it an honest wheel? It was the only one he'd ever played where he'd never caught them fixing the bet; in all likelihood that was as good a definition of honest as he'd ever get.

He pulled the envelope Danny had given him from his pocket. Fifteen thousand pounds. Half his mother's life insurance policy. Half of what her life had been worth.

He pulled the money from the envelope. Slapped it on the table. The croupier studied him carefully, shrugged, took the money, stuffed it into a slot. Slid Fitz a stack of chips.

Fitz took the chips. Lifted one, turned it over in his hand.

Black.

Or red.

Fitz was going to make his mother a millionaire.

He took hold of the chips, slid the entire stack back across the table.

Red.

The croupier spun the wheel.

The moment stretched out forever. Every little clink and

bump of the ball across the wheel was a punch in the heart for Fitz. And that was what it was all about, the heightened sensation, the expectation, the hope, the desperation, the buzz.

More to it this time, of course.

The ball landed on red.

Fitz's stack of chips doubled in size.

Fitz turned to a little man in a dark suit playing the wheel beside him. 'Thirty thousand. That's the sum total of my mother's life. The value of my mother's life. Thirty thousand pounds.'

The man looked at Fitz for a moment, then lost interest and resumed placing his own bets.

Fitz smiled. Lit up a high tar. Sucked hard. Blew smoke. Slid thirty thousand pounds' worth of chips onto black.

'No more bets please.'

The wheel turned. The ball juddered from one slot to the next.

Fitz wheezed and shuddered.

The ball stopped.

Black.

And Fitz grinned once again at the man beside him. 'Sixty thousand pounds. I've doubled the value of my mother's life in seconds. Do you think there's anything immoral in that?'

The man edged away from Fitz.

Fitz looked at the croupier. Slim. Beautiful. Sharply dressed in a tight suit that showed off her body to its best advantage. 'How many men have stood here, lost the lot, gone home and topped themselves? You think it's got nothing to do with you? The suicides, the broken homes, the sheer bloody despair?' Fitz didn't wait for a reply, slid sixty thousand pounds' worth of chips onto red, continued, 'It has got something to do with you. Because you know what they think when they stand here facing you? The more they win, the more chance they've got of screwing you. Isn't that what they're meant to think?'

The croupier looked straight through Fitz. Totally professional. No reaction at all. The wheel spun. The ball juddered and Fitz's heart juddered with it.

Red.

He smiled at the croupier. Was that the tiniest hint of emotion on her face? What was it? Anger? Lust? Did he really care? 'I've quadrupled the value of my mother's life. I could walk away with a hundred and twenty grand. But there'd be this question gnawing away – how far could I have gone? Could I have made it to two forty? Quarter of a mil? Give or take.'

The croupier glanced around the table, ignored Fitz totally. 'Place your bets, please.'

And Fitz studied the table. All of life. A simple choice. Guilt or innocence. Judith or Panhandle. Live or die. Black or red.

He pushed one hundred and twenty thousand pounds' worth of chips onto black.

The wheel spun –

All of life.

A simple choice.

– the ball juddered –

Guilt or innocence.

– slowed –

Judith or Panhandle.

– flipped over a last division to come to rest.

Live or die.

Black or red.

Red.

Fitz pursed his lips. Felt the chemical dance of adrenalin in his brain shudder to a stop. Gone. All gone. His mother was gone. She was gone. She was dead.

The little man in the dark suit beside Fitz leaned closer. 'Good system, buddy.'

And Fitz grinned then, the sparkling grin of a man who has won, not wealth but understanding.

To the little man he said, 'The money's gone. Mum's gone. While the money was there she was alive and I couldn't let her go. Now the money's gone and I know in my heart she's dead.'

The little man looked at Fitz as if he were utterly mad.

Fitz didn't care. Guilt or innocence. Judith or Panhandle. Live or die.

Two choices made.

He turned to leave the table, found Penhaligon waiting for him.

'How did you find me?'

'Don't be silly, Fitz.'

'Do you want a drink? You'll have to buy it.'

'No, Fitz. I don't want a drink. I want you.' Fitz waggled his eyebrows suggestively but she ignored him. 'Jimmy Beck's gone off the deep end. He's got a gun. And David Harvey. He picked him up after we released him. He's on the top of the old Egerton engineering works. He says there's only one way he's coming down.'

And Fitz's grin widened. Finally it was all making sense. Guilt or innocence. Judith or Panhandle. Live or die.

Only one choice left to make now.

TWENTY-SIX

Jimmy Beck stood on the edge of the world and the edge of the world was crumbling.

In one hand the gun, in the other a fist full of David Harvey's collar. Five storeys below him was the ground, visible only where the headlights of police cars split the darkness. Above him the moon was rising. A thin crescent bisected by umber clouds. Men had walked there leaving footprints in dust older than life on earth. No wind would ever stir them or cover them. The little silver world was at peace. The peace of death. Beck felt as if a similar calm had enveloped him. All the voices. All the voices were the same now. Bilborough. Penhaligon. Even Fitz. And his own, of course. All the same. And they were fading, all fading to leave just one.

David Harvey.

Begging for his life.

Beck swung Harvey a little closer to the edge. Harvey made a strangled noise and shut up. That was better. Now he could think. Now that he didn't have to shout above the voices he could explain it.

'Look,' Beck told Harvey reasonably. 'Bilborough wanted him punished. Penhaligon wanted him punished. My friend and my lover. How can I let them down?'

Harvey said nothing, slipped on the crumbling concrete lip of the roof.

Beck tightened his grip on Harvey. He was about to continue when there was a sound behind them. The door to the elevator service room opened with a creak. Someone came out, a pale face in the moonlight.

Penhaligon.

She called back through the door. 'Come on, Fitz. Hurry up!'

She turned and Beck felt her gaze on him. Painless for the first time. Because he knew. He knew what she wanted. He explained it to Harvey. 'They're here now. Bilborough. Penhaligon. You won't be able to see Bilborough, of course. He's dead. But he's still my best friend. I loved him, you see. So I know what he wants too.'

The lip of concrete crumbled a little more beneath his feet. Harvey lurched in his grip. Beck struggled to maintain his balance. From inside the metal door behind Penhaligon, the sound of footsteps ringing on metal. Distant but getting closer. Fast. Like the moment. The moment of decision. No. That was wrong. The decision had already been taken. The moment of action then. Yes, that was better. The moment of action was approaching.

'Jimmy –' A pigeon erupted from the roof, disturbed by her presence. Startled, Beck lurched, managed to regain his balance with a huge effort. Not yet. Not quite yet. Harvey squealed with fear as he slid an inch closer to the edge.

The door opened again. Fitz. Eyes black in the night. High tar burning like a coal in the darkness. He leaned against the lift blockhouse, winded. 'Jesus. Those stairs. And my piles. Hope to God the twain will never meet again.'

Beck said nothing.

Fitz regained his breath. 'Coppers. Marksmen. Paramedics. It's like an episode of *The Bill* down there.'

Beck smiled.

Fitz moved closer, stood next to Penhaligon, touched her briefly on the shoulder, moved past her.

Beck pointed the gun at him.

Fitz stopped. Sucked on his high tar. 'Cigarette, Jimmy?'

Beck laughed. 'Bad for your health.'

'So's a five-storey swan dive, I should imagine. No prizes for best triple somersault and half twist when you're spread all over the pavement, am I right?'

Beck said nothing.

'I know you think David Harvey should be punished. We all do. But not like this. He's unimportant. An irrelevancy.'

'*I am not a fucking irrelevancy!*' Harvey's voice was a hysterical squeal in the darkness.

Beck snarled, 'That's right, you little shit. You're not irrelevant. You killed someone didn't you? Shoved a chisel into her and ripped her open! Fucked her with that chisel! Didn't you?'

A long pause. The wind gusted quietly, rocking him towards the edge and back again. Beneath his feet the ledge crumbled.

Fitz said, very quietly, 'Tell me about it, Jimmy. Tell me why.'

Beck shrugged, ignored Harvey's terrified whimper, felt the man grip his arm even tighter, smelled sweat, felt the heat of him through the sleeve of his suit.

'Jimmy. Tell me why. I'd like to know.'

Why not?

Beck tightened his grip on Harvey, began to speak. 'There was a copper used to walk up and down our street. That was when you could walk up and down the street. Big man. You kept your nose clean, you'd be all right. Step out of line and you'd get a clip round the ear. Everyone respected him and I wanted to be just like him. I wanted to be that man. But I can't be that man. There's no-one like that man. Not these days. They've all gone. Give 'em a clip round the ear these days and you'd end up in court. Those days have all gone. Those men have all gone. A life for a life. Kill and you hang. Those days have all gone.'

Beck looked up then. Clouds covered the moon. It was dark. As dark as it had been inside the building when he'd tried to find Old Barney. Had that only been two days ago?

A lifetime. That's what it was; further away in time than the policeman he had so wanted to be like as a child.

Fitz moved slightly closer, his feet shuffling along the roof. 'Jimmy. You don't want to die. If you did why did you radio in your location? It's a cry for help, right? Well, I can help. I helped you once, I can help you again.'

Beck tried to make Fitz out in the darkness. No chance. Voices in the dark. They were all just voices in the dark. 'Did you tell her? Did you break the seal of the confessional? Never mind. It's not important. What is? Objectivity. That's what is important. That's what the law demands. But you can't be objective unless you understand. You can't weigh up crime and punishment unless you understand the crime. I understand. I've lost people I've loved. I've made cups of tea for the widows. I understand murder. I'm objective about murder. For murder you should hang.'

Well, that seemed to go over well enough. Fitz hadn't responded. Was he thinking about it, trying to work out a clever way of twisting the situation to his advantage? It wouldn't do him any good. The decision had been made and the moment was approaching. And it was time for another voice in the darkness. 'Mister Harvey. Did you kill Jean McIlvanney?'

'Yes! Oh God, yes, I killed her, the edge is crumbling, please let me go, I've got children. I killed her. I killed Jean McIlvanney. I did it!'

'You see, Fitz? Trouble is – and you know it as well, I'm sure – is that a judge'll throw it out. Confession under duress. No chance in a court of law. That's what it's like these days. Everything's designed to get you off.' Beck hesitated, addressed his next words to Harvey. 'That's a wonderful ... what's the word I'm looking for Mister Harvey? Ah. Irony. There's a wonderful irony there, isn't there? Because everything's designed to get you off from murder, you're going to have to die. You do appreciate the irony, Mister Harvey, don't you?'

248

Harvey began to cry.

Well, that wasn't going to change anything. Beck had shown his one moment of compassion and that one moment of compassion had killed his best mate. And anyway it was getting harder to hear Harvey because of all the voices. The voices in the night. Coming back again, slowly. Bilborough. Penhaligon. Fitz.

Especially Fitz.

'Jimmy. Listen to me. I want to talk to David. Not Harvey. Bilborough. I want to talk to David Bilborough for a minute. Can you hear me, David?'

Beck thought about that one. Why would Fitz want to talk to Bilborough? Oh well. It didn't matter. David was his mate. He wouldn't let him down. No matter what Fitz said.

'This is evidence.' That was odd. David Bilborough's voice seemed to be different from that he remembered. It was deeper. A tinge of Belfast. 'This is a dying man's statement. Get this man for me, Jimmy. For me and Catriona. Get this bastard, Jimmy.'

And Fitz said, 'That man is in jail, David. Jimmy caught him for you. He bottled him and kicked him, broke his nose, practically killed him. He's in jail. He's going to rot there.'

That's OK then.

'You hear that, Jimmy? You've punished the man responsible for Bilborough's death.'

No. That's not true. He's here. Here in the darkness. Here with David Harvey.

'It's true. His name was Albie and he's serving life. Thanks to you. He's been punished.'

Beck was confused. That was wrong. The man responsible for Bilborough's death was still at large. Was here. But Fitz was right. Albie had been arrested. Beck had arrested him. David's wish for his death to be avenged had been granted. By Beck. Oh, this was confusing. Had the man responsible for Bilborough's death been punished or not? Was he still at large or not?

It was so hard to think, to decide.

And the gun was heavy. Almost as heavy as Harvey. And it was no use pointing it at Fitz. With the moon gone he couldn't see Fitz. They were all just voices in the night, blown by the wind, loops and whirls of confused thoughts and words.

Beck decided he didn't need the gun any more.

He dropped it.

There was no clunk when it hit the roof.

Over the edge. He must have dropped it over the –

A noise then. Metal on metal as the gun bounced from the roof of a car, discharging a single bullet into the night. Voices. Curses. A scream. The shouting. 'No! Hold your fire, he dropped the gun! It went off by accident!'

Beck dismissed this from his mind. He lowered his arm. That was better. Now he could hold Harvey much more comfortably. Hold him while he decided whether the guilty man had been punished or not.

And then, before he really had a chance to think, another voice in the darkness.

Penhaligon.

'Jimmy . . . No one wants you to do this.'

And Beck felt the confusion coming back then, with the voices. Louder. And louder. Bilborough. Penhaligon. Fitz. Harvey. Albie. Wise. And they were all shouting at him now. Screaming. *Punish him. Don't punish him. Punish him.*

'What do you mean?' He made no attempt to disguise the confusion in his voice. 'You told me you want him punished! Why are you lying to me? How can I believe you if you lie to me?'

'I was wrong. I've changed my mind. I was wrong.'

And Beck was thoroughly confused now. 'How can you not want him punished? After what he did to you? After he raped you?'

'I forgive him, Jimmy. He has to be punished by the law.'

'And he will be. But not by you.'

And with those words it all became clear. Very clear. And he took the last step he would ever take. Him and David Harvey and David Bilborough. Together. And it really was clear. As clear as the night between himself and the ground. As clear as David Harvey's dying scream as they fell together from the building, as clear as David Bilborough's whispered *Thanks Jimmy*, as clear as the dazzling headlights which rose to meet him in a storm of shattered glass and crumpled metal and blood and shattered bones and –

– Jimmy Beck tried to scream but there were no voices any more.

No voices to scream with, no voices to hear.

Not Harvey's, not David's, not Penhaligon's.

Not even his own.

TWENTY-SEVEN

The combined mass of David Harvey and Detective Sergeant Jimmy Beck falling at terminal velocity folded the bonnet of the police Rover in half on impact. Both headlights were crushed. Broken glass and shattered plastic fragments of the air filter littered the ground. All in all it was surprisingly little damage when you considered the condition of both Beck's and Harvey's bodies.

Fitz gazed for a long time at the wreckage, both machine and human. He wondered about a great many things. Eventually he became aware of someone standing beside him.

Penhaligon.

'He said "Did you tell her?" Did you tell me what?'

'I promised.'

'You promised a dead man.'

'He raped you. He admitted it. This act was his apology.'

'Jesus.' Penhaligon leant against the passenger door of the Rover. Fitz watched her for a moment. She seemed lost in memories of an earlier experience. She looked up. 'I had a gun in his mouth. I pulled the trigger. The gun wasn't loaded. He looked at me and laughed. He laughed.' She looked over the front of the car, past the folded bonnet, the blood-soaked engine block, to the bodies. 'Even when he admitted raping me, he admitted it to you. I never did get even.'

Fitz felt his heart lurch. Hadn't she got it yet? 'Healing isn't about getting even.'

And she looked at him then with heart-stopping frankness, her hair and face backlit by the line of police cars behind. 'Don't you think I don't know that, Fitz? But God. It's so hard. So hard. When you've been violated and every cell in you is crying – screaming – out for revenge. And then when it happens it doesn't mean anything at all. Because it hasn't magically cured you. You're still the same. It's all still the same. Don't you think I know that?'

Fitz reached out a tentative hand for her. He moved slowly, expecting rejection, but instead she grabbed the hand, pulled herself closer. And she cried. Tears soaked his shirt, seemed to penetrate to his very heart.

And he said, 'I can help.'

She nodded. 'I know. I know you can help.'

'Will you let me?'

And he waited a long time for her answer. He waited while the police cars backed off, the ambulance responded to a call from Manchester Central to attend the aftermath of a pub fight, he waited while the forensics team had examined Beck and Harvey and bagged them, and driven them off to the mortuary. He waited because this was the moment. The most important moment since they'd met. The moment which would determine if they could remain friends or whether circumstances and selfishness and stupidity had driven them an irreparable distance apart.

She looked at him. After a long time she nodded.

His heart lurched. Joy. He smiled. He looked over her shoulder at the bloodstained mess where Jimmy Beck had died and whispered something.

'You what?'

'I said, "We keep passing unseen through little moments of other people's lives." '

She smiled tearfully. '*Zen and the Art of Motorcycle Maintenance*.'

He grinned. 'Actually I read it on a Waterstone's bookshop bag.'

She laughed then, let him lead her away from the battered Rover and back to her Volvo. He opened the driver's door for her. Laughed suddenly as she was about to climb in.

'Care to share the joke?'

'The Rover. What do you think they'll write on their insurance claim? "Act of God"? That's what they normally write when things drop out of the sky.'

And she laughed then, laughed as he held her briefly, then walked around to the passenger door to get into the car as well. She was still laughing as she started the engine and drove away.

And that pleased Fitz. Because for both of them the laughter was the first step on the road to recovery.

EPILOGUE

Mummy was singing again. But that was OK. He liked to hear Mummy singing. In the carrycot, in the living room. Her voice buoyed him. Her voice had been his first contact with the world. Now she jogged his rattle and sang again.

> 'How much is that doggie in the window,
> The one with the waggly tail?'

Then she stopped, interrupted by a man's voice. Daddy's voice.

Tense. Tired. Angry.

'Judith, please! If you sing that song even once more I swear I'll go stark staring cuckoo!'

Then there was laughter.

He wondered how long it would last this time.

ACKNOWLEDGEMENTS

End Titles

Cracker: Brotherly Love
Composed by Jimmy McGovern
Bristol Remix by Jim Mortimore
The MC Pete-ey Thoroughly Ruthless Edit

Starring: Trees (who isn't), Paul Hinder (who doesn't), Mum and Dad, Jop and Andrea, Jo and Steve, Timbo, Kurt, Andy, Lynne and Lizzie and anyone else who has ever signed contracts for two novels in one day and then realised they were both due for delivery on the same date some eight weeks later and *then* been told there's no video for one and *then* contracted serious food poisoning for three weeks and *then* had to drive a hundred and twenty miles with a thrombosed pile with someone so they wouldn't fall asleep at the wheel and miss their flight to Japan by killing themselves on the M4 on the very day they were due to finish the main character's suicide scene.

Thomas and Gizmo don't appear, but apparently I have to mention them again because I didn't pay them enough royalties last time.

The thrombosed pile is real. It's mine. It's agony. I *hate* it. (Won't stop me earning money from it though.)

So until *NEXT WEEK*, same *TIME*, same *CHANNEL* . . .
Be excellent to each other and . . . *PARTY ON DUDES!*

Outta here –

Jimbo

CRACKER

**Cracker novels are available from all
good book shops, but in case of difficulty you can
order them directly from Virgin Publishing.**

Each book costs £4.99. Please add for postage and packing:
– in the UK / BFPO / Ireland: £1 for the first book and 50p for
each additional book;
– overseas: £2 for the first book and £1 for each additional book.

You can pay by cheque, made payable to Virgin Publishing Ltd,
or by credit card.

Send your order to:
Cash Sales Department, Virgin Publishing Ltd,
332 Ladbroke Grove, London W10 5AH

- -

Please send me the following Cracker novels

                                                               Quantity

The Mad Woman In The Attic	by Jim Mortimore	....
To Say I Love You	by Molly Brown	....
One Day A Lemming Will Fly	by Liz Holliday	....
To Be A Somebody	by Gareth Roberts	....
The Big Crunch	by Liz Holliday	....
Men Should Weep	by Jim Mortimore	....
Brotherly Love	by Jim Mortimore	....
Best Boys	by Gareth Roberts	....
True Romance	by Liz Holliday	....

Please tick one box and complete the spaces

☐   I enclose my cheque for £ ....

☐   Please debit my Visa/Access/Mastercard account

      (please delete those not applicable)

      My card number is ....

      and its expiry date is ....

Please send the books to: Name ....

                                      Address ....

                                      ....

                                      ....

                                      ....